TOP SECRET
FOR YOUR EYES ONLY

SUBJECT: Geoffrey Gallowglass, second son of SCENT agent Rod Gallowglass, the High Warlock of Gramarye.

BACKGROUND: Father landed on feudal planet Gramarye, his mission to help establish a democratic government. With the aid of Fess, an artificial intelligence in the form of a horse, became recognized as a warlock (see *The Warlock in Spite of Himself*). Despite going native, agent has been successful in laying the foundations of democratic institutions (see files *King Kobold Revived*, *The Warlock Unlocked*, *The Warlock Enraged*, etc.).

CURRENT SITUATION: A second generation of Gallowglass family now coming of age. Children all possess psychic talents, inherited from Gallowglass and his wife, the "witch" Gwendylon (see *Warlock and Son* and *A Wizard in Absentia* for recent mission files on eldest son, Magnus. See also *M'Lady Witch* for latest information on Cordelia, Gallowglass's daughter).

PROJECTION: Geoffrey, now a young man, has great promise, possessing both fantastic strength and skill with weapons, as well as impressive psi abilities. Also has a growing reputation for "wenching" (frankly put, Geoffrey has a weakness for attractive females). Expect antidemocratic forces—namely sultry SPITE agent Finister—to attempt seduction and matrimony, effectively putting enemy within legal reach of throne (see current file, *Quicksilver's Knight*) . . .

QUICKSILVER'S KNIGHT

CHRISTOPHER STASHEFF

ACE BOOKS, NEW YORK

This book is an Ace original edition,
and has never been previously published.

QUICKSILVER'S KNIGHT

An Ace Book / published by arrangement with
the author

PRINTING HISTORY
Ace edition / August 1995

ISBN: 0-441-00229-3

ACE®
Ace Books are published by The Berkley Publishing Group,
200 Madison Avenue, New York, NY 10016.
ACE and the "A" design are trademarks
belonging to Charter Communications, Inc.

PRINTED IN THE UNITED STATES OF AMERICA

10 9 8 7 6 5 4 3 2 1

CHAPTER
~1~

Geoffrey had decided that it was very boring being the son of a nobleman—especially the second son, even if the first was away from home. It was even more boring if the only thing you were really good at was war, and nobody was obliging you by attacking your king. He would have settled gladly for even a nice pocket war, a tidy little rebellion in some distant corner of the kingdom of Gramarye, with a few good battles, some privations to endure and trials of will and muscle, feasting and celebrating after the victory—Geoffrey had no doubt that, with him on the King's side, the rebellion would end in victory.

Unfortunately, the rest of the kingdom seemed to have no doubt about that, either—or perhaps it was just King Tuan's twenty-five-year record of winning every battle he had fought, especially with the Gallowglass family on his side. If Geoffrey couldn't win single-handedly, his parents, brother, and sister could certainly tip the scales in his favor.

So, all in all, it wasn't too surprising if nobody wanted to start a war—and, to keep himself from going crazy with inaction, Geoffrey had volunteered to be royal trouble-shooter. When the King didn't come up with enough troubles to shoot, he took to the roads as a knight-errant. Again, though, his bad luck held—all he had to do was ride into a county, and the bandits instantly faded away into some other district. The lords began a startling program of reform, ceasing oppression and moving toward enlightened government; they stopped exploiting the peasants and began just and humane rule.

Which left Geoffrey with nothing to do but indulge himself in his only other really strong interest—wenching.

Which is why he was currently in the hayloft with a particularly luscious and tempting morsel named Doll, caressing experimentally, to determine which stroke elicited the largest number of gasps, and beginning to coax her out of her bodice. Of course, he was minimizing the possibility of her objecting by seeing to it that her mouth was fully occupied with his own, and was distracting her with a particularly ardent kiss as he began to untie her lacings when a voice like the mew of a seagull called, "Young warlock!"

The girl froze, and so did Geoffrey, cursing darkly within his mind. Then he lifted himself away, giving her a tender and reassuring smile—rather necessary, since she was staring up at him with incipient panic as the voice called again, "Warlock Geoffrey! Come, sir, speak!"

"You are a warlock, then?" Doll whispered.

"I am," Geoffrey sighed.

She relaxed, eyes half-closing, her smile returning, sultry and inviting. "Then work magic upon me, young sir." She wriggled to emphasize her words.

Geoffrey caught his breath, and was about to accept the

invitation when the voice demanded, "There are folk in need, Sir Geoffrey! Remember your oath of chivalry!"

"A warlock, and a knight too," Doll murmured.

"A double curse," Geoffrey sighed, "if it must take me from your arms. Bide, though, and let us see if I may not send this small messenger packing."

"Small? How can you know that?"

"By the quality of his voice." Geoffrey rolled away from her and sat up in the hay, looking about.

"Up here, knight!"

Geoffrey looked up, and there upon a roof beam stood a foot-high mannikin, only a few feet above his head in the loft. The girl gasped and wrapped her arms about her torso, even though she was still fully clothed.

"Oh, be at peace, child! We of the Wee Folk have seen it all—so many times as to be wearied with it," the elf said with disdain. "Warlock, I am sent to summon thee to The Chief."

"The King of the Elves?" Doll gasped.

"Nay, only The Chief," the elf corrected. "He hath action for thee, warlock, an thou dost wish it."

"I was engaged in action that I did wish to pursue," Geoffrey grumped. "Can he not wait an hour or so?"

Doll glanced from the elf to the warlock and back, looking very wary and not entirely sure about the enterprise. She was past second thoughts and heading into thirds.

Geoffrey saw, and his hormones beat all the harder. "Surely whatever's amiss will not miscarry worse for a few minutes' wait!"

"Mayhap not, but The Chief will," the elf reminded him. "Thou dost know his moods."

Geoffrey smiled up at the elf, amused. "Do you say I should fear the Puck?"

The girl gasped and flinched away from him.

"A pox on this mode of speech that hath afflicted thy generation," the elf sighed. "Canst thou not say 'thee' and 'thou' like an honest citizen?"

"Perhaps I can say them, though as to my honesty, you shall have to judge for yourself," Geoffrey countered. "Surely one who honors Robin Goodfellow as chief would not be overly concerned with truth."

"We are, though not in the fashion in which you mean it," the elf snapped.

Geoffrey nodded slowly. "No wonder you think that I should fear him."

"*I* do," Doll assured him.

Geoffrey turned to caress her cheek gently. "Aye, poor lass! I have wronged you, to seek your favors when I was such a fearsome beast. Nay, here will I leave you, that you may have no fear of the Wee Folk further."

"I do not mean that you should go," she said in alarm.

"But I must," Geoffrey sighed, "or the Puck shall blame you for my tardiness—and I would not wish his ill will on any mortal who has no defense of magic. Perhaps we shall meet again, pretty wanton. I shall hope for it, for my body rages at me for breaking off this encounter."

"As does mine, Sir Geoffrey!" She caught his hand with both of hers, pulling. "Nay, bide awhile. I will risk the Puck's wrath, for the delights we may share!"

Her tone made Geoffrey's blood pound in his veins, but he summoned his warrior's self-discipline and disengaged her hands gently but firmly. "Nay, for I'd not forgive myself for what he would do to you. When your ardor has cooled and clear judgement has returned, you shall thank me for leave-taking. But I go to danger, I always go to danger, so do not await my return."

"You must not go, then!" she cried, reaching for him again.

"But I must." He avoided her grasp deftly, then knelt suddenly to kiss her—fleetingly, arousing more than he soothed. "Yet if I should chance to come back, and you are still unwed, perhaps we can begin the dance anew. Farewell, sweeting! Find a strong husband, for he'll need great endurance!" And he was gone before she could plead another excuse for delay—he was gone, leaping over the side of the loft into a mound of hay below, and striding out the door of the barn, still buckling on his swordbelt.

Doll glared after him, slamming a little fist into the pile of hay beside her. Now that he was gone from sight, she let her temper have its full, savage sweep, pummelling the mound about her, leaping up to lash kicks at the unoffending straws, not daring to shout her curses and imprecations for fear he would hear, but loosing them in a steady stream of hisses.

It wasn't just a release of a surge of frustrated hormones, though there was much of that to her vehemence—it was also anger and fury at one more plot that had miscarried, once again due to the interference of the Wee Folk. Handfuls of hay went flying through the air, but without the aid of hands, for Doll was an esper, gifted with quite a few psionic talents, among them telekinesis. She could move objects just by thinking at them, and in her rage she moved quite a few. Milking buckets and old horseshoes went clattering against the walls; a pitchfork hurled itself with such vehemence that it buried its prongs in a beam. She was having a full-fledged tantrum, and it felt very good.

Doll was really Central Agent Finister, the head of the Gramarye office of the Society for the Prevention of Integration of Telepathic Entities. SPITE was Geoffrey's hereditary foe, since it was the enemy of his father—but it was nothing personal; SPITE was really just the enemy of everything his father stood for.

For Finister, though, it was very definitely personal. Her interest in the Gallowglass family amounted to an obsession, but her interest in Geoffrey was very definitely a vivid example of lust adulterated only by hatred. Taken all together, it made him fascinating.

The clanging and clattering stopped; the cow ceased her terrified mooing, and the chickens sought their roosts again. Finister knelt in the hay, panting, hair dishevelled, amidst random straws that slowly drifted down into the mow. Slowly, clear thoughts returned, foremost among them being the fact that the yeoman who owned the barn was bound to come running in alarm to see what all the commotion had been. It would make things easier if she were not there.

She ran to the ladder, swung down to the earthen floor, then dodged out the small door at the back, where Agent Grommet was waiting with her cloak. He was looking considerably happier than when she had left him. "No luck?" he asked cheerily.

Finister was used to her male agents' suppressed sexual jealousy; she couldn't really resent it, since their desire was so useful for keeping them in line. That didn't mean, of course, that she couldn't torment them a little. "A great deal of success," she countered, and waited just long enough for his disappointment to harden into a wooden mask before she let him off the hook: "Until some weasel of an elf called him away for a conference!"

Grommet relaxed—relieved, Finister saw darkly. Like herself, he was a "home agent"—a local recruit, who had been found on the doorstep of an agent who had a reputation for taking in foundlings. In fact, it was his primary role in the organization, and he did it very well, raising local Gramarye children to believe in the goals and methods of SPITE, while nurturing their resentment against the society that had abandoned them. In Finister, that resentment had deepened into hatred, and the Gallowglasses had proved the perfect target for it. Her adoptive father had also recognized her psionic talents, and proved very adept at helping her train them, though he himself had none. He had turned her loose as a mature agent of SPITE at sixteen, and she had risen rapidly, being given her first assignment to hamstring a Gallowglass at the tender age of nineteen.

Grommet draped her cloak over her shoulders, grumbling, "I don't see why you have to pay so much attention to that musclebound oaf, anyway."

The reminder of Geoffrey's muscles stirred a thrill of desire in Finister, making her a bit more snappish than she needed to be as she answered, "Yes, you do—to make sure the influence of that viper, Rod Gallowglass, won't keep going after his death."

"Well, yes, I understand that," Grommet griped. "But why do we have to do it by making sure none of his children reproduce?"

"Because we've tried every other way," Finister fumed. "Assassination, rebellion, poisoning his mind with a psychoactive drug—and none of them worked. Between that horse of his and that *wife* . . ." She made the word an obscenity. " . . . he's just too well guarded."

She could have added the elves to the list of Rod's guardians, but she preferred not to think of them just now.

Rod Gallowglass was an agent for the Society for the Conversion of Extraterrestrial Nascent Totalitarianisms, an organization dedicated to promulgating democracy by sniffing out dictatorships and other forms of oppressive government, and steering them onto the road toward democracy in one of its many forms. As such, Rod was the bitter enemy of all SPITE's agents—because this planet of Gramarye was absolutely vital to the future of democracy. By a fluke of genetic selection, it contained more active telepaths than all the rest of the Terran-colonized planets combined—and if those telepaths could be swayed toward believing in democracy, they would become the communications system for a galaxywide federation of democratic governments.

In fact, that was exactly what had happened—or would happen, in the future. Centuries down the timeline, an interstellar democratic government ruled the Terran Sphere, with Gramarye's telepaths as its communications network. The anarchists had lost—as had their equally virulent enemies, the future totalitarians—so both groups had sent agents back in time, to try to change their own past and Gramarye's future, by swaying the planet toward anarchy on the one hand, or totalitarianism on the other. As Rod Gallowglass and his local allies had frustrated one plot after another and used each challenge to put the planet more firmly than ever on the road to democracy, the futurians had become less and less picky—they no longer cared much what kind of government Gramarye had, so long as it wasn't democratic.

In fact, both organizations had pretty well resigned themselves to having lost the fight, as long as Rod Gallowglass lived. The totalitarians were biding their time, plotting for the day after he died—but the anarchists, under Finister's leadership, were taking action *now*.

"How else do you think we're going to keep Gallowglass from polluting the future with his asinine democracy?" she demanded.

Grommet was silent for a few strides, face darkening. Finally, he had to admit, "Not much else I can see."

Finister felt a stab of vindictive satisfaction. "No other way at all—and so far, I haven't done too badly."

"Well, you made a good start, anyway," Grommet admitted, "and I can't deny you were the perfect agent to assign to the Magnus Gallowglass case."

"Yes, I certainly was," Finister purred. In three separate encounters, she had given Magnus such a nightmarish view of sex that it was highly doubtful he would ever do more than think of reproduction, and that only in the most clinical way. In fact, he had left the planet to get away from her (at least, *she* was sure that was the reason), and she thought it was all for the best. His siblings had to be much less effective without him. He was the eldest, after all, and the one they all looked up to, though she knew Geoffrey would have hated to admit it.

Cordelia would have, too, being the second child and the only girl. Finister's eyes flashed as she thought of the moralistic chit, and it didn't help that Grommet chose just that moment to mutter, "You didn't do too well when it came to Cordelia, though."

"Of course not! She's female, after all!"

"True," Grommet grated, and started to say something else, but caught his tongue in time.

And a good thing, too, Finister thought grimly—especially if he'd been about to remind her that, though Cordelia *might* not have been susceptible to Finister's wiles, her fiancé, the Crown Prince Alain, *certainly* was not. "I almost had him," she said between her teeth, "but the bitch used some kind of witchcraft on him that I don't know about."

Not surprising that she didn't, Grommet reflected, since the magic in question was called "love." From personal experience, he knew that Finister equated the word with "sex," and thought everything else associated with it was sentimental hypocrisy. She didn't really have the concept, and Grommet wondered why. He knew she had had a rough childhood before being dumped on the SPITE agent's doorstep, being batted back and forth from one relative to another, then to foster parent after foster parent, before someone had finally remembered that there was a couple in one village who seemed willing to take all and any children, no questions asked. Fortunately, the SPITE agent's cover identity as a merchant let him support all those hungry mouths with no one wondering where the money came from, though there had been plenty of gossip about how well the grown-ups could have lived if they hadn't had such an expensive hobby. The local lord must have realized that there was enormous untapped potential for taxation there, but they were solving a problem for him that might otherwise have cost him even more, directly or through the Church's charities, so he had left the brooding couple alone.

Grommet did know, from personal experience growing up with Finister, that she had always thought talk of love was silly. She had become fanatically loyal to her adoptive parents, but even that seemed to be more out of a sense of survival than from any tender feelings. She had also realized the importance of status to survival, and had understood the effects of her burgeoning charms at a startlingly young age, using them to keep the boys firmly on her side, ensuring her dominance over the other children, even the girls who were four and five years older than herself.

So he wasn't terribly surprised that Finister could not understand how Cordelia had won Prince Alain's affections against every curve that Finister could throw. "You're going to have to work awfully hard," he said. "The Home Office still says there will be an alarming number of successful brats issuing from Cordelia's marriage to Prince Alain."

"You don't have to remind me!" Finister rounded on him. "Unless you want to spend the rest of your life watching the lack of events in some village out in the boondocks?"

"No, no," Grommet said quickly. "You know I want to be as near you as I can, Chief."

"Yes, I know," Finister said, gloating. She could see how her tone twisted inside Grommet, and felt a glow of satisfaction—and pleasure. She turned away, pacing as quickly as she could toward the forest. "They don't ever seem to remember Magnus having had any children, though."

"No," Grommet admitted, "but we here can remember that he did. Only because the old Chief Agent wrote it down, of course, just before he died."

Finister suppressed a quick shiver of delight at the memory of how the old man had passed away. The prelude hadn't given her much pleasure, but his dying had—and had given her a great deal of power, too, since he had named her as his successor. Of course, by that time, he would have said anything to win some time alone with her.

Foolish or not, Grommet was in the mood for revenge. "The future is still saying that, only a generation down the timeline, one of Cordelia's children becomes king with extremely republican ideals."

"Yes, I know," Finister hissed, "and worse, all his siblings will have been raised to be intensely loyal to him—once they're grown up."

Grommet didn't like the sound of that last. "Of course they'll grow up!"

"Not 'of course' at all," Finister corrected. "That can be changed."

"What?" Grommet stared at her, aghast. "Their growing up?"

"Of course." Finister gave him a saccharine smile.

That shook Grommet down to the laces in his boots—but he was even more appalled to discover that, no matter how much of a monster she suddenly appeared to be, he still would have killed to get into bed with her. His loathing turned inward.

"So, for that matter, can Cordelia's marriage," Finister informed him.

"Can what?" Grommet stared.

"Be changed. Of course."

Grommet suddenly understood—and also understood that there was a great deal of Finister's self-esteem at stake here. He would have to tread carefully. "But they're engaged . . ."

"Yes," said Finister, "but the wedding is still three months away, and while there's bachelorhood, there's hope."

Grommet gave a humorless bark of laughter. "Chief, with your talents, even *after* the wedding, there's hope."

"Yes, there is, isn't there?" Finister said, preening. "Marriages can always be wrecked."

"And if you don't mind my saying so," Grommet said, "no one's better fitted for the task than you."

"You say the sweetest things, Grommet. Yes, I *am* well suited to the task, aren't I? Which is why I have to take charge of Geoffrey Gallowglass's case personally."

Grommet looked up in alarm, to her satisfaction. Had he really thought he had sidetracked her? Yes, none of her agents had anywhere nearly as good a chance of ensnaring Geoffrey as she had— she shivered at the thought of how she would go about that ensnaring. Certainly that was the reason—or one of the reasons, anyway; the shiver summed up all the rest.

In her natural form, Finister was a voluptuous, striking beauty—striking anyone who could be lulled into lowering his guard to her charms. But she depended on artifice more than nature, appearing to the Gallowglasses in a host of disguises, which made her appear even more beautiful than she was. She was a projectile telepath, and therefore skilled at casting illusions. She was also skilled at stimulating men's ardor, both telepathically and otherwise.

"So you've taken a personal interest in the case?" Grommet asked, with irony.

"Personal in more ways than one," Finister countered. "He's escaped me once already. Curse the fool! Doesn't he know I can see how badly he wants me?"

"From what you've told me, he hasn't made any effort to disguise how much he desired you," Grommet said shortly.

"No, he hasn't," Finister agreed, "but he seems somehow to be infuriatingly proof against my spells!"

Forget the spells, Grommet thought—her physical charms were enough. "He must be the only man you've ever met who is."

"Definitely the only one." But Finister reflected grimly that Geoffrey was also the only man who might be capable of enjoying her favors without being captivated by them. "It's a challenge I can't resist."

Nor could she, really, resist Geoffrey himself. She could not explain this obsession—he was handsome enough, surely, but there were men who were more handsome still; Geoffrey was certainly not what she would call a gorgeous hunk of male animal. Oh, he was male enough, to be sure, and a hunk—she had seen him without his doublet, and knew that he was muscular enough to make Adonis blush

13

for shame; his chest and arms were magnificent, and the way he wore tights was distinctly unfair to every unattached female in his vicinity—and perhaps to some of those who were attached, too. Still, there were men enough with handsome displays of pectorals and biceps, and many of them were even more handsome than Geoffrey—so what was it about him that sent pangs of covetousness coursing through her whenever she thought of him? She could not make sense of it; she only knew that she had to have him, and *would* have him, some day.

Have him permanently, if she was bewitching enough—and she knew she could be.

"But what are you going to do with him once you catch him?" Grommet asked.

"What?" Finister looked up, startled at his words having matched her thoughts so well. Grommet was no telepath—but even if he had been, she was very adept at shielding what she was thinking. Covering her surprise, she snapped, "What am I going to do with him? I'm going to light such a flame of lust in him that it will never die down! Once I've done that, I can transmute it into what fools like him call love, even though it's just an obsession surging up from the gonads." She saw, with satisfaction, that Grommet was suffering. "Once I've done that, he'll realize that he absolutely *must* have me with him always."

"Meaning that you intend to marry him," Grommet said softly.

"Of course." Finister tossed her head, "I'm every bit as good as any of those highborn trulls he might be thinking about, when he gets old enough. In fact, I'm a lot better!" Was that a groan she heard from Grommet? Well, maybe a very soft one.

"You know that and I know that," Grommet said, his voice low, "but his parents don't."

Finister shrugged. "They'll object to my class, of course—peasant girls are all very well to bed, but not to marry. When the time is right, though, I'll reveal that I'm really the long-lost daughter of some forgotten earl who secretly married a woman who conveniently died in childbirth."

Grommet nodded; the device came as no surprise. "So you'll be legitimately of the nobility, but since you won't be competing with anybody for inheritance, you won't make enemies out of the dead lord's heirs—and, of course, you'll have a marriage contract and a statement from the priest who married them, just in case they want you to prove it."

"Of course," Finister agreed sweetly. "After all, we have the best forgers in the country, don't we?"

"The best we know about, Chief—so even the High Warlock and his wife won't be able to deny you."

"No, they won't. What good would it do them, anyway? I'll have their son so emotionally hog-tied that saying no will only make him elope with me."

"They'll disinherit him," Grommet warned.

That struck a qualm within Finister, making her angry at herself—she knew it for the mere instinctive response that it was. So she took it out on Grommet, speaking harshly. "What difference does that make? With his sword and my magic, we'll carve out our own fortune fast enough! But I don't think they *will* cut him off—their children mean too much to them, the fools! They won't be able to deny me, either. No one will."

"Least of all Geoffrey," Grommet said darkly. "So you'll live like a duchess, with all the respect and kowtowing that goes with it."

"Yes, I will," Finister said, gloating, but she thrilled inside at the thought of the less public rewards that would go with marriage to Geoffrey. She hid it, though. "I'll be in an excellent position to sabotage the government of King Tuan and Queen Catharine, too."

"Very subtly, of course," Grommet said sourly. "Can't risk your cover, can you?"

"Only as far as making sure I don't have any children," Finister assured him. That was no great sacrifice—she hated the little monsters anyway, especially babies, and wasn't about to go through that much inconvenience and pain, to say nothing of the damage it would do to her figure—or to her relationship with Geoffrey; the enforced abstinence of pregnancy would weaken the power she intended to have over him.

"How are you going to hold onto him if you don't give him the children he wants, though?"

Finister flashed Grommet an angry glare, then followed it with a lazy smile, stepping closer. "The same way I hold onto you, little man, and make sure you do exactly as I want. Could *you* dream of disobeying me?"

Grommet turned away, his face scarlet.

Finister gave him a low, gloating laugh, then turned away and tossed her head. "Don't worry, I'll have a grip on him that no infant could match—a grip so strong that he'll *have* to be faithful to me, whether he likes it or not."

"A compulsion," Grommet breathed. He knew it would not be completely natural.

"Yes, a compulsion—and don't worry about his defenses. Psi or not, he can't stand against *this* form of projective telepathy. He's a man, after all, and this is *my* area of psionics."

Grommet didn't doubt it for a second. With Finister around, testosterone haze would cloud Geoffrey's psi abilities to the point of disability.

"I'll see to it that he can't even *think* of leaving me!"

Finister's eyes glowed. "He'll be so ecstatic that he'll never regret the children he doesn't have—at least, not for any longer than it takes to come near me."

"He doesn't exactly seem to be the fatherly sort, anyway," Grommet grumbled. Then he saw a chance to get a little of his own back, and took it. "But even *your* charms can't last forever, Chief."

Finister tossed her head as though she didn't care, but inwardly marked Grommet for a long and painful revenge. "There's always the poison bottle."

"Why don't you just kill him right now and be done with it?" Grommet muttered.

"Because I can't get close enough to him for long enough, of course! I have to win his confidence first, so that he's willing to drink what I give him. We've already tried all the other ways—several times, too. The man has an uncanny knack for knowing where the knife is coming from."

It was a good excuse, but she and Grommet both knew the real reason—that she hated to see such a good hunk of manflesh go to waste. Finister intended to take her pleasures of Geoffrey first; there would be time enough to kill him later—and it would be far easier when his wariness had been blunted by love and trust.

In the meantime, if he could give her the power and status she had always craved, so much the better.

"It's just a matter of time, then," Grommet said.

"Yes," Finister echoed, "just a matter of time." Time until she had her way with him, time until she wed him—time until she killed him.

"Of course," Grommet said spitefully, "there's always the chance that there might not *be* that much time."

Finister suppressed a surge of rage—because she knew the man was right. Every day that passed increased the chance that Geoffrey might meet the wrong woman—wrong for Finister, anyway—and fall in love. He was at that atrociously dangerous age—one of the characteristics that made him so fascinating. He was twenty, which was old for a peasant to marry, just right for a lord. He might well hold onto bachelorhood for another ten years—or he might surrender it tomorrow.

"Don't worry," she assured Grommet, with her sweetest smile. "I can frustrate any romance he might develop—and it's more fun after it's started. First I lead him into infidelity, then I make him forget the woman he thought he loved."

If that failed, of course, she had an excellent team of assassins, and though Geoffrey might have proved immune to them, his ladylove certainly would not.

"You failed today." Grommet was becoming reckless indeed, in his jealousy. "You might fail, period."

"Don't be ridiculous!" Finister snapped. "You know I would have had had him today, if it hadn't been for that blasted elf!" For a moment, she let her anger boil over, picturing the little fellow screeching through all manner of delightful torments, then shut the picture away with a shudder of pleasure and turned her mind back to Geoffrey, who quite frankly held much more of her attention than an enemy should. She would never admit it aloud, but she knew Grommet was right—Geoffrey was a tougher target than any she had ever faced. She would have to be very industrious in her seductions.

Well, she had failed to captivate him again—but it did not much matter that the elf had destroyed this opportunity for her. "I'll find another chance," she assured Grommet, "or make one."

Grommet knew she would. Finister excelled in the use of makeup, so none of the Gallowglasses had ever seen her in the same guise twice. A discerning eye could see which facial features Doll had in common with the Faerie Queene, or the Hag of the Tower, or La Belle Dame Sans Merci—but when she appeared to one of the Gallowglass boys, their minds were scarcely discerning.

"I'll meet Geoffrey Gallowglass again," she breathed, "in one disguise or another—and I'll know him when we meet, but he won't know me."

CHAPTER
~2~

If Finister had thought about it, she might have wondered why Geoffey didn't have to follow the elf back to "The Chief." Of course, by the time she came down from the loft, he was long gone, so the thought never crossed her mind.

What crossed Geoffrey's mind was the need to get out of that farmyard before the farmer happened to come by. He strode out the gate, totally unaware of the haystorm going on in the loft, and veered into a grove of trees. There he stopped and called out, "Well enough, Puck, I am come! What is your pleasure?"

There was an instant's pause—no doubt Puck had been shadowing his every footstep, but it still took him a moment to catch up—then a brawny, foot-and-a-half-high form detached itself from the shadows under the leaves, and a deep voice chuckled. "Well asked. We know what *thy* pleasure was, lordling!"

Geoffrey's mouth tightened with annoyance, as much at the stilted "thee" and "thou" speech of the older generation (in Puck's case, a *much* older generation) as at the jibe. "You could indeed have chosen a better moment for your summons, Robin!"

"Nay, never one more apt," the elf retorted, "The look on thy face alone must have been worth a king's ransom."

Puckish humor indeed; Robin Goodfellow was ever the prankster, as who should know better than a young man who had suffered Puck as a babysitter? But Geoffrey remembered the top elf's notions of chastisement, too, so he forced back the irritation and sighed, 'Well, it's done, and the lass fled, no doubt."

" 'The lass?' " said Puck. "Dost not even know her name?"

Geoffrey shrugged irritably. "It is of no importance now. Was the matter truly so grave that it could not have waited another hour, Puck?"

"Nay, I suppose," the elf agreed. " 'Twas only more enjoyable in this fashion."

Anger sprang, but Geoffrey remembered how ugly he had looked as a toad, the last time he had let himself be angry with Puck, and schooled himself to patience. "Well, then, what was this errand that could have waited, O Friend of All Who Are Wary?"

Puck chuckled. "Thou hast learned thy lessons well, lad."

"But school is out," Geoffrey countered. " 'Tis a mission now, not homework. Come, tell me of it. Is it your notion of fitting work for me, or His Majesty's?"

He didn't mean King Tuan, but rather the King of the Elves. He didn't *know* who that individual was, exactly, and had never *officially* seen him—but he had made some shrewd guesses.

"Be easy in thine heart—'tis His Majesty's," Puck said, with studied nonchalance, "and 'tis he who bade me summon thee at once, saying thou must needs drop whatever else thou hadst in train."

"Then I am glad you did not catch me a few minutes sooner, when I had caught the wench up in my arms. What is this matter of supreme importance?"

"A warlord," Puck replied, watching Geoffrey closely. "An outlaw who had conquered several parishes, nigh onto a whole county, has but only now defeated the army the Count sent against him. He has established sway over the peasantry, and rules them like any lord."

Which meant exploitation and oppression. Geoffrey grinned with anticipation; giving such tyrants their due was one of the things he lived for. Unfortunately, legal excuses for it were rare. "What is his name, this warlord?"

"None know, nor have any seen him."

"What!" Geoffrey frowned. "Not even an elf?"

" 'Tis so. We have discovered his battle-leaders, but he himself has not even a tent. We do not know how he gives his orders to his warriors and battle-maids; we can only speak of their effect."

"Which seems to be massive." Geoffrey frowned. "Do they have no name for him, none of any kind?"

"Aye; they call him 'Quicksilver.' "

"An odd name, but fitting for one who cannot be found," Geoffrey mused. "And you say his army has shield-maidens as well as men?"

"Not shield-maidens, but warriors in their own right," Puck corrected. "He has a score of them, and score they do, for each seems to have a score of her own to settle, 'gainst men and, most pointedly, the Lord's men."

Geoffrey thought of the kind of hatred that bespoke and the ferocity that went with it, and frowned in thought. He had been trained never to strike a woman—but surely one who went in battle, and was trying to kill him, was another matter entirely. Still, it would be better if he could find this Quicksilver and bring him to justice—or death in battle, which was far more likely. With the head gone, the limbs would not know how or where to strike. "I may need to call for soldiers to gather up the leavings," he said slowly.

"An army the King must not send," Puck contradicted, "or this bandit Quicksilver may get notions above his station. 'Tis bad enough that he doth defy a count! If he should confront a king's army, we might have a full-blown rebellion afoot."

Geoffrey scowled; he knew what that meant. Lowborn or not, Quicksilver would become the focus of every disaffected lordling in Gramarye, and of any squire and knight who thought he had a score to settle with the Crown. It had been tried before, several times during the reign of Queen Catharine and King Tuan—but there was always the danger that the next try might succeed. It was a slight danger, to be sure, but a danger nonetheless.

What was far more likely was that estates and farmland would be torn apart in the battling, and that many peasants would lose their lives. "So. If His Majesty cannot send an army, he can send me."

"Do not preen thyself overmuch," Puck said with a jaundiced eye. "If thou dost think of thyself as the equal of an whole army, thou wilt shortly be dead."

Geoffrey shrugged off the comment; they both knew it was false. Still, for the sake of form, he said, "Do not worry, Puck—I am aware that I have only two arms and two legs. Still, though I might not face the whole army, I might find and defeat their commander—though 'tis scarcely chivalrous to slay a peasant."

"Then capture him if thou canst, but if 'tis his life or thine, do not hesitate to make it his. There is, after all, no loss of honor in slaying a peasant who hath defeated a count and his army."

"And great honor in freeing other peasants from a tyrant and brigand." Geoffrey grinned, his pulse quickening at the thought of real, genuine action. "Thanks for this good news, Puck. I was like to rot from inaction."

"In more ways than one," Puck muttered under his breath, then said aloud, "Ride swiftly, then, and with good heart."

"I shall," Geoffrey assured him, "for all laws of chivalry do agree on this being a noble and worthy quest. Thank you, Puck! I ride!"

And he did—he leaped on his horse and set off down the road. Puck watched him go, shaking his head, marvelling once again at the folly of mortals. Geoffrey was in such a hurry to meet a chance of death that he had not even turned to go home for a clean shirt!

Geoffrey had not gone home to pack because he always kept everything he needed for a mission with him, in his saddlebags. He had clean linen, hardtack, and a canteen which he could fill at the first stream he came to. Beyond that, he needed only his sword, which never left his side, and his dagger. He might indeed find a need for armor and a lance, though he doubted that—if he was going to take on a whole army by himself, mobility and secrecy would count for more than steel plate. If he did need it, he could always send for it—he could teleport home quickly enough, put on his armor, and teleport back. He saw no reason not to take full advantage of all his psi powers—there was no lack of honor in it, if he was to go up against a whole army. In fact, that was why the Elf King had sent himself, instead of a whole expeditionary force—that, and his skill at arms and talent for tactics.

Modesty? The need for it never occurred to Geoffrey. To believe himself capable of more than he really was would have been very bad tactics indeed. A general has to know the exact strength of his forces if he is to plan a campaign wisely, and Geoffrey had to know his own exact strengths and weaknesses for the same reasons. He was as wary of false modesty as of overconfidence. He would never make the mistake of underestimating an enemy— and for the same reason, he would never underestimate himself. To some people, conceit was a moral flaw; to Geoffrey, it was a military one.

On the one hand, he knew how to pretend modesty when the occasion called for it. He had learned that most people find truth distasteful, especially the truth about their own weaknesses and vices, and someone else's strengths and virtues. To others, a frank statement of Geoffrey's abilities counted as bragging, so he had learned to hold his tongue. Shortly thereafter, he had realized it was a good tactic, for it allowed possible enemies to underestimate him.

On the other hand, he knew himself for an arrogant idiot in any matter not relating to war or wooing—which, to him, were much the same; both involved the planning of a campaign, and both culminated in action. He was content to leave intellectual matters to Gregory, the care of others to Cordelia, and the rest of the galaxy to his absent brother Magnus. Governance he left to Their Majesties or, possibly, Cordelia—he knew he would make a botch of it if he tried. It had occurred to him, idly, that if he and his three siblings were all rolled into one person, they would make the ideal monarch. Since they were separate, however, he paid his allegiance to King Tuan and Queen Catharine, and when they were dead, he would pay allegiance to Alain—he had no doubt the prince would become an excellent ruler, with Cordelia beside him to guide and temper him.

That, however, was for the future. Today was for action. Geoffrey rode south with a light heart and a song on his lips. He was riding to battle—nothing else mattered.

Doll would have been highly indignant to learn that.

But it would have reassured Puck immensely. What the elf had not told Geoffrey was that his elves had been following "Doll" for some time, and had reason to wonder whether or not she would be good for Geoffrey. Puck certainly had no objection to two young folk merrily playing together, but he had other notions about entanglements, and though he was not sure exactly where Doll had come from, his agents had definitely overheard some remarks that were without question predatory, before she had taken up her station dallying by the wayside waiting for a dalliance—and knowing exactly who the next knight would be.

When Geoffrey came to a town large enough to have a fair, he stopped and bought a few items. He paid in gold, leaving the merchants goggling in his wake—not only because he paid generously, but also because the last thing they would have expected of a rough-clad knight-errant was to buy a burgher's robe and hat, not to mention the donkey and the load of odds and ends. But, when he brought the donkey back to his horse, he was amazed to find it gone, and a tall black stallion standing in its place—a stallion he recognized. He glanced around quickly, saw there was no one near, and muttered, "Fess! What are you doing here?"

"Waiting to serve you, Geoffrey," the huge black horse answered in a voice as low as his.

Fess wasn't a horse, really—he was a computer that could be installed in any number of robot bodies. This imitation horse was the one he had been inhabiting for the last twenty-odd years, ever since his master—Rod Gallowglass, Geoffrey's father—had landed on this planet of Gramarye to begin subverting its medieval monarchy into a democracy.

"I know, I know, you live but to serve!" Geoffrey said impatiently. "What happened to my horse, Fess?"

"An elf is riding him home this very minute. They seem to have established friendly relations."

Which was quite an accomplishment, considering that horses were usually spooked by close contact with elves. Geoffrey wondered how many apples and lumps of sugar it had taken. He sighed, resigning himself to accept the situation—there was no point in arguing with Fess, since he only carried out Rod's commands. "Why did Father send you?"

"Puck told him of your current mission, and both your parents became a trifle nervous over your confronting a small army single-handedly. They found it reassuring to think that you might have the company of a trusted retainer."

"Well, to speak truly, I do too," Geoffrey admitted. Not much—he knew that in a battle, Fess would fight with amazing bravery for several minutes, at which point the stress would take its toll, and the robot's faulty capacitor would discharge, tripping a circuit breaker that would turn him off to prevent his burning out. Fess was a cybernetic epileptic.

Nonetheless, Geoffrey felt quite cheered as he swung up into the saddle. There was nothing like the presence of an old family retainer to give you a sense of stability—and Fess had been with the family for five hundred years, give or take a decade or three.

However, Geoffrey braced himself for a few lectures. The "horse" he was riding might have been the friend of his childhood, but it had also been his tutor. Fess couldn't resist the chance to impart wisdom.

As they rode out of town, leading the donkey, Geoffrey drew many glances from people who exchanged very skeptical looks with their neighbors, shaking their heads and turning back to count their profits. What business of theirs was it if the young knight was a fool? The more fools *they* would have been, not to take the gold he offered!

But as soon as he had ridden into the woods, our young knight found a clearing where he could change his clothes—and a few minutes later, a young merchant was riding his way south through the woods, whistling and kicking his heels. His robe and hat were not rich or trimmed with fur, but he was clearly a merchant, with no armament except the dagger at his belt.

No armament visible, that is. The loose robe nicely concealed the sword slung across his back.

A lone merchant was, of course, too easy a prize for forest outlaws to resist, and at any other time, Geoffrey would have been delighted to battle any one of them, or even all together—he had done so before, when he became really bored; chivalry always allowed him to clean up a few menaces to public safety. But this time he was after bigger game, and couldn't take the time to knock out and bring in every petty outlaw who came his way—so Geoffrey kept his mind open, picking up their greedy thoughts as soon as they sighted him, and managing to insert a little apprehension, then nourishing it. After a few minutes, even the most hardened bandit turned away with a shudder. There was something about this young merchant, something eldritch, some shadow of menace that overhung him. Tempting his donkeyload of goods might be, but not so tempting as to defy whatever force it was that shadowed him.

When he came into County Laeg, though, Geoffrey dropped the aura of dread that he had been projecting and rode along looking as innocent as possible. Now he *wanted* to attract bandits' attention—but only that of the right bandits. Still, from what Puck had said, he suspected that any bandits here would be the right bandits—he didn't expect that Quicksilver would allow any small fry to go poaching on his domain, any more than Count Laeg had.

He did not stop by the castle to tell the Count he was here, though by the laws of chivalry, he should have. Since that would have given away who he really was, though, he let it slide—he had a notion the Count would overlook the rudeness, if Geoffrey brought in Quicksilver.

Finally, he felt a surge of interest in a mind not far from the trail—but he was surprized to discover that it was less an outlaw's greed than a sentry's wariness. Still, larceny was definitely there, and Geoffrey heard the bird calls with which the sentry summoned his captain.

The blood began to sing in Geoffrey's veins as the minds about him became more numerous. He faked a yawn and reached up to scratch his back—and clear the collar of his robe from the hilt of his sword. Excitement gathered; it was time for action!

He rounded a bend and found a dozen outlaws blocking the path, quarterstaves at the ready, the leader with his sword raised.

Geoffrey stopped, feigning shock—and noticed the dozen more outlaws who stepped out of the brush to block the road behind him. These bandits, at least, didn't believe in taking chances.

He was amazed at their discipline, but even more amazed at the state of their clothing. Here were no patched tunics with cloaks of untanned hides, but jerkins and hose of good stout broadcloth, in the green and brown that blended so well with the forest foliage. Only the leader wore a hat, but it looked new, and was decorated with a bright red feather. His sword was bright, not rusty, and not honed down from decades of sharpening. As outlaws went, these were very affluent.

"Well met, stranger!" the leader called, and one of his men chuckled. "We have met him well indeed, Ostricht."

"Be still, Tomkin!" Ostricht snapped, then to Geoffrey again, "Be sure you may ride our pathways in safety, young merchant—if you pay our toll."

Geoffrey forced himself to look casual and heaved a sigh. "Ah me, how the cost of doing business keeps rising! Very well, forester—how much toll does your lord demand?"

At the word 'forester,' the outlaws all began to snicker. Ostricht glared them down, then smiled at Geoffrey. "A half of all your goods, young merchant."

Geoffrey stared. "A half! Nay, sir! That is far too high a tax! If I were to pay that at every toll gate, I would have nothing left to sell before I came to the next town!"

A soft rustling sounded all around him as archers drew their bows.

"True," Ostricht admitted, "but we shall see to it that there *are* no other tolls—and if you do not pay us half, you will not live to sell the other half."

"Oh, I think that I shall," Geoffrey said quietly.

He rolled off Fess and down, below the archers' aim. For a second they stood, realizing that their arrows might very well hit one another—which gave Geoffrey just enough time to spring upward, whipping the sword out from behind his back and lunging at Ostricht.

Surprized, the leader nonetheless managed to parry, but not well—Geoffrey's blade grazed his left arm. He howled in anger, but Geoffrey was already crowding him, sword flickering in and out, pushing him back and back among his own men. A ranker broke out of the paralysis of surprize and swung his quarterstaff with a snarl; Geoffrey chopped it aside, thrust into the man's thigh, hearing the bellow of pain as he collapsed and Geoffrey turned to catch Ostricht's blade on his own, then riposted quickly to thrust at the bandit leader's face. Ostricht flinched away, and a quarterstaff cracked across the back of Geoffrey's shoulders. He grunted with pain and half-turned, just far enough to lash a kick into the stomach of the man who had struck him—a foul blow was fully justified, when an assailant struck from behind. Then back he spun, to catch Ostricht's blade in a bind and step up *corps à corps*, backing the bandit leader into a tree. An arrow whistled past his ear to bite into the trunk, and Geoffrey snarled, "Fool!"

"Fool!" Ostricht agreed in a bellow. "Put up your bows! Do you mean to slay *me*?" Prudently, he didn't wait for an answer, but shoved hard, trying to push Geoffrey far enough away so that he could disentangle his blade . . .

It was like trying to shove a boulder.

A quarterstaff caught Geoffrey across the back of the knees.

He grunted and threw an arm around Ostricht. The bandit leader saw his chance and shoved, hard, and Geoffrey fell . . .

. . . with Ostricht right on top of him.

Even so, Geoffrey managed to twist as he fell, and rose up with his dagger at Ostricht's throat, sword sweeping up to knock aside the quarterstaves that struck at him as he bellowed, "Hold! Or I'll cut his throat!"

The bandits froze.

Then an ugly, bearded one snarled, "Do, and we'll crush you to jelly!"

Geoffrey's hand twitched, and a drop of blood appeared on Ostricht's throat. The bandit leader went rigid, eyes wide in horror.

"Crush away, then," Geoffrey hissed.

The bandit glared at him, but held his staff still—and his tongue.

"Away!" Ostricht grated. "Put down your bows! If he falls, he's like to slit my throat as he topples!"

"Wisely said," Geoffrey agreed. "Bid them back away now, a good ten feet."

"Do as he says!" Ostricht snapped.

Reluctantly, the bandits gave ground.

"Now," Geoffrey said, "put down your bows."

He did not even look, only kept his gaze locked with Ostricht's, his lips thin, hand rock-steady.

"Obey!" Ostricht groaned.

There was silence. Then one bow dropped, and all the others clattered down beside it.

"Now," said Geoffrey, "take me to your leader."

Ostricht stared at him, and his men growled and muttered. "I would sooner die!" the bandit leader snapped.

"You have chosen." Geoffrey swung the sword-tip down, right above Ostricht's eyes.

The bandits howled, starting forward, then froze.

"Thrust," Ostricht grated. "I shall not betray my chief!"

"Thrust," growled one of the bandits, "and we shall slay *you*."

But Geoffrey ignored him, frowning. "What manner of

bandit chieftain is this Quicksilver, to inspire such loyalty in you?"

"A leader worth a thousand of the lord who claims the right to rule us," Ostricht snapped. "Strike, and be done—but I shall not betray Quicksilver!"

"Then we shall carve up what's left," another bandit growled.

"Carve!" Geoffrey snarled, and leaped up and back, kicking Ostricht aside as he did. He stumbled back, his knees not yet fully recovered, and the bandits roared and closed in. But Geoffrey had aimed well; he fell back against a tree. Quarterstaves rained down at him, but he blocked them with sword and dagger. Sticks exploded against his ribs, drubbed his shoulders, pounded his thighs, for he could not block them all—but by the same token, the bandits were too closely packed to be able to get much of a swing. Geoffrey's knees were strong enough for kicks, though, and suddenly all but two of the bandits were rolling on the ground, howling in pain, and the remaining pair were streaked with blood from Geoffrey's sword.

He shouted, "Havoc!" and leaped at the one on his right, chopping and thrusting. His knees held, and the man howled, falling back with a gash in his thigh. Geoffrey spun in time to parry the staff that struck down from his left, then riposted and grazed the man's ribs. He swung back to the front just in time to parry a thrust from Ostricht, then advanced on him, thrusting so quickly that the man scarcely had time to parry, and certainly none to riposte. He gave ground, and none of his men could help him now—until a tree suddenly struck his back, and Geoffrey caught his sword in a quick circling movement of his own blade. Ostricht's sword went flying, and he stood at bay, bloodied and gasping for breath, staring wildly at the blade whose point touched his throat.

"Now," Geoffrey called out, "one of you who can still walk, lead me to Quicksilver!"

"I am here," said a voice behind him.

Geoffrey spun about, leaping aside to keep his point near Ostricht's throat even in his amazement at the sound of that voice. He stared at its owner.

She was long and lithe, slender and supple. If Helen's face would have launched a thousand ships, Quicksilver's figure would have wrecked them, for the helmsmen would not have been able to keep their eyes on the sea ahead. Her auburn hair was caught by a gleaming headband, but fell loose about her shoulders in a swaying mass. She wore a copper-colored surcoat, but not the armor it should have covered, giving her, in effect, a long split skirt over girded loins, and a bodice that tied about her neck and just below her breasts, binding them as firmly as any brassiere. Her buskins were soft leather, almost moccasins, but cross-gartered up over her calves.

And her face . . .

Wide across high cheekbones, narrowing to a small, firm chin—a small, straight nose, huge dark brown eyes, a high unlined forehead, wide mouth with full, ripe lips . . .

Geoffrey caught his breath. His thoughts spun, seeking refuge, some defense against this goddess whose mere presence seemed to demand his homage, the total devotion of every fiber of his being, and found it—in the errant thought that he had, most surely, seen faces more beautiful.

But not bodies . . .

Perhaps one or two faces more beautiful, but this one had a compelling quality, some strange attraction that made every cell within him scream to feel her touch, her embrace, fought for some action that would bring him into contact with her, no matter how brutal that action might be.

Chivalry clamped down on instinct. Geoffrey caught his breath, and his presence of mind. Somehow, the magnificent creature facing him seemed to dwindle a bit, into a mere mortal woman, not the goddess she had seemed in the first shock of seeing . . .

But still fantastically attractive.

Charisma, he thought crazily, she had immense charisma—and Ostricht slipped aside from his blade, then sprang back beside his chief, panting and glaring at Geoffrey, bloodied but still ready to try to tear him apart with his bare hands if Geoffrey so much as raised a finger against his female leader.

Very female, immensely female—and every iota of his being clamored in response. He stood still, rooted to the spot, but felt as though his whole body was nonetheless straining to be closer to her—and she responded, he could feel the intensity of that response as her eyes glowed into his, seeming to swallow him up, yearning to devour every shred of his being and meld her substance with his . . .

Or was this only the effect she had on all men? Was he nothing exceptional to her, only another male foe to be captured, subverted, enslaved by his own emotions? Lust was too mild a word for the feelings she inspired in him; covetousness might have begun to cover it, obsession to enwrap it, but no word ever made could encompass it, could begin to describe the height and depth of it.

The thought slid by, irrelevant and irreverent, that he might be facing a woman who had great psionic power, but who was unaware of it.

Unaware? No, surely not; surely there had never been a woman who could have been unaware of her effect on men, not a woman like this, no, who could make a very stone to groan with longing.

He forced himself to some rough facsimile of poise. "I had not known you were a woman."

Her lips quirked in the faintest of smiles. "Do you doubt it?"

"Nay, surely not," Geoffrey breathed, and she seemed to swell in his consciousness again, becoming once more larger than life. He thrust her down to normal size in his mind, remembering himself by sheer will alone. "I have heard only the name, and thought a bandit chieftain must be a man."

"Who could better lead men than a woman?" Quicksilver demanded.

Geoffrey felt instant sympathy and total agreement—a woman like this could have led any man anywhere. In fact, she probably had. "You are very aptly come, on the cusp of the moment to rescue your men."

"My sentries are everywhere throughout this county," Quicksilver returned. "As soon as you demanded to see me, word sped to me—and I sped to you, for I fight for my men even as they fight for me."

Geoffrey could understand why men would fight for her—he felt like doing so himself. But he strove for sanity and, to remind himself of the true state of affairs, protested, "You are no lady of rank."

"You are no merchant," Quicksilver retorted.

The overly obvious observation restored Geoffrey to some sense of self-possession. He smiled. "You are perceptive."

"What are you, then?"

"A man."

"Aye, you are," Quicksilver breathed, and for a moment, her eyes seemed to swell, to drink him in; he felt that he had to brace himself against that pull, or be sucked into the maelstrom of her presence.

Then it receded, and she was only mortal again—but Geoffrey could understand how men would follow her blindly, and understand even more clearly how they would be willing to die rather than betray her.

There was a rustle and a clank of metal around her, and for the first time he realized that she was flanked by a bodyguard of a dozen women, perhaps more—but what women! They were tall, nearly six feet every one, and corded with sleek, firm muscles. Each was dressed as Quicksilver was, though with different colors; each had her hair bound out of her way in a loose tail at the back of her head. Most were beautiful, some were not—but all their faces were hard, very hard, as though they yearned for him to raise a hand against their chieftain, so that they might have an excuse to chop him up and feed his bonemeal to the fishes.

But beauty and perfection of form notwithstanding, all paled into insignificance beside their chief.

Which amazed Geoffrey, because he realized that several of them, objectively, were more beautiful than Quicksilver. The thought occurred to him that other men might not find her so irresistible, that perhaps it was only he himself who thought her the most fascinating woman in the universe—but, no; he remembered how completely she seemed to command the loyalty of her bandits; surely they must find her as compelling as he did ...

She was saying something. He yanked his concentration back to her words, then was horrified to realize that, while he had been distracted by her beauty, any man could have stepped up behind him and run him through. Even that thought made him miss her words, though; she was frowning at his silence, and he did not want her to frown ...

"I said, 'Who are you?' " she demanded.

There seemed no good reason to lie. "I am Geoffrey Gallowglass."

A murmur of shock and surprize passed through the bandit host, even the bodyguards, and their eyes narrowed. Quicksilver seemed to stiffen, and her stare was somehow wary; Geoffrey only now realized that it had been confident, almost contemptuous, before.

It was significant that no one said, "The son of the High Warlock" or "The son of the arch-witch Gwendylon!" or even, "So you are of *that* tribe!" Geoffrey had built a reputation of his own, even though he was only twenty—and among warriors like these, that reputation blazed far more brightly than that of his mother or father.

Quicksilver's gaze held steady, boring into his own. "The King and Queen have sent you, have they not?"

"Yes," Geoffrey said, but didn't feel obliged to tell her the rest of the truth.

Quicksilver's gaze didn't waver a millimeter. "Why are you come?"

"To arrest the bandit chieftain Quicksilver," Geoffrey said plainly, "and take her back to Their Majesties for trial."

The bandits went into an uproar, but the bodyguards shouted, "Assassin!" and leaped forward, swords flashing out . . .

Or almost leaped forward; but Quicksilver held up her hand, and they jarred to a halt. Her lips curved in a slight smile, and her eyes glittered. "Do you think you can pluck me out from the midst of my band and live to tell of it?"

"No," Geoffrey returned. "I think that first I shall have to kill them all."

The crowd went into an uproar again. He raised his voice just enough for his words to bore through the commotion: "But if I were to fight them all, I might have to slay you, too—and I would be very loathe to do that."

"Braggart," she breathed, and the whole band quieted to hear her response.

Geoffrey shook his head. "It may seem so, but it is not. I shall not brag—and I never threaten. I will, however, give notice of what I intend to do."

"Not a warning," Quicksilver qualified.

"Nay," Geoffrey agreed. "Only the facts, as I see them."

"I cannot help but think that you see a bit too much of yourself."

"Oh, no," Geoffrey said, his eyes glowing into hers. "Not when all I can see is *you*."

The bodyguards snarled and lifted their swords again, but Quicksilver actually blushed. "My mother taught me to beware of men with sweet words."

"Beware of me indeed," Geoffrey murmured.

The whole band went silent, staring at their chief in amazement—and the bodyguards seemed almost in shock.

Had no one ever tried to woo this woman?

Perhaps not, Geoffrey realized—perhaps none had dared.

"Do you hope to beguile me into surrender, with naught but sweet words?" Quicksilver asked.

"I might hope," Geoffrey answered, "but I would be a fool to think I could."

"And are you a fool?"

"Perhaps for you," he agreed, "but not so great a fool as to let you continue to flout the King's Law."

"Do you threaten me, then?"

"No," Geoffrey said quickly, before the Amazons could start to growl again. "But I tell you frankly, that I will take you back to Runnymede, to await Their Majesties' justice."

The bodyguards howled, flourishing their swords, but again Quicksilver held up her hand. "Withold. He is a warlock."

The Amazons stilled, not because they feared magic, but because Quicksilver had told them to.

Geoffrey nodded. "You are wise. There is no shame in using magic when I am so greatly outnumbered—for I can see through the trees that your band now continues to gather; there must be hundreds—and I would be loathe to hurt women."

"Loathe?" Quicksilver demanded. "But you would do it?"

Geoffrey nodded. "She who takes up weapons forfeits her rights to the protections of chivalry—for a knight must defend his life."

"Yet even so, he must do no more damage to a female than he needs," Quicksilver reminded him.

Geoffrey's eyes gleamed again. "Who are you, to lecture me on the rules of chivalry? Are you nobly born?"

"Only the daughter of a squire," Quicksilver returned, "but thereby did I learn of the Knights' Code."

"Then do you live by it?"

"So far as a woman may."

"Why, that is completely," Geoffrey said, frowning.

Quicksilver finally smiled in amusement. "Yes, that is so—and that is how far I do live by it."

Geoffrey's eyes burned, but his voice sank to a caress. "Yield yourself, I pray—for I would be loathe indeed to hurt you."

"And if I do not," Quicksilver said, equally softly, "you will shatter my army with witch-power."

"I shall," Geoffrey confirmed.

"Why, then, the fight must be between the two of us, and we two alone." At last, Quicksilver reached up to draw the broadsword that was slung across her back, and stepped forward from among her women. They cried out in alarm and leaped forward to stop her—but she waved them away. "I shall fight without my band, if you swear to fight without your magic."

"Why, that is honorable indeed!" Geoffrey said, the glow in his eyes spreading across his face. "I swear I shall work no magic, if you forbid your troops to fight!"

"I forbid you all to fight in my defense!" Quicksilver called out. "This is my fight, mine alone, for this man is my meat!"

Eighteen of her bodyguards cried out in protest—but the other two stood silent, staring at their chief in understanding. Slowly and reluctantly, they sheathed their swords and waved their sisters back.

Quicksilver stepped forward, sword on guard, a lioness stalking her quarry, a panther readying herself to spring.

Geoffrey lifted his own sword and stepped forward, ignoring the weakness in his knees.

CHAPTER
~3~

Reluctantly, the outlaws drew back, the bodyguards most reluctantly of all, leaving a bare circle of ground fifty feet across with Geoffrey standing near its center. Quicksilver stepped out in a fighter's crouch, sword in both hands, and began to prowl about him. Geoffrey caught his breath; she was a magnificent figure, red gold in the sunlight, her movements fluid and sinuous. Geoffrey watched her as a good warrior should, trying to watch her whole body but still notice every slightest movement—and notice them he did, for something within him thrilled to each tiniest quiver. He had heard it said that it was the female's movement that caught the male's eye, and if that was so, this was certainly the most intensely feminine being he had ever seen.

But she was a feminine being with a sword, and its edge was whetted and glittering.

Finally, Geoffrey realized that she had no intention of

striking the first blow—she would wait for him to do so, and try to take advantage of any opening he might reveal. Well, that was fine with him—he was more than glad to wait, too, and watch her move.

It must have shown in his face, for she flushed, then suddenly struck in a blinding blur of swordcuts, hammering and pounding at him from every angle with unbelievable speed. He retreated a couple of steps, stunned by her skill, struck by the beauty and precision of her attack. He parried every cut, of course, but had no time to riposte until she leaped back, eyes smouldering, sword at the ready, breast heaving with the exertion. He stared, and knew, with a sinking heart, that he could not possibly risk hurting this gorgeous creature.

Then she was on him again, so quickly that he scarcely saw her advance, only knew that her blows were raining about him again, so that he seemed to be inside a smithy, inside the anvil itself, with a hail of blows clanging about him. This time she did not leap back, but stayed and kept slashing and cutting. The technique worked; he parried every cut, but some by a very narrow margin, and when she finally leaped back with a cry of satisfaction, he knew she had struck first blood.

She was easily the most skilled opponent he had ever met with a sword. He had fought stronger, but what she lacked in strength, she made up for in speed and deftness—and precision. "You are excellent," he breathed.

She must have known how he meant it, that he meant it in every way, for she blushed and snapped, "Come, sir, where is your skill? Where is the vaunted swordsmanship of Geoffrey Gallowglass? Can you not match me blow for blow?"

He felt the taunt stab home, but he knew the game, which was to make him attack in anger, losing his own precision. He grinned instead and said, "Your sword may be sharp, but I have not yet felt its edge."

"Be assured that it has felt your flesh," she snarled, then suddenly leaped forward again.

But Geoffrey was ready this time—when she landed, he wasn't there, but had skipped nimbly to the side. She whirled even as she landed and parried his cut with an oath, then thrust without riposting—a risky move, but effective, if he had been there. But he flinched away, sword-tip flicking out to test his own reach against hers—and sure enough, her blade was inches away from his waist, but his tip nicked her shoulder.

He knew he could not bring himself to strike lower.

A shout went up, rage at seeing their chief's blood, and Geoffrey was suddenly alert for the blow from behind—but it did not come, for Quicksilver, in a rage, leaped in to shower blows upon him. Geoffrey blocked and parried, waiting her out, sure that she was nicking him in a dozen places, giving ground slowly.

Then a cut swung under his guard and thrust straight for his heart in a full lunge.

Geoffrey barely managed to slip aside in time, and felt the sword score his ribs instead of severing his aorta—and a chill seized his vitals, for he knew without a shadow of doubt that she had meant that thrust to strike home, to slay him completely. She might be attracted to him, every ounce of femininity in her might be aching for him, but she would nonetheless kill him if she could, skewer him like a trout, slay him without regret. Well, not perhaps without regret—but she would slay him nonetheless. He wondered if she treated all her suitors this way—then felt the realization strike him, with the force of a body blow, that he was indeed a suitor!

He leaped back out of her reach, to recover from the

shock of the discovery—but she mistook the move for weakness and pressed in with a shout of triumph. It was a mistake; he parried the thrust automatically, then with equally unthinking skill counterthrust without riposting, scoring a trickle of blood across her upper arm. The scarlet thread was almost a physical pain to him, too, but habit as well as the chance of death made him keep on, thrusting here, there, high, low—but never too close to the center, never too close to her torso, always at her arms or shoulders or, Heaven help him, her thighs. She howled with anger, blocking and parrying, matching him blow for blow but too quickly to be able to riposte or attack. She gave ground, face pale with fury, then suddenly caught his sword in a bind, thrusting it up just long enough to slam a kick into his stomach.

Geoffrey saw it coming and rolled with the blow, but it still drove the breath out of him, and he fell, rolling along the ground. He heard her shout of triumph ringing in his ears, saw her boots pound close, and rolled aside just as she stabbed down, then rocked back a split second before she stabbed again. His lungs clamored for air as his belly strove to pull, to inhale—and finally the first breath came, finally oxygen flooded in again, and he surged up to his feet, inside her guard, sword arrowing straight for her throat—but the tip veered aside to nick her shoulder instead. She cried out in alarm and leaped back; the delay had been just long enough for that, but not long enough to recover. Geoffrey pressed the attack, raining cuts and thrusts at her from all sides, keeping her sword too busy parrying to be able to stab at him, for he realized with a sick certainty that the only way he could win was to disarm her; he could not bear to do anything else—but she could, and would.

He did not intend to let her.

Her sword was slowing just the tiniest bit, but his was not—yet, though it soon would. His blows were coming closer to her body now; the sphere of safety about her was shrinking. Geoffrey saw, and rejoiced—if he could slow her enough, he could catch her sword in a bind. She knew it, too—or knew that she would be at his mercy, for she was tiring faster than he, and she glared her hatred at him.

Then, suddenly, she leaped back to give herself a second's breathing space. Her left hand shot up to the nape of her neck and loosed a knot—and her halter fell away, revealing her naked breasts, full and golden in the morning sunlight.

Geoffrey stared, frozen for an instant of sheer admiration—and in that instant, Quicksilver struck.

Here was no testing rain of cuts—here was only a single, clean, full-body lunge; her whole form seemed to straighten into a single line of steel that culminated in a point to lance straight through his heart.

The streak of silver snapped Geoffrey out of his daze; he stepped aside and parried, then leaped in close, wrist circling to catch her blade in a bind—but she leaped in, too, *corps à corps*, body to body, each long quivering muscle of hers against his, thigh to thigh, arm to arm, breast to chest . . .

For a moment, he froze; but she had outsmarted herself, for she froze, too, and their gazes locked. For an instant, it seemed to him that he could see all the way to the depths of her soul, so clear and pure it was, and he could not take his gaze away . . .

Then her lips writhed in a snarl, and that clearness filled with fire.

She leaped back, sword cutting and thrusting—but he parried and waited, for the thrusts were slower and slower now, though he must keep his eyes resolutely on her face, his gaze on hers, taking in the sword but never looking squarely at it, for her torso would be behind it . . .

Then she thrust, but just a little too slowly now, and he caught her blade in a circle again, a double circle twisting hard against her thumb, and the sword snapped free from tired fingers to go spinning through the air. Her whole band shouted, but even now he did not trust himself to look down to her heart, only touched his sword to her throat, rested the tip against the delicious hollow at its base that he longed to kiss and taste, but held himself back, panting, and said, quite clearly (which amazed him), "Yield!"

She stood frozen, her chest heaving as she panted, glaring murder into his eyes, but not daring to move.

"Yield yourself unto me," he said more gently.

"I must, must I not?" she said, with full bitterness.

"No!" cried the chief of her bodyguard, and the Amazons shouted as they leaped, their swords out. Her whole army pressed forward with one mighty shout.

"No!" she cried, but not quite quickly enough; the earth erupted in a ring all about them, blowing up in a cloud of dirt that flung outward with a huge booming, and the outlaws cried out in fear and alarm, crowding backwards just long enough for Quicksilver to shout again, "No! I gave my word!" Then, never taking her eyes from Geoffrey's, "If you strike, he is freed to use his witch-power—as he has done even now; but where only dirt flew up here, he could bring flame! Could you not, sir?"

"I could," Geoffrey called loudly and clearly, but wondered how she knew. Had she fought a warlock before? Was that the source of her bitterness?

"Then rain fire!" the leader of her bodyguard shouted. "We will die before we leave her to you!"

The whole army roared agreement and pressed in.

There was only a moment to begin slaughter, or find a way out—and Geoffrey stepped right up against Quicksilver, caught her body up against his and bent all his attention on a little glade by a river that he had studied, a dozen miles away. The double crack of imploding and exploding air battered their eardrums, and his concentration slipped; he could only hold it for a split second, with that wondrous body pressed against his, especially as it began to writhe; but Quicksilver raged, "Let me go! Oh, let me *go!*" and wrenched herself free, leaping back.

Automatically, Geoffrey brought his sword back up to her throat.

She ignored the threat, only glared into his eyes. "What have you done with my band?"

With peripheral vision, Geoffrey registered the presence of the glade he had pictured, of the absence of battle cries and rattle of steel, of a silence broken only by the purling of a brook and the calls of songbirds. "They are where they were. It is we who have gone, not they."

Her voice shook. "What warlock's trick is this?"

"Only teleportation," he told her, "only moving myself, and whatsoever I clung to. It was the only way to arrest you as I said I would, but without hurting your people, as I said I would not."

"So you have kept your word," she said bitterly, "and I am your captive. Have your way with me, then, since I cannot prevent you—but never dare turn your back on me, or I shall slay you!"

"Nay," Geoffrey replied. "I have never forced a woman, and shall not do so now. Yet I wish you were not an outlaw and a murderer, for I would rather woo you than arrest you."

"I am what I am," Quicksilver snapped, "and what men have made me."

"Yet it was not I who made you so." Geoffrey lowered his point, frowning, still exercising every jot of willpower to keep his gaze on her eyes. "It was not I who gave you cause for grief. Why then do you hate me so?"

"Because you fight for *them*, you fight to enforce the law that upholds them, though it allows them to commit sins that would be high crimes, were a peasant to seek to behave so to a lord's daughter! Yet I am only a daughter of a squire, so the law you claim to enforce will not protect me! Aye, and I do not doubt that you would have done as they did, if you'd had the chance!"

"I would not." Geoffrey's voice lowered. "And certainly never against you."

Quicksilver's lip curled. "Oh assuredly, you would not! And how can you prove that, sir?"

"Why," said Geoffrey simply, "because I have the chance now, but will not do it."

For a moment, there was stark fear in Quicksilver's eyes, and she flinched away a step—but Geoffrey made no move to follow, only kept his eyes on her face and said softly, "Do me this courtesy, at least—make it less trying for me to keep my resolve. Bind up your halter again; cover yourself, so that my blood may rage less fiercely through me, and my own loins may not rage at me for a fool."

For a moment, she stared at him in surprise. Then a smile spread slowly, and she said, "Nay, I think not—since it causes you pain."

"Why, as you will," Geoffrey groaned. Then a thought struck him. He dropped his gaze, letting himself drink in fully the sight of her naked breasts, letting the feelings inspired thrill through him, like the sweetest of wines in his blood, and breathed, "Though truth to tell, it gives me great delight, too."

Quicksilver stared, taken aback, then blushed furiously and caught up her halter to tie it behind her neck again in quick, angry movements.

"I thank you," Geoffrey sighed in relief, "I think . . ."

"Treasure the memory, sir, for you'll not see them again!" Quicksilver snapped.

"You shall haunt my dreams, I assure you," Geoffrey groaned. "Take pity, cruel wanton . . ."

"I am no wanton, but a swordswoman!"

"Then you are one who does not mind behaving at least a little like a wanton," Geoffrey clarified. "Nay, take pity—distract me from thoughts of desire. Tell me what score this is that you hold against men—though I gather 'tis noble men, not common, whom you hate."

"For the common I have contempt," Quicksilver said, frowning, "or at least, for their weakness and crudeness. For the noble, I have hatred for the ways in which they sought to exploit me—but for their weakness, too; there's not a man I have met who can stand against me."

Geoffrey looked up sharply, then held his gaze steady on hers. She did not waver a trace, but after a minute admitted, "Till now."

"I thank you for the courtesy." Geoffrey inclined his head, then sat down beside the brook—though warily, since she might take the chance to flee or attack. "Come, sit down beside me, and tell me the manner of it—for I am sworn to uphold the Queen's Law, and if any have broken that law in wronging you, I shall bring them to justice, too."

"Oh, I am sure they did not," she said sourly, but sat beside him anyway—sat gingerly and lightly, as though ready to flee in an instant, and well beyond his reach; but she sat nonetheless. "I am sure they did not, for it is truly the King's Law you uphold, not the Queen's."

"Only Catharine is monarch by right of birth," Geoffrey told her. "Tuan's claim is by marriage to her. It is she who makes the laws; he does only as she asks, which is to enforce her precepts, and keep her barons in order."

Quicksilver frowned. "I have heard no word of this."

"It is not noised abroad," Geoffrey told her, "but those who do know the Court have thought through that much for themselves."

"Nevertheless," Quicksilver said, "the Queen's Law was made by kings—her father and her grandfather and ancestors. Has she transformed all its provisions that allow women to be used and tossed aside?"

"All she has encountered," Geoffrey qualified.

"Which means there is one law for noble women, and another for their commoner sisters!" Quicksilver held up a hand to forestall his answer. "Nay, sir, hear what I have learned from living—then tell me if you can deny it."

"If I can, I will prove it on their bodies," Geoffrey said, frowning, "they who have hurt you. If I cannot, I will petition the Queen."

"But if you believe me, yet find that what they did to me was legal, you will nevertheless not seek revenge for me."

Geoffrey gazed at her a long moment, then said, "I have not that right—for you are not my sister, nor my wife, nor my fiancée."

"And you have no wish for me to be," she said with a sardonic smile.

Geoffrey just sat there gazing at her while the tumult of emotions swirled within him, and she gradually lost her smile.

Then, finally, he said, "Not upon such short acquaintance—and you must admit, our first interchange has scarcely been friendly. Nay, tell me your tale, that I may ponder the case."

She looked at him as though it were on the tip of her tongue to demand which case he meant, but she thought better of it, and composed herself to tell him the story. "I am called 'Quicksilver' now, but I was born plain Jane, of the village of Dungreigh. My father was a squire."

"A squire?" Geoffrey looked up. "But never a knight?"

"No," she said sharply, "but there was no shame for him thereby, for he was not nobly born, nor even the son of a knight, but only a serf who followed the plow."

Geoffrey nodded. "He was a serf pressed into service by his lord."

"Aye, service for a knight bachelor, the son of Sir Grayling, who held the village of Dungreigh and the farms about it as his fief. Sir Dunmore, his son, was newly knighted, and had need of a squire."

"But was himself too young, too poor, and too green to sponsor a young knight's son as his squire," Geoffrey interpreted.

"I see you know the ways of chivalry well. Thus it was, and therefore Sir Grayling bade my father Perkin to follow after Sir Dunmore—though he was not my father then, of course . . ."

"Of course," Geoffrey agreed. "If he'd had a wife and bairns, his lord would never have thought to send him travelling so. Tell me, was he wed?"

"Nay, though he and my mother already regarded one another with fond and admiring eyes, or so they told me. Being young and without bonds, Perkin was glad to ride with Sir Dunmore, to buckle him into his armor, then polish it after the fight, and to bear his sword and shield."

Geoffrey smiled. "He went willingly, then?"

"Aye, even eagerly, for what young man does not dream

of seeing something of the world beyond his own village? Or what young woman either, for that matter, though we are not like to have the chance," Quicksilver said bitterly.

"Be fair," Geoffrey urged. "Few young men have the chance, either."

"There's some truth in that, at least for a serf," Quicksilver admitted, "and my father Perkin was very glad of it. He followed Sir Dunmore from one tournament to another for five years, while Sir Dunmore accumulated honor, glory, and some wealth."

"He was an able fighter, then," Geoffrey noted. Tournament knights made money by ransoming the arms and armor of the knights they defeated.

"Aye, though he had need for my father to pull him out from the press of bodies in the melee more than once," Quicksilver said, with a touch of pride, "so Father gained some little wealth too, in reward. Still, both longed for a real war."

"With real glory," Geoffrey murmured, "and real loot."

"Even so. It was the Barons' War against Queen Catharine, which your father won for her . . ."

"Well, not he alone," Geoffrey hedged, though he had to admit his father had been surprizingly adroit in welding together an alliance of the oddest sorts of soldiers to stand up to the barons. Really, he was quite surprised at the old fellow. He had made a careful study of that battle, from the reports of those who had been there, and knew just how well his father had done—but was also sure that though he might know, his father didn't. "But Sir Dunmore was the son of a southern lord, and the vassal of Count Laeg, who was himself vassal to Lord Loguire—or to the son who usurped his rank, I should say: Anselm, who did raise the rebellion against the Crown. How did Sir Dunmore come to fight for the Queen?"

"Because Sir Grayling his father was prudent," Quicksilver explained, "and sent his son to fight for the Crown, so that no matter who should win, the family would not lose."

Geoffrey nodded—it was a common enough stratagem, though it cost father and son dearly in anxiety and, frequently, grief and guilt. "Your father went with Sir Dunmore, of course."

"Aye, and from that came five years in the Queen's service. Then Sir Grayling died, and Sir Dunmore and Father came back to Dungreigh, to marry and become landholders—for Sir Dunmore inherited his father's estate, and thereby had means enough to bring another knight's son to his court as his squire. My father thereby retired from the field and found he was no longer a serf, but a man of means—for he had prudently saved what Sir Dunmore paid him, and some prize money of his own, from enemies he had captured in the field. He bought several farms from Sir Dunmore . . ."

"Bought! Do you not mean that he held them enfeoffed?"

"Nay, for he is a squire, not a knight. But you have the gist of it," she said bitterly. "If he died without heir, his lands reverted to Sir Dunmore, or *his* heir."

Geoffrey wondered at the bitterness, but was sure he would learn the reason for it. "Surely there was money enough for a wedding also."

"Aye; he wed the prettiest lass in the village—or so he assured me, though my mother denies it . . ." For a moment, her face lapsed into a fond smile that was tinged with longing, but stern discipline quickly erased it. "He built a large house, for her to fill with children. I was the middle child of five, and the older of the two girls—but there were two brothers elder and one younger, so I learned early that a girl must stand up for herself, or be pushed aside."

"And you were not of a temperament to be pushed aside."

Quicksilver smiled with relish. "No, I was not."

"Surely you did not learn swordplay from chastising your brothers!"

"No, but they did afford me great practice at fighting with my bare hands."

Geoffrey remembered his own childhood. "Thus it is with brothers and sisters, when they are small."

"True," Quicksilver said, "but my father saw, and determined that I should never be at their mercy. He gave lessons in swordplay to all his children, not the boys alone. He also taught us to fight with wooden knives, and quarterstaves, and taught us archery."

"Your mother must not have been pleased with such unladylike pursuits."

"She was not. She retaliated by teaching us all to clean and cook, reminding us that we were, after all, of peasant stock, and that his sons might yet be glad of a few skills that would make them more valuable to their lord, as stewards if as nothing else."

"Or as squires," Geoffrey said softly.

Quicksilver nodded, gazing off into the past. "So he noted; so he told them when my brothers complained of having to do 'women's work.' Father told them of his labors for Sir Dunmore, told them so often that they ceased fussing to avoid his lectures."

Geoffrey grinned, feeling a bond with boys he had never met. "It does not sound like a noisome childhood."

"Oh, it was not," Quicksilver said softly. "Noisy, perhaps, but never noisome. We quarrelled and we played, we fought and we rejoiced—but there was never true bitterness or enmity. However, every childhood must end."

Hers had ended when her body underwent the magical transformation into womanhood. She blossomed into amazing beauty, and the village boys took notice. "I loved the life I lived," she told Geoffrey, "though your fine court ladies might sneer at it as provincial and boring—but I could think of no higher purpose than to become a wife and mother, like all the grown women I knew; I could think of no greater vocation than that, for it is the making of people and the rearing and training of their minds and souls, and surely there can be no life that serves a higher purpose."

"No, indeed," Geoffrey said, awed, "when you think of it in those terms. Yet you seem to have been called to a vastly different role, damsel. Why did you not marry?"

"Why, because I was revolted at the thought of climbing into bed with any of the boys I knew!" she told him.

The boys, of course, had not been revolted at the thought of climbing into *her* bed—and they set about trying to achieve just that.

CHAPTER
~4~

"Come, sweeting!" one callow swain breathed, clasping her sharply to him one moonlit night. "You are not so far above me in birth that you should look down your nose at me—and am I not a fine figure of a man?"

"If you can call an 'eight' a fine figure!" Angrily, Jane tried to push him away. "You are far too round above, Lumpkin, and rounder below!"

True, but he had too much bulk to be easily pushed away, and he laughed, almost nauseating her with bad breath. "Come, I know you jest! We are alone, here in this moonlit wood, and who is to know if we share a kiss?"

"Share your own kisses, then!" Jane hooked a foot around Lumpkin's ankle and shoved hard as she kicked back. Over her would-be lover went with a squall, and Jane was away, fleeing down the moonlit path. By the time he had climbed to his feet and come lumbering after, she was gone from sight.

She never told her brothers, though—she knew what they would do to the uncouth youth, and did not wish to see any of them tried for murder. After all, accidents could happen. Besides, Jane was quite sure she could handle any one such lumpen suitor by herself.

But she had not bargained for three of them to catch her alone, nor in her own father's wood!

Her first hint of their presence was the stifled chuckle from the thicket. Instantly, she was on her guard; still, she was somewhat surprized when a hulking plowboy stepped out from the underbrush in front of her, grinning and asking, "Well, now! And what is such a pretty morsel doing alone in the woods at night, eh?"

"Coming from tending Granny Hacken, who is sick abed!" Jane snapped. "Step aside, Rogash, or this 'pretty morsel' will stick in your craw!"

"Oh, I think not," Rogash said easily, "not when there are three of us to take you in small nibbles. Shall we taste, lads?"

"Aye, we shall see if she is as hot a dish as she seems," Lumpkin chuckled from behind her, and "Not hot, for she is a sweeting," said the nasal voice of a third village boy whom Jane recognized as Barlein.

"Would you seek to harm a virgin, then?" Jane managed to keep her voice steady, masking the anger that covered the fear.

"Virgin!" Rogash sneered. "Nay, what virgin would be abroad in the wood by night, and alone?"

"A virgin who has mercy on a poor old woman, and stays to see her asleep before she leaves to go to her home! But even if I were only a virgin who likes to follow the song of the nightingale, you would still be most wrong to accost me!"

" 'Accost,' forsooth! What a grand word, for a lass who

is only the daughter of a squire who was born a peasant!" Rogash nodded to Lumpkin and Barlein. "Let us 'accost' her well then, lads."

"Hold, fools!" Jane snapped. "I have three stalwart brothers, who will flay the hides from your backs if you dare to touch me!"

"Not when they learn you were not a virgin," Lumpkin said, gloating, and Rogash added, "For no virgin comes by night to the woods where men might lurk."

Jane knew her brothers would never believe such a charge; she knew they would very probably kill these three clods; but she also knew that would be far too late for her. There was, however, a strong chance that her brothers and father were already abroad searching for her, so she screamed as the three youths closed in. Jane screamed again as she stepped inside Rogash's reaching hand to slam a small fist into his gut with all her strength, screamed once more as he folded over his pain and she whirled away from him to lash a kick into Barlein's stomach. She missed; the kick went low, and Barlein crumpled with a gargling scream. Somehow, though, Jane felt no guilt about it.

But Lumpkin's fist slammed into her cheek as he snarled, "Vixen!" Pain seared through the side of her face, stabs of light obscured him from her, and she leaped back but not fast enough; his rough hand closed over her arm, yanking her off her feet. The ground rushed up to slam against her, but training came to her rescue—she tucked her chin in as she fell so that her head did not strike the ground. In fact, she managed to fall on her side, reached out to grasp the leg in front of her behind the knee, and pulled as hard as she could. She must have hit something she didn't know about, for Lumpkin screamed, a high and whinnying cry, as he toppled. Still dazed, she managed to push herself to her feet, her head clearing enough to see Rogash just beginning to get his breath back, glaring murder at her as he straightened—as much as he could.

Jane leaped back into the underbrush, then twisted aside, and Rogash blundered past her, bellowing, "Come back here, vixen!" Moving with the silence of one born to the greenwood, Jane searched among last year's fallen leaves until she found a broken branch, three feet long and still sound.

Rogash came blundering back, calling, "Where are you, trull? Come out and get what you deserve!"

Jane stepped out in front of him and swung the branch two-handed.

Rogash howled with pain, falling back with a crash— but Jane heard a retching gasp behind her and turned to see Barlein coming toward her, still hunched over his pain, but with a dagger in his hand and blood in his eye.

Jane swung her improvised club in a feint. Barlein reached up to catch it, lunging with his knife . . .

But the branch wasn't there to catch; it circled around to smash against his knife hand. He screamed again, dropping the knife, then went silent as the branch cracked against his head.

Suddenly, the wood was awfully still.

Fear of another sort seized Jane, for she had never killed any man, and had no wish to begin. She glanced at Rogash, but he began to groan, clasping his head, and Barlein at her feet was breathing, at least. She stepped back into the roadway, club ready—but Lumpkin was scrabbling in the dust, trying to regain his feet. All guilt vanished, and Jane raised her club . . .

Feet pounded through the underbrush, many feet, and Jane leaped back with a scream that was as much anger as fear, her club swinging high, ready to strike . . .

"Nay, sister, I pray thee," Leander said, startled.

Jory and Martin stepped up to either side of him.

Jane just stared at them, still holding her club as she gave a sobbing gasp. Then she dropped it and leaped into her eldest brother's embrace, throwing her arms about his chest in a hug like that of Death.

"Nay, sister, 'tis well, 'tis well,' he soothed. "You are safe now—we will not let any harm you."

"She seems to have little enough need of us," Jory told him, and there was definite pride in his voice.

"No need! See how she trembles, brother! Nay, sister, what did these cattle seek to do to you?"

"What do you think, Leander?" Martin snapped. "Brave fellows, to come at a poor weak lass three together!"

"Fool that I was, to ever let you go alone in the woods!" Leander groaned.

"You did well, sister," Martin said with admiration.

"Well, but not enough." Leander disengaged himself from Jane. "Come, brothers. Let us finish what she has begun."

"No!" Jane cried in panic. "I would not have you hang!"

"Peace, sister." Now it was Jory's arm around her. "We shall not be hung—but neither shall they."

"No, no!" Jane cried. "Nothing that will not heal!"

"You are too kindhearted, sister," Martin sighed, "but we shall honor your wish." He dropped to one knee to yank Lumpkin's head up by the hair. "Did you hear that, bag of offal? It is only by our sister's mercy that you shall not lose more than your life."

"Nor even that!" Jane cried.

"Well, as you wish, sister," Jory sighed, dragging Barlein back into the trail and throwing him down on the ground. "Up, swine! For I shall give you one chance of fair fight, though 'tis more than you gave my sister."

But Barlein knew better than to risk it; he scrambled to his feet, trying to spring past Jory.

Jory kicked his feet out from under him. "You do not wish the chance, then? Sister, turn your head!"

"Aye, Martin, take her home," Leander snapped. "The two of us are more than a match for what is left of the three of them. Do not beseech greater mercy, sister, for they deserve none."

"True enough." Martin turned her away with a consoling arm about her shoulders. "Come, sister, home to safety. You do not wish to see what follows."

He was right—she didn't. She was sure of that the next week, when she happened to see Lumpkin going out to the field to work. The bruises had faded, but he was still limping.

She had no trouble with the village boys after that— but apparently, word of her spread to the manor house, for it was Sir Hempen who stopped her next—Sir Hempen, the son of Sir Dunmore, the knight whom her father served.

Sir Hempen leaned down from his saddle to catch her wrist, saying, "Hail, pretty maid!"

Jane's heart quailed within, for knight's son or not, the glint in his eye was the same she had seen in the eye of the peasant Lumpkin. "Say, pretty maid, have you seen a fox?"

"Several times in my life, sir." Jane gripped her staff more tightly— she never went without one, now.

"Aye, but have you seen one *today*? I am hunting vixen."

"I have not seen one, sir, not this week past."

"None?" Sir Hempen feigned surprize. "Not even when you have looked into the waters of a still pond?"

Jane stared at him, startled, then twisted her wrist out of his grasp in anger. "Nay, sir, but I have seen an ass, not two minutes past!"

His hand cracked across her cheek, and she fell back, biting down on a cry of pain, pressing her left hand to her cheek, then glaring up at him—but the young knight lolled back in his saddle, face easing into a wolfish grin. "Why, then, if you have seen an ass, so shall I! Come, wanton, will you be bought? Or will you be forced?"

"I am no wanton, sir," she retorted angrily, "not for any man's buying or beckoning!"

"That is not what I hear from the village boys. Nay, think, pretty lass—there shall be gold for you, and for your child."

A sudden certainty crystallized within her, and she did not know where it came from, for it must have been building a while. "I shall never bear any child, sir, not yours nor any man's!"

But he misunderstood her completely. "Barren? So much the better, then!"

"Nay, sir, I am a virgin!"

"Then how could you know you were barren?" He reached down again. "Come, I am not your first, nor shall I be your last!"

She stared at the reaching hand for a horrified instant, realizing that Lumpkin and his friends had certainly had their revenge. Anger glared into rage, anger at them and this presumptuous young knight. She snatched the groping hand and spun about, yanking hard. She heard Sir Hempen's cry of surprize and fear, then saw him fly past her to slam full-length into the ground. His horse neighed and backed, alarmed—and Jane felt satisfaction glowing within her.

Then Sir Hempen heaved himself up, glaring murder at

her, and with a sick sense of certainty, she saw in her mind's eye a gallows, with the bodies of her three brothers swaying in the wind—for to revenge your sister on a peasant was one thing, but to take that same revenge on a knight's son was quite another. The certainty grew and the sickness faded as she lifted her quarterstaff in both hands, with grim conviction—for though Sir Hempen might have charged her brothers with assault, she knew he never would complain of a beating from a girl, for the very shame of it.

If she could—for a peasant was one thing, but a knight trained in fighting was another.

"You shall regret that, my lass," Sir Hempen grated, "regret it now, and in my bed!"

"I shall never come to your bed, sir," she retorted. "They who did hint that I might, did slander me most sorely."

"Most sore shall you be," he retorted, "but I doubt that you were slandered." He gathered himself and charged, reaching.

She spun aside and swung her staff.

It caught him on the back of the head with a hollow knock, and he went sprawling.

Jane stepped back and waited. A single blow and a quick flight would not serve this time, she knew, for word might still reach her brothers, and fools of honor that they were, they would seek Sir Hempen out. Worse, he would pursue her still, if not today, then another time, until they were bound to come against him. The only chance was to stand and fight, and best him at his own game.

Sir Hempen came slowly to his feet, his eyes chips of ice. "What sort of a virgin swings a staff like a soldier?"

"A virgin who is determined to remain so," she countered.

He snarled and came for her again, drawing his sword.

Fear stabbed her at the thought that the sword might, but she stood her ground, circling around him, ready. He began to smile, enjoying her apprehension, then suddenly advanced, slashing.

She parried with the left end of the staff, then the right, then the left again. He lost his smile and swung his sword high—but she stepped in and swung the staff up to knock the blade aside.

He caught the staff with his left hand, though, and held it high as he turned the sword and, using the hilt as a knuckle guard, drove his fist into her stomach.

She fell back, unable even to cry out, and he wrested the staff from her as she fell, then pounced upon her—but even with the breath driven out of her, she had presence of mind enough to roll, and roll again and keep rolling. He had to scramble back to his feet, and it cost him just enough time for her to roll into the underbrush where she could catch herself to a sapling and use it to haul herself back to her feet, sucking in one tearing breath, then another—much more quickly than he would expect, for her whole body was in far better shape than that of any of the village boys she knew, from her daily sword drills.

Cursing, Sir Hempen blundered into the thicket after her.

Jane backed away from him, pulling the sapling with her, hand over hand until she was holding it near the top, its trunk bent into a steep curve. Sir Hempen was too enraged to notice; he only came for her, hands outstretched, lips writhing back in a snarl.

Jane let go of the sapling.

It slammed full into Sir Hempen's face. He staggered back with a squall, groping for something to hold him up, missed, and fell, rolling on the ground, his hands pressed to his face, groaning.

Jane leaped past him, watching him as carefully as though he were a snake, stepping back to the roadway, where she caught up his fallen sword. There she stood and waited.

It was only a few minutes before he came staggering out of the brush, saw her, and jolted to a halt, startled. Then his eyes narrowed. "Put it down, slut. You will hurt yourself."

"Not myself, Sir Cur," she retorted.

His head snapped up at the insult. Then he snarled again and came for her.

She stepped back, whipping the sword through a quick series of slashes and circles. He should have taken warning, but he didn't; he kept on coming, and she stepped nimbly aside as she swung the blade.

It sliced open his doublet, tracing a thin line of red across his chest.

Jane felt her stomach sink; she had cut deeper than she had intended.

But it must have been only his skin that she had cut, for he looked up at her again, his face stone, and took another step.

She swept the blade down and around.

Even Sir Hempen had sense enough to jolt to a halt with a sword's point aimed right at his belly.

"You shall regret this, wanton!" he grated.

"No wanton, but a maid!" she flashed. "And I intend to remain so! Now get you out from this wood, Sir Knight, while you can still walk!"

His eyes narrowed. "You would not dare to harm a belted knight!"

For a moment, her heart quailed within her, for she suddenly realized what would happen if she did—prison at the least, hanging at the worst. But hard on the heels of dismay followed inspiration, and she retorted, "I would dare to tell your father what you sought to do, to his old squire's virgin daughter—and be sure the wives can seek and verify that I am indeed virgin!"

"At twenty?" he scoffed. "Twenty, and unmarried? How could the daughter of a peasant still be a virgin?"

"The daughter of a *squire*! No matter his birth! And as to the how of it, 'tis simply that all the village boys are such clodpolls that I can feel only contempt for their callow uncouthness! Aye, and for their weakness and clumsiness, for there's not a one of them can stand up to me—no more than can you, knight or not! Nay, none have the quality to win my love, and none have been strong enough to force what I have no desire to give, when none give me desire! Be sure I am truly virgin, and that your mother and mine shall both ascertain it, if they must!"

Sir Hempen kept his glare, but the first trace of doubt began to show. "Give me back my sword."

"Ride away," she told him. "When you are out of sight, I shall leave it leaning 'gainst an oak at the edge of the wood, so that you may come back and find it—but you shall not find me."

"Nay, for some poacher might chance upon it and steal it ere I come! How should a knight explain that he has lost his sword?"

"How shall you explain that loss if I keep it?" she countered, and waited just long enough for the flush of his embarrassment to redden his face. "You may come back for the sword, sir, or you may ride off without it—but I shall not give it back to you while you are near me, save between your ribs!"

Sir Hempen brayed harsh laughter. "Between my ribs? Why, foolish maid, how would you explain my death?"

Again, dismay—and again, inspiration. "I would not," she said simply. "Who would think an unarmed maid could have slain you—*if* they found your body?"

Sir Hempen reddened again, but this time, he said only, "The huge old oak that stands by the carters' path, where it enters the wood."

"When you are out of sight," Jane said, by way of agreement.

Sir Hempen favored her with one last glare as he turned on his heel and strode away to catch his horse.

Jane watched him go. As soon as he had disappeared among the leaves, she disappeared into the underbrush at the side of the path. *Then* she let her knees buckle, let the sobs come.

He found his sword—she watched from hiding as he took it up—and rode away. She was sure he was determined to have revenge, but she was equally determined that he should never have the chance. She never went alone by night again, but always asked one of her brothers to escort her. They, at least, were as skilled with weapons as she.

It was a pity they were her brothers.

But there were other ways of having revenge. Other young knights came riding, to flirt with her—only their flirtations were crude and demanding. She sent them away with sharp words, but when the third came by, she realized that since Sir Hempen had not been able to ruin her, he had ruined her reputation. She would have to put an end to that, she knew—and as always, she was determined not to put her brothers in trouble.

So when the next young knight came by, she batted her eyelashes, laughed low in her throat, and told him to meet her by the great oak that stood by the carters' path, where it entered the wood. When he came, she gave him the same instruction in the strengths of the quarterstaff that she had given Sir Hempen, and bade him come back to the oak for his sword.

It occurred to her that she should start a collection—but she understood, in some fashion, that swords were so important to knights that if she kept them, they would *have* to seek revenge on her, to the point of trial for witchcraft, or some such. She had to leave them something, or they would leave her nothing.

But she came home to find her mother and sister in tears, and her brothers looking glum instead of grim, and learned how little they really had.

They followed their father's coffin to the churchyard, then took their mother home. In the days that followed, they labored their way through grief together, trying to understand why God had taken their father away—though at sixty, he was certainly an old man. Nonetheless, his loss struck deep, and Jane was shocked to realize how much he had been the rock on which they all stood.

She realized it all over again at the end of the month, when Sir Dunmore ordered all three of her brothers to join his entourage as he went to make a show of force along Count Laeg's border with his neighbor, whose soldiers had been committing a series of petty thefts.

"All three?" Mother stared, taken aback. "Can he not leave me even one of my sons to care for me?"

"Count Laeg has ordered Sir Dunmore to take all three," the squire told her. "His reasons are not for us to question."

"No, surely not," Mother agreed, her gaze straying.

But Jane realized why Count Laeg had given the order, and felt her heart sink within her. She tried to tell herself that she was being silly, that she was seeing evil intent where there was none, but she found she couldn't believe that. She knew Count Laeg had seen her on one of his recent visits to their village, and apparently taken notice of her, as he noticed every pretty young girl in his demesne—the lecherous old goat! Surely that was all; surely Sir Hempen would have been too ashamed to mention his encounter with her to Count Laeg's son, or to any other young man—and surely the other knights would have been similarly too embarrassed. Surely none of them would have spoken of her at all.

But if that was so, why did a knight with a dozen men-at-arms come to fetch her, instead of one squire?

"My daughter Jane?" Mother held to the doorjamb as though she would herself be the door that kept them out. "Why would His Lordship require her attendance?"

"To serve him and his household." The knight couldn't quite meet her eyes. "He has a wife and daughters, and need of lasses to serve them."

Her mother's face went slack with foreboding; even she had heard the rumors of the sort of attendance Count Laeg required.

"Why, how kind!" Jane forced herself to show a bright cheeriness that she did not feel. "Maidservants are well paid, after all, Mother. Surely the Count knows of Father's death, and has taken this chance to give us some money—he must know we will be in need of it." But she realized that the Count had indeed known of Father's death, and realized even more, with a stab of fire, that it was only the old man's presence that had kept her safe from the Count's grasp. Her father's presence, and her brothers', of course—but it had been easy enough for the Count to get them out of the way for the time being. Anxiety churned within her—surely Count Laeg would not have them slain in some contrived border skirmish! But if he did not, what would happen when they came home? A vision of bloody swords stabbing flashed before her mind's eye, and with grim resolve she determined that no matter what happened to her, her brothers would not learn of it.

"It is true," said the knight who led the troop of soldiers.

Jane looked up, startled and frightened. Had he heard her thoughts?

"Count Laeg will give you silver," the knight assured her.

Silver, when what he meant to have was far dearer than gold—dearer than life!

But her mother's face had smoothed with the fiction Jane had given her, for she wanted desperately to believe there was no danger to her daughter. "Of course! But you must be presentable for the Countess and her daughters, my dear. Run and pack your things—quickly now, and I'll see to it that Gertrude fixes you some food to take on the journey."

Jane could have protested that the journey would take less than a day, and in any case, she had no appetite—but she knew her mother needed to believe it was all innocent, and that Jane was delighted at the prospect of serving the Countess and her daughters, so she turned and tripped gaily up the stairs, pretending for all she was worth.

In her chamber, she dropped the mask and let the grimness show in her face. Hot tears burned her eyes, but she blinked them away angrily as she changed into travelling garb and made a bundle of her four dresses and other clothes—but in the center of the bundle she packed the dagger her father had given her, so long ago.

Then, forcing herself to seem cheerful again, she went to join the soldiers.

The men-at-arms treated her with courtesy, at least—whether it was out of sympathy, or because they knew better than to seek to taste of their lord's sweetmeats, she didn't know. She was only grateful for one less worry.

As they rode, though, she burned with fury inside. Who was Count Laeg to order her about at his whim, especially to so vile a usage? Having defeated four young knights, she had lost respect for them—they were no better than the village boys in what they wanted and how they chose to get it. Oh, they were better fighters, it was true, for they knew swordplay—but not so well as Jane herself, it seemed. They were certainly of no higher quality than she was, and somewhat less, for all she could tell, in both swordplay and morality. No better than her village swains indeed! By what right were they knights? By what right was this corrupt old Count Laeg a lord, while she was only a commoner?

Why, by right of birth, of course—or by accident, rather; for if they were no better than Jane or her brothers, it was only accident that they were born of knights and ladies, while she was born the daughter of a mere squire and a peasant woman. Perhaps she should be a lord herself, if all it took was a quick blade and quicker wits.

He offered her silver, did he? Well, she prized her virginity more dearly than that! Better dead than bedded, she vowed silently—but she knew her surest way out was through His Lordship's chamber.

Sure enough, that was where they took her, as soon as they had come to his castle—come to it through a postern gate, and led her up a back stairs. Apparently, none were to know of her arrival except the knight and soldiers who had brought her. Oh, she did not doubt she would wait upon the Countess and her daughters—when the Count was done with her! After all, he had to have some excuse for having brought her to his castle—but he could not let his wife see her before he had used her, or the Countess might grow suspicious. No, straight to his chamber she was brought, and there given water to wash away the dust of the journey. She was given a little food, too, and wine—a whole bottle of wine.

The door closed behind the soldiers, and she glared at the bottle with contempt. She did not doubt that the poor girls he had summoned here before her had drunk themselves senseless in hope of diminishing their fear and pain—but she had need of a clear head.

However, she did not want Count Laeg to know that.

So she poured half the bottle into a chamber pot, then opened her bundle of clothes just long enough to take out the dagger.

There was a sumptuous dressing gown laid out on the bed, but no linen to wear beneath it, so she kept her own linen on, though she doffed her travelling dress to put on the gown—and hid her dagger beneath it.

Then she waited while the sun went down, growing more and more apprehensive, more and more tense.

Finally, the door opened, and His Lordship came in—smelling like a winery, and like decay. He smiled through his yellowed beard as he came up to lay a hand on her waist. "Well met, sweeting!"

Jane forced herself to smile, though she felt like gnashing her teeth. "Good evening, my lord."

He chuckled. "So the vixen Rumor speaks of is so easily tamed as this! My captain tells me you are quick for silver."

"Quick enough, my lord," she said, seething.

"Are you truly! Come, let us see!" And he swept her

into an embrace with an arm that was still strong enough to surprize her, swept her up against him, fondling with the other hand, and lowering his mouth to hers.

Noisome though it was, she forced herself to bear his kiss, for she needed his mouth muffled. She slid one hand up behind his neck while the other slipped the dagger out from beneath her robe and plunged it into his chest.

He cried out, but her hand tightened on his neck like a vise, forcing his mouth to stay tight to hers, muffling the scream. Then his whole body went slack, dragging down, and she loosed her hold, letting him slip to the floor. She stared down at the crumpled body and the spreading pool of blood, hardly able to believe he was really dead—but he did not move and, bending down to look, she saw his eyes had glazed. So much, then, for the debaucher of maidens! She felt not the slightest qualm of guilt; he had deserved a violent death a hundred times over. In fact, she found room to regret that it had been so quick.

Moving deliberately, she lifted the goblet; *now* she could allow herself a swallow, though she used it to rinse her mouth first, then took another mouthful to drink. Then, without hurrying, she changed back into her travelling dress; she knew no one dared disturb the lord at his pleasures, so none would come looking for him until morning. Finally, she pulled her knife from his chest, turned away so that she would not see the blood that must come pumping out, wiped the blade, and tucked it away in her sleeve. Then she opened the door.

The guards outside looked up, then frowned to see the clothes she wore.

"His Lordship requires more wine," she said, slurring her words and blinking blearily.

One guard smiled, relaxing, and nodded, moving away.

"So you drank it all, and saved none for him?" the other guard asked, chuckling.

"Aye . . ." She stared at his halberd, blinking stupidly as she listened to the other guard's footsteps fade away. "Why do you hold that . . . that . . ."

"Halberd," he supplied. "To protect His Lordship, little miss."

"How will it do that?" she asked, taking hold of the shaft.

He chuckled indulgently and let go, letting her have the weapon. She took a staggering step backwards . . . then swept the butt around with blinding speed and unerring accuracy. It cracked on bone; the guard crumpled.

Quickly, Jane caught him under the arms and straightened up, heaving. Staggering, she managed to drag him back inside the Count's chamber and closed the door. She bound the guard with his own belt, gagged him with a strip from his own tunic, then rolled him in a bedsheet, so that he would not be able to see the Count's body when he waked, and would perhaps be a little less frantic to call for help. Then she went back to collect her bundle and ran to the door. But she paused in the portal, considering, then reflected that it was hanged for the kid, hanged for the goat—if her life was forfeit for killing a nobleman, what mattered the punishment for stealing his sword? She hurried back to his dead body, unbuckled the swordbelt, and fastened it about her own waist. Then, with no further ado, she hurried out of the chamber.

She closed the door firmly behind her, turned the key in the huge old lock, then tucked it into her bundle and was off.

She knew where to go—they had brought her in that way, after all, to avoid notice. She avoided notice again as she slipped out, down the back stairs, through the servants' door, and across to the postern gate. If anyone saw her, they took no notice—least of all the guard at the postern, who knew only that there were suddenly a great many more stars than usual, then a deeper darkness. Jane slipped out, closed the gate softly behind her, and was gone into the night.

CHAPTER

~5~

"So you are still a virgin?" Geoffrey asked.

"I am," Quicksilver replied.

"Then most definitely I shall not touch you, though I shall tell you truly, the urge to do so burns and rages within me. Lessen my strain, I beseech you—distract me with your tale again. Tell me how you came to rule a county."

Quicksilver gave him a long, gauging look, as though measuring just how much turmoil he was hiding, and whether or not it was enough to satisfy her thirst for vengeance. Apparently what she saw pleased her, for she gave him a slanting smile and turned half away, to take up her history again.

"I had bought some time, for none would intrude in the Count's chamber until morning, and the sentry in the garderobe was not likely to be discovered unless someone should wake in the night. His fellow guard would think him fled after a wench, like as not, and would surely wait long before searching for him. I had at the least some hours, at most till mid-morning."

"Then, though," said Geoffrey, "they would be after you in earnest, with dogs and horses."

"Oh, they were," Quicksilver said softly, "as I knew they would be. But it was my county too, look you, and I knew its fields and woodlots better than any lord. Nay, I was into the trees within the hour, and buried in the depths of the greenwood before the air turned chill to wait for dawn. There I sat me down in the hollow of a huge old oak, to wait and plan—for I had thought no further than flight."

"Small wonder there," Geoffrey said, with a taut smile. "It was amazing you thought so clearly as you did, and so far ahead. Few men would have had the courage to plan so, let alone to carry out those plans."

"I . . . thank you," she said, surprised. "Yet what choice had I?" She must have thought it was a rhetorical question, for she went right on. "I knew there were dangers awaiting me that, though not as bad as the Count's men, would be bad enough. I hid to catch what sleep I could, then woke to find the sun up and the forest filled with its light, straying through the leaves in scattered beams. There I laid my plans."

"Did not the dogs find your trail?"

For answer, Quicksilver only flashed him a hard smile.

"Of course," Geoffrey said slowly. "You knew the ways of the wood, and how to hide all evidence of your passage."

"Far better than any dog, I assure you, whether he had four legs or two. Nay, I came out for my morning's ablutions, then was amazed to find that I was a-hungered. I ate of the food my mother had packed, then went back to my hollow to plan. I knew that I had become an outlaw by my night's work, for a dead lord is far more proof than is needed to hang a squire's daughter—and hang I would, if they caught me. I knew some anxiety for my brothers and my mother and sister, that the Count's son—the new Count, now—might seek to revenge his father on them; but I could not deal with it all, and had to take what fights came first."

"A sound plan," Geoffrey agreed.

"It was no plan at all," Quicksilver said tartly. "I began with what I knew—that I was dead if caught, probably torture first and hanging later; that I would have to live outside the law, where my life was any man's who wished to take it."

"The more fool he," Geoffrey grunted.

"Oh, I had no doubt he would come," Quicksilver said softly. "The world is filled with men who are fools. I bethought me how I should deal with them when they came, and was glad I had taken the Count's sword."

"How long did it take the gentlemen of the greenwood to find you?" Geoffrey asked.

"Call them not gentlemen, but men of the midden, for they were the refuse of manhood if ever I saw it. They came at noon, for they were more clever at following a trail than the Count's men—or, at least, the trail I had laid just for them, which began not at the edge of the wood, but only some few hundred feet from where I waited in hiding."

Geoffrey nodded judiciously. "So you chose the time and the place for the battle. Wisely done. Where was it?"

"A clearing," Quicksilver answered, "only a clearing in the woods, perhaps fifty feet across. I stood at the southern edge, screened by brush . . ."

"So the sun would be behind you, and in their eyes."

"Even so. They were a ragtag bunch, unwashed and unkempt . . ."

The bandits halted in the middle of the clearing, looking about them, puzzled. "She came this far," said one.

"You see well enough, Much," the biggest bandit said impatiently. "Who cannot see those prints of tiny shoes? Aye, she came this far—but how did she disappear?"

"Perhaps an eagle lifted her up and took her away, Bulin," one of his cronies suggested.

Bulin backhanded him across the mouth, but with a weary negligence that allowed the man to duck the blow easily; he seemed quite adept at it. "Be still, Tolb," Bulin growled. "She may be small, as women are, but far too big for any bird to carry."

"She may have hidden her tracks," another bandit said. "The village folk do say she is keen for woodcraft."

"Aye, Lambert, and that she had oft gone a-poaching by herself, in the little Home Wood."

"She will be well poached surely," Bulin grunted, "as the game, not the hunter. She is in the forest now, not some little Home Wood."

"Still, let us go warily about this poaching," Lambert counselled. "The village lad told us that she slew the Count!"

"A mishap," Bulin grunted, "and like as not he died in the throes of ecstasy, for he was very old. How else could so slight a girl slay a lord?"

"With a dagger." Quicksilver stepped forward from her screen of brush.

The outlaws' heads snapped up; they gawked. They had been prepared for a grimy urchin in clothing torn by brambles; they had expected anything but a lady in a good broadcloth travelling dress, though it was hiked up to her knees to give her more freedom of movement. Still, she was clean and, frankly, more beautiful than any woman any of them had ever seen.

Bulin recovered from his surprize and smiled, a curve of the lips that widened into a wolfish grin as he said, "Well, then! You have seen that you cannot live in the greenwood without a man to protect you, eh?"

"Oh," said Jane, "I think I can manage."

"Then why did she draw us?" Lambert grumbled.

"Be still, fool!" Bulin snapped. "You do not think she would admit to her need, to you? Nay, need of a man in more ways than one, by the look of her."

Jane's lips tightened. Why, she wondered, did men seem to think that the prettier a woman was, the more she needed a man's caresses?

"Even one man alone will not protect you well enough, lass," Bulin informed her, "for there are many bands of outlaws in this wood, and no one fighter can stand against them. Nay, you are wise to seek out a band to join with—and ours is the strongest band in the forest!"

Jane hoped that it was true—it would make her task simpler—but she doubted it. "To have a band about me seems wise. But what is the price of your protection?"

Some of the men snickered, some chuckled, and some guffawed. "Why, what do you *think* the price would be?" asked one.

"Cooking and nursing, like as not," Jane said airily.

"There is that," Bulin conceded, "and making beds."

"And sleeping in them," one of the men said with a chuckle.

"What, all?" Jane widened her eyes in mock innocence.

"Well, not all in one night," Bulin conceded. "Nay, each night you would have a new bed."

"Why would I need so many beds?"

"Come, do not play the fool!" Bulin snapped. "You would share each man's bed, and couple with him!"

Now Jane could let her brows draw down in the anger she really felt. "Nay, I like not the sound of that."

"More's the pity, then," Bulin grunted, "for if you will not come willingly, you will come by force—but you will come to bed, pretty one, be sure of that."

"Have I no choice, then?"

"To come willingly, or by force." Bulin grinned, and several of his men chuckled, gloating, as though they would prefer the second. "Those are your choices."

Jane fought to keep her voice from shaking with the anger she felt. "Well enough, then—you have named your price. Now I shall name mine."

"I had thought you might," Bulin said smugly. "Women are quick enough, for silver."

"Nay, I am quick to fight," Jane said, "and my silver is here." She brought Count Laeg's sword out from behind her skirts.

The bandits lost their grins and exclaimed to one another in a roar of confusion. Bulin, though, only kept his grim gaze fixed on Jane and held up a hand to quiet them. They did, and Bulin said, "You had best give us that toy, lass, ere you hurt yourself with it."

"Not myself," she assured him. "Have the villagers not told you why the soldiers seek me?"

"For killing the Count," Lambert said, frowning. "I doubt not 'twas because you were too frisky in bed . . ."

"Nay." Jane's tone was ice. "I slew him with this." She flourished the dagger in her left hand. "This sword was Count Laeg's—but by right of conquest, it is now mine." She moved her feet slightly, bending her knees just a little, and stood guard in a stance that any practiced swordsman would have recognized—but these men were peasants, and had never been taught proper swordplay. Bulin only frowned. "Then what is your price?"

"Your head," she answered, and leaped at him, sword slashing through a triple arc.

Bulin stepped back with a shout of anger, brought his own blade up to block hers—and left his midriff wide open. Jane pivoted, thrusting her dagger into his belly. Bulin stared at her in horror as he folded over in sudden agony, his lips moving but unable to form words. Jane called up a vision of what he had meant to do to her and thrust the sword through his chest, giving him a mercifully quick death that she thought was probably much more than he deserved.

Then she leaped back, yanking her sword clear. Bulin's lifeless body rolled on the ground.

The outlaws stared down, dumb with horror.

"Who else would seek to bed me, then?" Jane demanded, her voice still cold as ice.

That brought them out of it. Every head snapped up; every pair of eyes stared at her, suddenly afraid.

She stepped forward with swift precision, and the outlaws fell back with shouts of alarm—all except Lambert, who stood stiff as a rail, not daring to move, because the sword's tip was under his chin, at his throat. Jane nudged a little, and his head lifted; he dared not move his jaw, but a whine of fear came out his nose.

"Shall I slay your friend, then?" Jane demanded.

They glanced at each other, and she could see it written in their faces that they were on the verge of fleeing, and leaving Lambert to his fate—but one bowman plucked up the courage to draw an arrow from his quiver.

Another outlaw knocked it out of his hand. "Nay, fool! Draw that bow, and she'll slay Lambert!"

"Why, Stowton?" the man demanded.

"Because it would be one less fool that I would have to slay," Jane snapped. "Be sure that I can cut his throat even as I leap aside—and do you truly think that the ten of you together could stand against me?"

They stared at her, but they could tell by her tone that she meant every word. A few at the back began to edge away.

"Hold!" Stowton cried. "The fewer of us there are, the more we're apt to fall before another band! We must be all together—and we're already less by one!"

"Aye, and the one with the brains, I dare say," Jane told him.

They muttered, not liking the sound of that, but none denied it. "Spare our mate, mistress," Stowton pleaded. "We have done you no harm."

"Nay, but you would have! Perhaps I shall spare him after all—if he swears to obey me." She twitched the point, and a trickle of blood ran down Lambert's throat. He stiffened even more, whining in terror. "How say you, Lambert? Will you obey my commands?" She drew the sword back an inch. "There! Room for you to move your jaw, enough to say yes or no."

"Yes," Lambert muttered through his teeth, not daring to open his mouth. "Yes, mistress—spare my life! For I see that we have misjudged you, and you are a lady of quality!"

"I am the daughter of a squire, and reared to fight," Jane told him grimly. She lowered the sword . . .

Then she heard the footfall behind her.

She leaped aside, dropping into a crouch, and the quarterstaff whizzed by above her head. She stepped in for a quick thrust, but the tall outlaw parried her blow with one end of his staff, then struck sideways at her skull. She dodged again, leaping upright, and the blow missed her head, but cracked into her waist. Pain flared through her hip, but she ignored it and stabbed down at the hand on the staff with her dagger.

The tall outlaw howled and dropped his staff, clutching his hand and staring at the blood in disbelief.

Jane lunged, and ran him through.

She knew there was no room for pity here—that was why she had killed Bulin, not even trying to spare his life. If she gave these thugs the slightest sign of softness, they would fall on her in a mass, and bear her down by sheer weight. Her only chance was to intimidate them thoroughly and quickly, and that meant death—theirs, or hers.

She yanked the sword out and leaped back, glaring at the outlaws, bloody sword and bloody dagger upraised. "Is there another coward who would come at my back? And I a weak woman! Look upon him, and see the price of treachery!"

They stared down in shock. "How did you know he was there?" Lambert mumbled.

"I told you I had been reared to the ways of war," Jane snapped, "and it is clear that none of you have! Nay, you shall be cat's meat for any band that chooses to chew you up! But I think I shall take pity on you, and be your captain."

They all stared up in indignation and, finally, some anger.

"Ah, they have remembered they are men!" Jane crooned. "But I have not given you a choice in this—I have told you!"

"A woman for our chief?" the tallest outlaw said, aghast.

"Even so! Henceforth I shall command, and you shall obey!"

"And if we do not?" The tallest narrowed his eyes.

"Why, then, I shall slay you!"

The tallest kept his glare, though she could see he was unnerved. Jane wondered if she would have to kill him, too.

Inwardly, she was amazed at herself—amazed, and horrified. Something shrank within her, in loathing—but she held her stance grimly. Before she slew Bulin, she'd had the choice to strike or to be raped; now, she could kill or be killed.

She did not intend to die.

"And if we obey," Stowton said carefully, "what will be our reward?"

"Your lives," Jane said, "and gold and silver, for there shall be rich takings indeed, if you but do as I tell you."

The bandits glanced at one another. "She must sleep some time," one of them said.

"Not where you would ever find me," Jane snapped. "Come, will you be my liegemen? Or corpses?"

The tallest licked his lips, but nervously. "She cannot stand against all of us together," he said. "Indeed, she must lie down."

"No, *you* shall!" Rage seized her, and Jane leaped forward, feinting three times to draw his guard down, then lunging to stab him through the vitals. She leaped back, watching the blood spread and the dead man topple, and still inside her something watched in horror—but it was deep inside, for most of her felt only a grim satisfaction. She did not doubt that the man would have done as much to her, if he could have—after he had done worse.

She looked up at his fellows, who were staring in shock. "You are no use to me alive," she said, and stepped toward them.

"No, no mistress, withold!" Stowton held up his hands,

backing away. "We shall be your men, we shall ward your sleep!"

"Wisely chosen." Jane let her sword's point lower a little. "And you shall not regret it, for if you do as I bid you, there shall be more loot than ever you have seen. You shall have silver from fat merchants—or the silver of my blade." She lowered the sword's point almost to the ground, and waited. But the bandits did not try to jump past her guard, as she would have done in their places— they nodded, and Stowton doffed his cap. "You are quick with that silver, so I shall wait for the other. Quick silver is not for the taking."

"Why, then, Quicksilver I am, and never forget that I am not for any man's taking," Jane said with a grim smile. "I see that you have some trace of wit, fellow, which is more than your friends have."

"Thank you, Mistress Quicksilver."

" 'Quicksilver' will do, for I am no man's mistress." Jane was rather pleased with that. "And since you have sense enough to know it, you shall be my lieutenant over this ragtag batch. Now, all of you, lead me to your camp!"

The bandits turned away, but Jane heard someone mutter again, "Sooner or later, she must sleep!" She was about to demand who had spoken, but Stowton said sharply, "None of that! There has been little enough loot for us; let us see what she may bring. Aye, she must sleep, but 'tis myself shall guard her slumber!"

"And so shall we," said a familiar voice.

Jane spun about, scarcely believing her ears. But it was him, it was really Leander! With Martin and Jory coming up behind him. "Brothers!" she cried, dropping her sword and throwing herself into Leander's embrace. His great brawny arm closed about her, and for a moment, she let herself go weak, let herself be vulnerable again, for she knew she was safe—for a little while.

"If any man should dare harm our sister," Martin informed the bandits, "we shall set out his giblets as bait for the crows. From this time forth, two of us shall stand guard while the other two sleep."

"But how . . . how!" Jane looked up at him. "How is it you are come?"

"A friend brought us word of what had passed at the castle, and we thought it best to leave Count Laeg's army before his son took it into his head to arrest us and hold us hostage for your own surrender."

"Hostage!" Jane stepped back, hand coming to her mouth, eyes wide. "Oh, Mother, and little Nan!"

"We are here, daughter." Her mother stepped out of the thicket, behind the watchful eyes of her sons, their hands on their swords as they smiled brightly at the bandits.

"And little Nan!" Jane leaped forward to hug her little sister.

"Not so little any more," Nan said, with all the authority of thirteen.

"Nay, surely not!" Jane laughed, then sobered suddenly, looking up at her mother, wide-eyed. "But our house! And your featherbed, and all your . . ."

"All that truly matters is here." Mother patted a large sack she was holding. "Mementoes of your father, and of your childhoods—and my rings are on my fingers. All else?" She shrugged. "The life is far more important than the furnishings."

"Oh, you speak bravely!" Jane hugged her. "How can you ever forgive me for bringing you to this, Mother?"

"It is no fault of yours, but of the men who sought to use you," her mother said with asperity. "You have done only as I wish I had been brave enough to do if I had been in your place, daughter, and my pride in you outshines all I have lost. In truth, I would not have you do otherwise for the world."

But Jane knew that the loss of all her household goods, all her treasured possessions, must truly grieve her sorely. "I shall have it all back for you, Mother, and more!"

But Mother shook her head. "It is only furniture, my dear, and can be bought anew. Your virtue could not, nor certainly your life!"

"Then that shall be our first prize!" Jane turned back to her new band with sudden resolution. "Quickly now, before the sun rises and Sir Hempen comes to confiscate! Bury these dead dogs and march quickly!"

Apparently the bandits had never had much love for their dead leader, for not one of them showed the slightest sign of rancor. Indeed, they were delighted to scoop out a shallow grave and plant the bad seeds, then to follow Jane—or Quicksilver, as they called her—on her first foray. After all, it was night—and it was only a house.

But Sir Hempen had been there already.

Quicksilver surveyed the vandalized remains of what had been her childhood home, and a sick horror filled her. She felt something die within her, and knew it was the girl Jane. But over that grief flooded a tide of cold anger, and she knew that something else had been born—the outlaw Quicksilver.

"It is well that Mother and Nan waited in the greenwood with Jory," Leander said softly.

"Well indeed," she replied.

"Where is the loot you spoke of, Quicksilver?" Stowton said softly at her elbow.

"In Sir Hempen's manor, I doubt not," she returned.

"Ay de mi!" Stowton sighed. "How shall we bring it out from such a stronghold?"

"Why, by seizing it!" Quicksilver snapped. "He has taken my house, so I shall take his!"

"Tonight?" Stowton stared, appalled.

"What better time? He will never expect us! Nay, like as not he and his men have taken the field, seeking for me in the Count's name!" She did not bother telling the outlaws that Sir Hempen had a score to settle with her. "If we go hotfoot to his manor house, we can strike and be gone ere he can return. Then on the way home, we shall steal his cattle."

"Steal a knight's cows?" Stowton looked up, wide-eyed. "Just like that? On the instant?"

"Why, would you have me send him notice? 'Tis summer, and the kine are loose in the pasture; I doubt that he will have set a guard over them. Have you no taste for beef?"

"Well, I do like the taste," Stowton admitted. "Come, my hearties! We shall breakfast on sirloin!"

And they did.

"That was only a raid, of course," Quicksilver told Geoffrey. "We did not seek to hold the manor, but took all my mother's household goods, and drove off all Sir Hempen's cattle and horses."

"You let them keep their own household goods?"

"Aye, for those belonged to Sir Dunmore's widow, and my quarrel was with Sir Hempen, not with his mother. Nay, *my* mother would have rebuked me sorely for stealing from her old mistress."

"Loyalty like hers is to be prized," Geoffrey agreed. "Why did you not seek to hold the manor?"

Quicksilver glanced up at him in irritation. "Do not mock me! You know well enough."

"I know why it would have been foolish to have held it," Geoffrey replied, "but I do not know if you had the true reasons, or only sentiment."

"So you wish to see if I knew as much of warfare as I thought?"

"Frankly, yes." Geoffrey leaned back on his elbows—an exposed position, but he was ready enough to use his feet, if Quicksilver tried to take advantage of it. She knew that, too, and glared daggers at him for tempting her. "Am I to amuse you by my foolishness, then?"

"I take great delight in hearing how your mind works," Geoffrey countered, "though amusement is too light a term."

She frowned at him, uncertain as to whether or not she had been complimented—so Geoffrey pushed a little harder. "The fruit of your tactics is battles won where no mere outlaw should be able to win, and strategy that has succeeded admirably till I hove into view. I cannot but admire such generalship—so give me reason to admire it more. Tell me why you did not seek to hold the manor, once you had taken it."

"Why, because we did not have enough men, nor enough arrows nor arms of any sort! In brief, because we had not prepared ourselves for such an undertaking—and because I was most unsure of the loyalty of my command."

"And of their quality." Geoffrey nodded with delight. "Exactly as I would have thought! Still, with all that against the undertaking, why did you do it?"

Quicksilver frowned. "I have told you that."

"No, you have told me the woman's reason. Surely the commander must have given it a thought, also."

"If you mean, before I said that we would go take back

my mother's belongings, had I thought of the issue as a commander? Had I paused to ask myself if we could do it and come away alive? Or most of us . . ."

"Aye, all of that—and if regaining your mother's property was your only reason for the raid."

"I saw that, if we won, it would secure the band behind me—if that is what you mean."

"The very thing! Did you think of that before the raid, or after?"

"Before, of course," she said, exasperated. "How could I fail to see it, when I dealt with outlaws? They are men who live by theft, after all, and nothing will earn you a bandit's obedience like good loot. There was also the matter of their seeing that I could plan an enterprise so that we could win, and that my brothers would not let them do other than I had commanded—for they were my captains, you see, one for each of the manor's walls. Nay, the men saw that I could plan a battle and win it, with only two of them dead and three wounded—and they durst not move against me after that."

Geoffrey frowned. "But you had been so careful to see that your brothers would not draw revenge for your deeds!"

"Aye." Quicksilver turned away, her face thunderous. "I failed in that. I know I should have let old Count Laeg have his way with me, so that my mother and brothers would not be hurt—but I saw instantly and clearly that my sister would be, when she came of age. Still, I make no excuse—it was only my own horror and loathing of the act that made me place myself above their welfare. It was selfish, I know—but it is done."

Geoffrey could only stare for a moment, shaken to his core by the idea of this beautiful, spirited warrior subjected to the clutches of an old goat—but shocked more by the thought that she should actually think she was in any way to blame for having defended herself. How could she believe there was any wrong in doing what was right?

He would have to make her see that.

CHAPTER

~6~

"I would not say selfish!" Geoffrey sat up, frowning. "A woman must never submit to such abuse as that, and your brothers and sister would have been the first to tell you so!"

"They have," she said, eyes downcast, "but if any of them come to grief, I shall blame myself eternally."

"What, blame yourself for Count Laeg's sin? Nay, surely! Besides, your brothers and mother came to you out of their own free will, and not from any constraint."

"None but that they saw the grief that would befall them, if they did not flee," Quicksilver retorted. "Since we were all outlaws, I saw that our only safety lay in beating young Count Laeg at his own game of tyranny, and that right quickly, before he could expect us."

"And you saw all that before you told your bandits you would take Sir Hempen's manor?"

"Aye, but it was not the careful and considered plan you make it out to be."

"No—the thoughts flashed through your mind, and you were instantly sure of their answer, were you not?"

Quicksilver's look became guarded. "How did you . . . ? Oh. It is even so with you."

"It is," Geoffrey agreed. "Your plans were excellent! Did your father teach you this?"

"Why—I really cannot say." Quicksilver spread her hands. "Some of it, I am sure he did. Most seems to come by common sense—though I will own I have learned some things by watching the commanders sent against me."

"Of whom the other outlaw bands were the first?"

"Oh, the outlaws!" Quicksilver dismissed them with a wave of her hand. "Bulin spoke truly—his band was the best, no thanks to him. He had bellowed and browbeaten them into doing what he wanted, but it was Stowton who had the sense to see what needed to be done."

"Bulin the strongarm, and Stowton the brain? How long did it take him to discover he could not make you front for him as Bulin had?"

"One night—that first raid. 'Do you not think we should break down the door with a tree trunk?' he asked, and I snapped, 'Nay, for they've crenels above it for pouring down boiling oil.' I pointed to the stonework above the entrance, then drew my finger down to point at the portal. 'Why do you think it is five feet above the ground?' I demanded. 'So that you must mount steps to reach it—and why do you think the steps are laid against the side of the wall?' 'Why,' he answered, wide-eyed, 'so that attackers must come right up beneath the crenels, where boiling water may be dropped upon them!' 'You are quicker than the rest,' I told him, 'but you must be quicker still, or you will be dead. We will seek out the postern whiles my brothers draw the defenders to the walls.' Then, when we had chopped our way in through the postern, Stowton said, 'I

shall take a band to bear away the knight's strongbox!'
But, 'No,' I said to him. 'We shall take only my mother's
goods, and Sir Hempen's horses and cattle. He shall be
wroth with us, and seek to punish us—but so long as we
stay within the greenwood and out of his way, he will be
content. If we take his gold, he will never hold back until
he has haled it back out, and us with it, that he may slit
our throats.' His eyes grew big, but he made no comment,
nor did he argue when I bade him take five men and bind
up the soldiers my brothers had knocked senseless. But he
did tell me that we should drive the cattle gently, so that
we need not make any great noise. I told him, 'What matters it, when we have made so great a hullabaloo here? If
a few villagers awake to watch us pass by, let them! They
will think twice ere they seek to enter the wood without a
by-your-leave.' He looked thoughtful at that, but he went
to drive the cattle. He never left off making suggestions,
and does not to this day—but I take his notions when it
will do no harm, and it keeps him content."

Geoffrey grinned. "Why, what a fox you are!"

"Do you not mean, a vixen?"

"I doubt it not," Geoffrey assured her, and managed to
restrain himself from telling her that he enjoyed hunting.
"But what of your brothers? Did they not find it galling to
take orders from their little sister?"

"Nay." There was a gentle amusement, perhaps even
tenderness, in her tone. "They knew enough of command
to realize that if they challenged my leadership, the outlaws would cease to respect me and would desert one by
one—and they knew also that it was better to have an outlaw band, than to be beset by one."

"Wisely thought," Geoffrey said, with approval. "Did
they tell you this?"

"Aye, when I demanded to know. 'Twas two days after

the raid on the castle, look you, and I had braced myself for them to come to me all three together to say, 'You have done bravely, sister, but now you may sit back safely and leave all to us.' "

"What would you have said if they had?"

"I would have told them that I had won the outlaws' obedience, through fear if nothing else, and that if I were to step aside, they would have to win that obedience all over again."

"You would have held onto what you had won, then."

"Aye." Quicksilver's smile turned predatory. "I had begun to enjoy the taste of power."

"It does whet the appetite," Geoffrey agreed. "Did not your brothers hunger after it?"

" 'Of course,' my eldest brother told me. 'Who does not? But we have discussed the matter, sister, and are all agreed that you will be our surest route to power.' "

"So simple as that?" Geoffrey asked, amazed.

"Aye. Mayhap they thought of me as a useful tool, but if so, they have not sought to master that tool. I think, though, that they were sincere—and I know they are proud of me." She smiled, a glow in her eyes.

"I doubt it not," Geoffrey assured her. "*I* would be proud of such a sister." He looked up, thinking over that statement.

"*Have* you such a sister?" Quicksilver asked.

"Aye, now that I think of it—though Cordelia fights with magic, where you fight with steel. And I *am* proud of her."

"But do you seek to rule her?"

Geoffrey gave a bark of laughter at the thought and shook his head. "I would never dream of it—but if I did, I would be grasping my head with the king of all aches in an instant."

"But you would *not* think of it."

"Nay, and I'd string out the guts of the man who did!"

"Then you should not find it hard to believe that my brothers do not seek to rule me."

Geoffrey thought that over, too, and nodded. "Even so. If Cordelia were to win what you have won, I would not seek to steal it, but would help her guard it, even as your brothers have done."

"Then why do you take me to the King and Queen, so that they may steal it from me?" Quicksilver asked softly.

That brought Geoffrey up short. "Because it is the law," he said slowly, "which I am sworn to uphold—and because what you have, you have stolen from its rightful owners."

"The county, do you mean? And are you so sure that young Count Laeg is its rightful owner?"

"He is, in the law," Geoffrey replied.

"But in morality? Does not the land rather belong to them who till it? Should not its fruits belong to those who have drawn them from the earth?"

"There might be right in that," Geoffrey admitted, "but it is the world as it perhaps should be, not the world as it is. I live in the world that is, and will let Their Majesties decide whether or not it is right or wrong."

"But what know they of County Laeg?" Quicksilver protested. "What know they of the ways in which the Count and his father and, aye, his grandfather, abused their office and their peasants?"

"Little," Geoffrey admitted. "But if you tell them, and bring them some sort of proof, they shall see the right of it and amend it."

"You have greater faith in Their Majesties than I," Quicksilver said bitterly. "But then, it is not hard to have more than nothing."

"I have just such faith, for I have known them from childhood," Geoffrey returned. "They are good folk, look you, and if you review the actions they have taken for the good of the land and the folk, you will be reassured."

"I would like to think so," she said darkly, "the more since I am going to appear before them."

Geoffrey frowned. "Are you so sure that you are so much better a ruler than the Counts Laeg?"

"I am," Quicksilver returned, "for I was close to the peasant folk, and knew their distress and their grievances. When I gained power over them, I saw to it those grievances were redressed."

"Tell me the manner of it," Geoffrey urged her.

"When three bands had sought to attack us, and been beaten for their pains," Quicksilver explained, "others began to give us a wide berth. But those we had beaten, we put to work hauling and hewing, for we had builded us a little village within the forest. However, when we went to raid Count Laeg's tax collectors, I placed them in my brothers' commands, though armed only with staves . . ."

"You did not put one band for each of your brothers!"

"Of course not." She gave him a look of contempt. "How great a fool do you think me?"

"None at all," he said promptly.

She colored a little, and looked away, but her voice ground on. "I split each band among the four commanders—my brothers and myself. There were never more than a dozen to a band, so what is four more among trusted and seasoned men?"

"Aye—eight trusted, and four new!"

"But each of those eight had beaten one or two of the others at practice," Quicksilver pointed out. "Besides, they had seen how well we lived, and were minded to give my captaincy a try. We captured the tax collectors and sent them back to Count Laeg with only their tunics and hose, for we kept their shoes, their gold, and even their robes. The new men sang my praises then, though they grumbled against me when I kept the greater part of the loot for myself. They might have mutinied, had I not sent some of them out with packets of money to help friends in the villages who were hard pressed for food to live on, since the tax collectors had taken nine parts out of ten."

"Did the poor ever receive the money you sent?"

"Most of it. I sent other men to make sure, as I had told the messengers I would—and if they kept a coin or two for their pains, I did not trouble myself about their hire."

"Surely not, since it bought their loyalty."

"It did," she sighed, "though I wondered at the worth of loyalty that could be bought, and still do."

"Surely they are loyal for better reasons now!"

"Aye—for winning." She gave him a sardonic smile. "But such loyalty lasts no longer than a few losses. Praise Heaven I have never had more than one loss at a time!"

"Heaven?" Geoffrey asked. "Or your own good judgement, in next choosing an easy target?"

"I would like to think there was some sense to my planning," she conceded. "But now that I myself am lost . . ." She flashed him a bitter smile. "Well. Now we shall truly learn of their loyalty, shall we not?"

Geoffrey felt his stomach sink, and wondered why he should feel guilty about doing his duty. What spell was this woman working on him? "So you conquered all the other bands in the forest."

"There was no need—one by one, they came and asked to join us. I made them swear loyalty, though I doubted their vows were worth more than the rags they wore. Still, I gave them good broadcloth clothes, and hoped their steadfastness would improve with their cloth."

"You must have prospered mightily," Geoffrey said.

Quicksilver shrugged. "I was an outlaw already, and dead if captured—and I had begun to think that I was more fit to rule than Count Laeg or his son."

Geoffrey frowned. "High thoughts, for the granddaughter of a peasant."

"You must not have met Count Laeg," she returned, "or Sir Hempen. I declared my rule over the forest, and sent men to pronounce it in every village."

Geoffrey stared. "In public? That was as good as a challenge!"

"It *was* a challenge," Quicksilver said with a hard smile, "and young Count Laeg knew it. Oh, he sent Sir Hempen after me first, but I defeated him and his band with a right good will. I sent them home all a-foot and bereft of arms, though I did regret the two slain in the battle, and the three of my own. But Sir Hempen I had scourged with a horsewhip besides, and sent him home without even his tunic."

Geoffrey frowned. "I thought you let your enemies keep their pride."

"Not him—he had cost me too much that was dear. I told him to thank his mother for his life—that if it had not been for the thought of her grief, I would have slain him outright. Well, no," she amended thoughtfully, "perhaps not 'outright.' Perhaps slowly . . ."

Geoffrey couldn't suppress a small shudder, and wondered why this woman still seemed fascinating to him. "He had to punish you for that, or lose the obedience of his peasants."

"That he had already lost. They began to come to me by twos and threes, young men and old, who had fallen a-foul of Sir Hempen's tyranny—crops and cattle taken as taxes, sweethearts and daughters taken as toys . . ." She shook herself, trying to dispel rising anger. "Faugh! What a dog is he! If I had not seen so much good, steadfast bravery and caring among my own band, I might have despaired forever of the breed of men!"

"I am glad that you have not," Geoffrey told her.

"Well, I nearly have, anyway," she told him, "for among the bands I conquered were women who were virtual slaves, forced to cook and clean, and fill the filthy outlaws' beds, and bear them brats which they then were forced to tend."

Geoffrey stared. "The sorry creatures! How had they come to such a pass?"

"Some had been kidnapped when they came to gather berries in the woods, poor innocents. Some had been captured from parties of travellers who were foolish enough to dare the wood without an armed guard. But most were those who had fled to the greenwood rather than bear the attentions of knights and their soldiers, or even of village bullies. Poor things, they exchanged bad for worse."

"But not when you found them?"

"If I had not needed the outlaws for an army," Quicksilver said bitterly, "I would have slain them then and there. As it was, I made to scourge them—but the women themselves actually begged me to desist, claiming that the men were their only source of livelihood and protection!"

Geoffrey closed his eyes in pain. "The poor bewildered creatures."

"So I thought," she said grimly. "I told them that I would provide their living henceforth, and their protection—but still they begged me not to punish their men overly much, for their captors were all they had."

"Why, they thought of themselves as wives!" Geoffrey said, astonished.

"So they did. I bade the men arise and treat their women gently and with respect henceforth, or it would go hard with them. I kept my word, too, seeing that any man who beat a woman received more blows than he had given. The females gained some measure of happiness then, tending their children and keeping house—but to my amazement, most of them continued to speak with the men who had been their captors, and even to bed with them!"

Geoffrey just stared at her for a second. Then he said, "Well, if they had come to think of themselves as wives, they must have thought of the men as their husbands."

"So it seemed—but I made sure each couple passed through a ceremony, when next a friar passed through the wood. I was most amazed that the men submitted with good grace, seeming even happy with the matter."

Geoffrey smiled. "Perhaps they were flattered to think that the women actually chose them, without being forced."

"There is that, and they did seem content with their company. I was forced to admit that I had not just an outlaw band, but also a village, a true one. Some of the women even asked their men to dig gardens, and began to grow crops. But there were others who rejoiced at their liberation, and wished to have nothing to do with any man again. These hailed me as their savior, and I was amazed when I woke one night and found two of them sitting up to watch my door, not trusting my brothers' vigil. I saw then that I must teach all women to bear weapons, and to fight with their hands, whether they would or no. I did, and there was never a wife-beating again—and my sentry-girls gave my brothers relief from their sleepless nights."

"Thus did your bodyguard grow?"

"Aye. They are a great comfort to me, for I know there is not a one of them would not rather lose her head than see an enemy come nigh me. Indeed . . ." Grief shadowed her face. ". . . three of them have died beside me, in battle. I could not ask for more worthy friends."

Geoffrey could sympathize, but he could also realize what those Amazons must be planning for himself, right at that moment. If they could find him . . . "And word of this spread? For surely, your men must have now and again stolen out to talk with old friends or kinfolk."

"They did indeed, though I did not realize it until village women began to come to me, one by one, then two and three together."

Geoffrey held his face carefully neutral. "Your men did not harm them, of course."

"Oh, certainly not," Quicksilver said softly, "for I had declared to all of them what *I* would do to the man I found hurting a woman. No, my sentries brought them in with courtesy and good cheer, and I welcomed them and bade my women shelter them. Then I taught them all the way of fighting, with and without weapons, and was amazed how many of them balked, and did not wish to learn. But I told them that they lived in a band of outlaws, and must be ready to help fight off the shire-reeves' men at any time. They took my meaning, and learned—and some among them chose to join my bodyguard."

"Did the others marry?"

Quicksilver shrugged. "There is no need—even if they do not, they shall be given food, drink, shelter, and fuel. Each must do her share of the camp's work, of course, and her own—but in my band, coupling will come from the desire of both, or not at all, and marriage will come from love, not from need. If there is anything left of my band in a week . . ."

Her face darkened, and Geoffrey knew only that he had to lighten it. Plague, he would *not* feel guilty about capturing her—it was she who had chosen to be a bandit warlord, and he who had chosen to be a royal knight! "Still," he said, "if Sir Hempen let your insult pass without punishment, he would have lost all power over his peasants. Did he not come again?"

"No, the King's shire-reeve came next, with a much larger force of men—in truth, half again as many as my band. My outlaws quailed at the news of their number, and would have faded into the forest leaves, had I not harangued them and shamed them and reminded them that this was *their* wood, and no man of the open lands could stand against them in it. They liked the sound of that, and took their stations where I bade them—though with my brothers keeping watch upon them, you may be sure. The shire-reeve rode in among the leaves, and walked out without his horse, as did all his men. Some chose to stay with us, under guise of having been captured and held hostage . . ."

"Holding peasant guardsmen hostage?" Geoffrey smiled at that. "Surely the shire-reeve saw that for the fiction it was!"

"No, I think he thought me so innocent as to actually expect him to offer a ransom for his men. When he did not, of course, I was able to keep them without his suspecting their treachery. So he left me a dozen of his men, and the rest of his band left us their armor and weapons, and five of their number dead. We buried them, though nowhere near the one of my men who died in the fight. My mother and sister led my officers in binding up the wounds of my men, then of theirs—I was enraged when I saw that the shire-reeve made no move toward tending his own wounded, and gave him a wound of his own for his pains, then forebade anyone to bind it for him. I relented at the last, when he had to set out walking, and knew he would have to come again, to recapture his arms, and his pride."

"You *wanted* to have them attack you!"

"Aye." She gave him a brittle smile. "To come against me here on my home ground, where I had the advantage of the terrain, and a great deal of cover. Finally young Count Laeg found he could not countenance this challenge to his power without losing respect and obedience among his own knights and squires, and surely among his peasants—so he led all his army against me, or almost all."

"With the shire-reeves and Sir Hempen among them."

"Oh, they led parties of knights themselves," she said softly. "That was a bloody battle indeed—ten of my band died, and twenty of his, with three times that number wounded. But when the fighting was done, it was Count Laeg who was chained and his men who were bound, and we who went back to his castle."

"This time," Geoffrey said softly, "you *were* prepared."

Quicksilver nodded, gazing off into space, seeing the battle all over again. "We were ready, and his castellan was not—his mother, I should say; but he had left her only a dozen guards to hold the walls, never thinking that we might come upon her. Come we did though, and my brothers raised a howl of battle all about the walls and the gatehouse, firing flaming arrows and hurling rocks from small catapults, but never coming close enough for the guards to pour oil on them, or have a decent chance of striking them with the crossbows that were their only weapons."

"While you forced the postern," Geoffrey inferred.

"Aye. We had brought a light skiff with us, and rowed across the moat to the little gate, a dozen of us, six men I trusted and six of my bodyguard . . . five of whom still live . . ."

Geoffrey saw the tear in her eye, and pushed her past the remorse. "No battle can be won without risk," he said

softly, "and to spare others from the grief and pain of a tyrannical lord is worth the gamble of a life."

"Aye." She lifted her head, giving it a shake. " 'Twas
nobly done! And while I ruled, the price bought good
worth."

"There was no guard upon the gate?" Geoffrey pressed.

"Aye, but he stood back and waited till we had chopped
through it. *Then* he shot his arbalest, and one of my
women died." Her face hardened. " 'Twas wrong of me, I
know, for he did no more than his duty—but I was afire
with rage. He drew a battle-axe, but I feinted once; he
swung, and I lunged, stabbing home. We kicked his dead
body out of the way and ran in, lightfoot, staying against
the walls, running silently in the darkness. The guards
were too busy howling insults at my brothers and firing
their crossbows at shadows to look down and see us. We
came to the gatehouse undetected, but found the windlass
guarded by a poor old lubber of a porter. He gibbered with
fright when my sword touched his throat, and my women
let the windlass go. The drawbridge fell down as my men
cranked the portcullis up. Too late, the guards realized
they had been invaded, and made the further mistake of
charging against us, leaving my brothers free to lead all
my men over the drawbridge and into the courtyard. There
they fell upon the guardsmen from the rear, where they
strove to wrest us out of the gatehouse—and we who had
been the quarry suddenly became the hunters, falling upon
them with steel and arrow. They were caught between two
forces, and threw down their weapons with cries for
mercy."

"Did you give it them?"

"Aye, for that time—though I held trials of the Count's
men all that next day, finding who had beaten and de-

spoiled the peasants and who had not. Two of those guards were hanged, along with five of the Count's army."

"Few enough, for the men of a tyrannical lord."

"Few indeed. The rest had friends among the villagers, and would not see them wronged—so they refrained from wronging others. Then I gave those who remained the choice of enlisting with me, or of exile. Most chose to stay; a score chose to go. I sent them with the Countess, and her son the new Count, to go where they wished. Then I entrenched myself in the castle and sent my brothers out and about the county, to put government to rights and see justice done. I cut the taxes in half and discharged corrupt magistrates—I knew them all by name, after all—and declared that no woman should be abused, most especially not by her husband, and that the workman was worthy of his hire."

"Your words have the sound of victory won, and enjoying its fruits," Geoffrey said, "but your tone is one of vigilance."

Quicksilver shrugged, her hands on her thighs, eyes downcast. "I have held myself, and my men, ready to fight any lord who may come against us—for I know that those born to rule will not abide an upstart squire's daughter to live without challenge. And, too, I had no knowledge of where the Countess had gone with her son."

"She went to Runnymede," Geoffrey said, "to Queen Catharine and King Tuan—and therefore no lord has come against you with his army, but only one knight, alone."

"One knight—who, Rumor says, is worth a whole army by himself," Quicksilver said bitterly. "If I had not been so chary of my outlaws' lives, and so wary of your magic, I would have tried the truth of that rumor."

"But it might have been true."

"It might," she said, though it pained her. "It might, and

my band of rogues and stalwarts dead. No, better to gamble my own freedom than their lives. But it is still better to chance my own death than your attentions!" Her hand reached automatically for the sword that wasn't there, then clenched in frustration.

"Rest easy," Geoffrey told her. "I am not one who takes pleasure from a woman's pain, no more than you delight in the torments of those who have not hurt you."

"Of those who have not, no," she said judiciously, "though I confess I take pleasure in seeing the suffering of those who have wronged me."

"Then you have not tyrannized the peasants?"

She frowned, unsure about the change in subject. "Ask among them, if you can disguise yourself so that they do not know you come from Their Majesties. I have."

"What?" Geoffrey demanded. "Gone among them in disguise?"

"Aye, and though they have many grievances, my rule was not one of them."

Geoffrey wondered if her disguise had really been all that good. "They found you fair, then."

"Do not you?" she demanded, with a vindictive smile.

Geoffrey stared, then realized the pun and reddened. He was appalled at himself—no woman had been able to embarrass him for years. He forced a leer and said, "Most fair, indeed—but I speak of your conduct, not your face."

"I know you speak not of my face," she said tartly. "As to my peasants, be mindful that I grew up among them—that as a squire's daughter, I was ever in converse with them. I know their grievances far better than could any lord who was born to his title. Mind you, I have dealt severely with those who seek to prey upon their weaker neighbors—and many men in my villages must smoulder with rage because I will not let them use the women as they would. To them, no doubt, I am a tyrant—but not to any good husband nor respectful swain. I doubt not there are many women who resent my seizing power, and decry me for an unwomanly rogue, but I do not seek to silence them."

"Here is no tyranny, then, nor any great oppression— but you are an outlaw, and have fought against the duly appointed nobility. I fear we must go to the Crown for judgement, no matter how wrong it may seem. Will you give me parole, or must I bind your hands?"

"Only while you sleep," she assured him.

CHAPTER
~7~

" 'Tis better, then, that you do not sleep," said a voice behind them.

Geoffrey spun about.

Three tall young men stood lounging at the edge of the clearing by the stream. They were broad-shouldered and handsome, with open faces that would normally have been friendly—but at the moment, their hands rested on the hilts of the swords by their sides, and their faces were grim.

Geoffrey studied them for a moment, then said to Quicksilver, "Your mother bore a handsome family."

"Lord Geoffrey," she said, "these are my brothers—Leander . . ."

The young man in front, with the broadest shoulders and darkest hair, nodded politely.

". . . Martin . . ." Quicksilver said.

The young man on the left, with the reddish hair, forced a smile; then it vanished.

"And this, I take it is Jory." Geoffrey nodded at the young man with the fair hair, on the right.

"You have a good memory," Quicksilver said.

"And we have a sister," Leander said. "We wish to keep her."

Geoffrey could fairly feel the tension thrumming through him, the mounting delight at the prospect of battle. "This is a family affair, then."

"Well, not quite." Leander made a beckoning circle with his hand, and the leaves beside him rustled as foresters stepped forward, some with arrows nocked, some with swords or axes in hand, most with nothing but quarterstaves—but Geoffrey could tell from the way they held them that they were skilled in their use. Even across the little brook, a score of men stepped forward—and the Amazons stepped up to circle protectively around their leader.

"Why, how is this, lady?" Geoffrey demanded, not looking at Quicksilver but at her brothers. "You agreed that it would be war between us two and us two only, and that your freedom would be forfeit if you lost."

"I did indeed!"

"But we did not," Leander said with a wolfish grin. "We find that we cannot abide the thought of our sister in chains, and verge on frenzy at the thought of her hanging."

Geoffrey winced at the picture that conjured up, but he held his ground. "Have you forgotten the purpose of our bargain?"

"To spare our lives?" Leander drew his sword. "We will chance it."

"But I will not!" Quicksilver darted between them. "Nay, forfend! If I must fight this man again, I shall—but myself alone!"

"Sister," Martin said, "it is we who should protect you, not you who should guard us. Nay, I think there shall be no need of fighting, for certainly this knight is wise enough in the ways of war to know a losing battle when he sees one."

Geoffrey nodded acknowledgement. "I have such wisdom—but I see no such sight."

Martin was taken aback for a moment; then he laughed. "Surely you do not think you can best our whole band!"

"With sword and strength alone, no," Geoffrey said, "but with magic, yes."

"No!" Quicksilver cried in panic. "You gave your word!"

"My word is void if yours is not kept."

"I have kept it!"

"But if we break your word for you, it is nonetheless broken." Leander nodded at the Amazons. "Take her in among you, ladies. I do not wish her near our fight."

Geoffrey's face went blank as he began to concentrate on the magical moves he was preparing.

"Have you not a sister?" Leander said, his voice low.

That broke Geoffrey's concentration and set him aback. "Aye—I have. Surely you know of that, if you know who I am."

"I do," Leander said. "Would you let some stranger knight carry the Lady Cordelia off to judgement and certain death?"

"Nay, of course not." Geoffrey's grin spread slowly, reflecting Leander's wolfishness. "I would die to prevent it, if I had to."

"And so shall we," said Martin.

"You shall not!" Quicksilver cried. "You shall live and protect your peasants and your men! I alone have brought down Count Laeg and his knights, and I alone shall pay for it!"

"No, you shall not," Leander said softly, his gaze still

locked with Geoffrey's. "Step aside, sister, for this has gone beyond you now."

"Beyond me! What . . . ?" Quicksilver glanced from Geoffrey to Leander and back. "Oh! It has become a test of strength between you, some foolish test of your manliness! A contest, an idiotic contest! Give over! It is not fit that good men should die only to prove their worth!"

"It is right and fitting," Geoffrey countered. "It is the way of Nature, beautiful lady, by which the strongest is chosen to strengthen the breed."

"You are men, not horses!" Quicksilver fairly screamed. "Put down those swords! I shall go to the King and Queen at Runnymede whether he brings me or not!"

"Not if I live," Leander said, and her two brothers gave a rumble of agreement that was picked up and carried around the circle of armed men. Quarterstaves rose, bows bent, and they all edged forward.

"Only I have drawn my sword yet," Leander said, but Martin and Jory both tightened the grip on their hilts.

Geoffrey scowled, and executed the first step in his magical defense.

The hilt twisted under Martin's hand, and he leaped aside with an oath, then realized the thing that had twisted had come with him.

The outlaws let out a shout and brought their weapons up.

The polearms twisted in the hands of a dozen or so, and they cried out, dropping their bows and axes—but the Amazons just clutched their swords more tightly, lips thinned, and moved in.

"Now *hold*!" Quicksilver cried with the first signs of anger.

The Amazons halted, but still glared daggers at Geoffrey.

"Craven!" Leander snapped. "Dare you fight me without your magic?"

"Dare you fight me without your army?" Geoffrey returned. "Nay, even all three of you together—so long as you bid your bandits hold their blades, I'll not use my magic!"

"This is nonsense!" Quicksilver stormed. "If you fight, you fight with all you have! If you fight to see who is stronger, fight with blunted weapons! Fight with swords of lath! But play me no boys' game of limits!"

"Boys are only little men, sister," Martin returned, eyes still on Geoffrey, "and if we limit our mayhem, 'tis to bring less disaster." He drew his sword. "Nay, make it squirm in my hand now, if you can! I will hold it fast!"

"Will you indeed," Geoffrey said softly, and the sword suddenly wrenched itself out of Martin's hand and flipped up high in the air, turned over, then stabbed down into the earth at his feet, where it stood quivering.

Martin blanched, staring at it. Then he looked up slowly, his face darkening.

"Bid your men stand," Geoffrey said softly.

"All of you, ground your weapons and stand fast!" Leander called out. "This warlock and I must settle our difference!"

"Aye, ground them!" Quicksilver shouted. "You too, brother mine! I would not see you slain!"

"I shall not be," Leander grated, but Martin wrenched his sword out of the ground.

Geoffrey drew his blade in a single clean motion and stepped forward, on guard.

"Not *either* of you! Hold! Put up your swords!"

" 'Tis even as your brother says," Geoffrey told her. "It has gone past you now." With that, he thrust. Leander parried; Geoffrey riposted and thrust again, then again and again, advancing.

"The young bulls are pawing the ground," the tallest bodyguard told Quicksilver.

"Nay, Minerva—they are done pawing, and charge at one another to lock horns! Separate them!" Quicksilver raised her voice. "Separate them, all of you!"

With a gleeful shout, the quarterstaff men hefted their staves and waded in.

"Hold!" Leander shouted, jumping back.

"Aye," Geoffrey agreed, and swept the bandits with one quick glare. The staff went spinning from one man's hand and knocked the staff from another's. Both men fell back with a cry, but Stowton shouted, "He cannot disarm us all! Charge him!"

A fallen staff leaped into Geoffrey's hand. He spun it like a baton, and all the other quarterstaves twisted in their owners' hands, trying to imitate Geoffrey's. They shouted and dropped their staves, some clutching bruised wrists.

The archers howled, brought up their arrows, and loosed.

"No!" Quicksilver shrieked, and leaped in front of Geoffrey.

The arrows all looped, curving, shooting back to their owners, who yelped with superstitious fright and broke ranks—but one arrow shot straight on to Geoffrey. He caught it and stabbed it into the ground. All the other arrows plunged down and lanced the earth in imitation.

The bandits crowded back, white showing around their eyes—but Minerva beckoned to her bodyguard and stepped forward, eyes cold.

Geoffrey didn't even notice. He was looking down at the beauty in front of him. "Thank you for your protection, but I will not see you pierced. Why did you leap to guard my body with your own?"

"Why ... why ..." Quicksilver stammered, and blushed, looking down. Then she spun about to him, chin up. "Why, because I gave my word! That none of my band would harm you! But I did not say that, once yielded, I would *stay* yielded! If any shall strike you, it shall be me!" She leaped back, holding out her hand, and Minerva slapped Quicksilver's own sword into that hand.

"You gave parole," Geoffrey reminded her. "You said you would not seek to escape."

"Aye, but I did not say I would not fight you again! On guard, warlock! This time, our fight shall have a different ending!"

"It shall indeed!" Minerva gestured and jumped in front of Quicksilver. Six other young women leaped in beside her, their swords raised.

"Brothers," Leander snapped, "it seems we are done with the ways of honor."

"Even so," Jory agreed, and stepped in behind Geoffrey.

Geoffrey opened his mind to awareness of them, of each tiniest motion they might make, as he kept his eyes on the bodyguards in front of him. The wolfish smile tugged at his lips; it would be a battle royal. True, he must not injure any of the women, at least not seriously—which gave him no compunction about using magic ...

A shout went up. Geoffrey swung about to see an arrow speeding toward him, knew it was already too close to divert, and was just beginning to duck when ...

... the arrow turned down and plunged into the earth.

It was almost a right-angle turn, not the drop of a smooth trajectory that was just a little short.

Geoffrey turned to face Quicksilver, blocking a blow from Minerva almost absentmindedly as his eyes met

Quicksilver's, and held with surprize on his part—but on hers, thin-lipped with the knowledge that she was unmasked. She raised her voice, crying out, "I bade you hold! I said that none of you should harm this knight!"

And she had kept her word, Geoffrey realized—for it was not he who had made that arrow plunge to earth.

Quicksilver, however, didn't seem to want her band to know that, because she said, "Adroitly done, warlock! But how did you know the arrow had been loosed?"

"My mind is alert to yours," he answered, "and to those of all your band."

It certainly would be from now on, for Geoffrey knew better than any that it was not his mind that had deflected that arrow. Still, it had been a great lapse on his part, to let himself be so distracted by the Amazons that he had ignored the rest of the band, and so had missed the archer loosing the arrow. Fortunately, Quicksilver had not.

Suddenly, he understood much better how she had managed to carve out her own little kingdom here in the forest, and expand it to include the whole county—because Quicksilver was herself an esper.

That did not mean she was any less a general, of course. She was still expert at tactics, and probably at strategy, too, though her campaign had been cut short before he could be sure of that. Certainly she was magnificent with a sword—but he suspected that she had made more than a little use of magic when she was outnumbered, and exercised it subtly but very effectively in her battles. More than anything else, though, it explained how she could be so effective a leader, why her fire and enthusiasm reached out to envelop her fighters. She was no doubt a projective telepath, at least in a small way, quite possibly in a larger. At the very least, it gave her a great deal of charisma.

And she knew that he knew. He probed with his mind

and came up against a mental wall—her shields were up—but felt also the questing alertness of another telepath, reaching out to him. He smiled, letting his mind be unshielded on the surface, letting her read not his long-range plans or deeper motives, but at least his current intentions and yearnings . . .

She blushed, and her gaze faltered for a moment, but came back to meet his with level candor. "You have broken your word, Sir Knight. You have used magic."

"Break causes break," Geoffrey countered, "whether it was your doing, or not." He turned to the three brothers. "Must I fight you all again?" He wasn't at all sure that he wanted to, now, though—his courage was so vast that he scarcely even noticed fear, but he knew a losing fight when he saw one, and battling might not be the best way to win this prize. Quicksilver might be able to counter all his magic with her own. At the least, she would slow him down so that he might well fall prey to the weapons of her outlaws—but he would take at least half of them with him, to death. He was struck with admiration at how adroitly she had prevented just that calamity, by persuasion and maneuvering. And he had not even known he was being maneuvered! How dextrously she had hidden her powers!

The chance of losing, or even of losing his life, would not stop him from battling, of course—not if the cause was worth his death. But he had a notion that Quicksilver was far more worth his life.

If she had hidden her powers so well, though, she could have taken him by surprise. Surely she could have defeated him with the loss of only a quarter of her fighters—and if she really hungered for power more than anything else, she would have done just that.

On the other hand, he did not doubt that she did want power—so why had she not ambushed him while she could? He felt a seed of hope sprout and shoot within him, but tried to ignore it; obviously there were things that were more important to her than power—but why should he presume that he was one of those things? Presumptuous indeed!

"Put up your weapons," he said to Leander. "Fall upon me again, and I will only steal her away again."

"Then we will only find you again!" Minerva said angrily. "There is not a foot of ground within this forest that our sentries do not see!"

"Thank you for the warning," Geoffrey said, with a courteous nod. "I shall take her far away from the greenwood this time."

Anger flared in the captain's face, but Quicksilver held up a hand to forestall her, saying quickly, "Peace, Minerva. I have no wish to ride *that* ghostly horse again! It was most unsettling, I assure you."

Minerva barked an order even as she sprang, and the Amazons were a sudden ring of muscle and steel enclosing their chief. "You must touch her to take her," Minerva snapped, "and if you attempt it, you shall die!"

Geoffrey stared at her for a second or two. Then his sword flashed out in three quick feints. Minerva parried the first two, then leaped to parry the third. Her women shouted and leaped out to surround Geoffrey—

And he sprang through the gap they had left, catching Quicksilver about the waist. But the feel of that supple body against him distracted him from his teleportation just long enough for Quicksilver to cry, "Hold!"

The bandits all froze where they were. Geoffrey wondered how often she could do that, before they ignored her command.

Then, to Minerva, Quicksilver said, "You may hold him off, my brave and loyal captain—or he may slip past your guard again, as he just has. I have no wish to feel the world turn inside out about me, or to have that blast deafen me. I gave my word, and I shall keep it!" She looked about her, eyes blazing. "So shall all of you! Aye, even you, my own brothers! I gave parole, and I shall go with him to Runnymede!"

"But he has broken his word," her brother protested.

Quicksilver disengaged herself from Geoffrey's arm and stepped back to give him a long measuring look. "You have," she said, "and because of that, I shall break my bond in this much—I shall still go with you, but if I see a chance of escape, I shall take it."

The outlaws cheered.

"Myself!" Quicksilver shouted into their din. "Myself alone! I shall escape with no peril to anyone else, or I shall not escape at all!"

The cheer subsided into mutinous muttering.

"Therefore begone!" Quicksilver commanded. "Back to the greenwood, and quickly, before the Crown's shire-reeve comes against you again, with a royal army!"

"If there is danger of that," said Leander, "we had best hold Laeg's castle, where we can defend ourselves better."

"Nay!" Geoffrey frowned. "It is Laeg's by right!"

"Right?" Martin sneered. "You speak of Laeg and right in the same breath? There was never anything right in Count Laeg's life, least of all in his dealings with his peasants!"

"That is no reason to deny his son his inheritance!"

"You cannot know if you have not lived here," Quicksilver snapped. "The son's deeds are no better than the father's; he is a true branch of the bad tree, and thinks the peasants are his cattle—aye, and we yeomen, who are children of a squire, too."

Geoffrey turned to her, frowning. "Be that as it may, the law is the law, and I am sworn to uphold it!"

"Even when it is wrong?" Jory jibed.

"The law was made by the lords," Martin said with scorn, "and it serves their ends, not those of us common folk."

"If there is truth in what you say, I shall be your advocate among the lords and before the Crown, to see the law changed!" Geoffrey declared.

"And while you are advocating," said Minerva, "what will they do to us?"

Geoffrey turned to her with words of reassurance on his lips—but found himself suddenly seeing her not as an opponent, but as a woman of the commoners, vulnerable to a lord's whims, and realized that behind the sword and beneath the armor was a very desirable body. It struck him as curious that he did not himself desire it, though he was sure he would have before he met Quicksilver. Nonetheless, the new Count Laeg no doubt would, and would use her own body to punish her. Geoffrey's bold words of faith in the law, died on his lips. Instead, he said, "Right or wrong, the law must be obeyed. If it is not, we will have chaos, with every man's hand turned against every other's, and the women caught between them in suffering."

"You say that to outlaws?" Leander scoffed. "Tell me, pray, what the difference is."

"And while you are debating it, Count Laeg will fall upon you," Quicksilver told them both. "Aye, brother, I think you will be safer in Castle Laeg while this bold champion debates our cause before the Crown."

"And tries your fate," Leander growled.

Geoffrey glared at him. "Will you not yield to the law?"

"Speak of that when the law has delivered its verdict," Quicksilver countered.

"What verdict?" Minerva demanded. "The only case that will be tried is whether or not you have slain a lord, Quicksilver, and stolen his lands—and we all know what the answer to that must be!"

The outlaws growled and pressed in.

"Yet you seem to think she was right in so doing!" Geoffrey called out. "Might not the King and Queen think so, too?"

The outlaws hovered, uncertain.

"Shall we not be tried with her, then?" Minerva demanded. "Even if we are not there?"

"We shall," Leander answered, "and an army sent against us if our sister is judged guilty. Nay, my sib, you must not go!"

The outlaws pressed in again, and Geoffrey gauged the distance between his arm and Quicksilver's waist. Looking up, he could see that Minerva was measuring it, too.

"I have sworn I will go with this man, and I shall!" Quicksilver called out. "Oh, I shall escape from him if I can—but I will not have you place your necks even further in the noose by assaulting a Gallowglass!"

"Hung for the sheep, hung for the flock," Leander answered, "even if the sheep was a rogue ram, and it was necessary to slay him to save our lives."

Geoffrey turned to him. "Is there a charge you would bring?"

Leander scowled. "What nonsense is this?"

"I have said I will be your advocate before the Crown—but I cannot be so, without a charge to prosecute or a cause to advocate! Do you accuse Count Laeg of breaking the law?"

A furious rumble went up among the outlaws, but Leander's eye caught fire. "Aye, we do, and our sister can give you a whole catalogue of his crimes—but the long and the short of it is this: that he has oppressed and exploited his peasants unmercifully, for his own pleasure and gain and not for their welfare, or the kingdom's."

"You charge, then, that he has been untrue to his vows as a knight, and as a vassal of the Queen?"

"As a knight, a thousand times over, for he swore to protect the weak from the strong, did he not?"

"He did," Geoffrey answered with full certainty.

"I charge that he has *been* the strong who has preyed upon the weak, and that his son has already done likewise! I charge that he has broken the law! And that in breaking it, he has left us no choice but to break it, too, or die at his hands! That the father has done this a thousand times in a thousand ways, and the son has already begun to follow his father's example!"

Quicksilver smiled, eyes glowing as she gazed at her brother, and even Geoffrey could feel the exaltation of her approval. Yes, the woman was a projective, and a powerful one, whether she knew it or not. For himself, he only nodded at Leander and said, "These are weighty charges indeed, and enough to justify unseating a lord—if they can be proved to be true."

Leander turned away in disgust, and Minerva flared, "Proved! What proof can peasants offer, against a thieving and rapacious lord?"

"Peasants cannot," Geoffrey told her, "but another lord can. Nay, I have said I will be your advocate, and I shall. This I swear—and I shall seek out what proof I can. Be of good cheer; this is no idle boast. I have agents who shall go among you unseen, for they owe me favors, even as I owe them. But I must ask you to trust me in this, for I cannot prove good faith until I speak before the Crown."

"At which time, if you break faith, it will be too late for

us," Minerva said, tight-lipped. "No, we must keep our chief here."

"I have said I will ride with this knight, and I shall!" Quicksilver snapped, beginning to be angry again. "For the rest of you, though, go back to Castle Laeg, and hold it for me! I must have a home to come back to, when I have escaped from this popinjay!"

"Oh, a popinjay, am I?" Geoffrey rounded on her, eyes glinting at the prospect of a good fight.

"Aye, a popinjay, and it is my lance for which you shall be the target!" Quicksilver stepped in to face him, fists on her hips. "Do not think to reverse that, for when did a popinjay bear a lance against a rider?"

A murmur of admiration and delight spread through the outlaw host. Geoffrey only grinned. "Beware, for your popinjay is truly a quintain, and equipped with a lance of his own!"

"My remedy, then, is to break it!"

"What then, will you break a lance with me?" Geoffrey purred, his eyes glowing into hers. "A valiant deed, and sport worthy of a true knight-errant."

Minerva stepped forward, alarmed, but Quicksilver only smiled with the same ferocious delight Geoffrey showed and answered, "I am not a knight, sir, nor even a squire, but only a squire's daughter."

"That may be so," Geoffrey conceded, "but you are every inch a lady."

Leander frowned. "What riddle is this you speak? A lady is the daughter of a lord or, at the least, a knight. A woman must be born a lady, or can never be one!"

"I must agree with that," Geoffrey returned, his gaze still on Quicksilver's, "but I have just discovered that a woman can be born a lady even if her father was *not* a lord."

The outlaws murmured in amazement, but Minerva cried in alarm, "Beware, mistress! He seeks to cozen you!"

"Of course he does," Quicksilver said. "When was there a man who did *not* seek to cozen every pretty maid he met?" But she was still smiling, still held her gaze locked with Geoffrey's.

"Sister," Leander said, a quaver in his voice, "I fear for you."

Geoffrey did not think he was talking about the noose.

"Some dangers I must face alone, Leander," Quicksilver told him, her gaze unwavering, "but the prize is worth the gamble."

"Not if the dice are loaded against you!" Minerva cried in near panic.

"Fear not, sweet friend," Quicksilver told her. "I have thrown with loaded dice before, and won."

Of course, Geoffrey thought—she was telekinetic. He wondered if he should read a double meaning into that, too. "You seem to forget," he said, "that riding with this woman is a gamble for me, too."

Minerva looked up at him in surprize. "I did not think you would realize that!"

"Oh, yes," Geoffrey said softly, "but I cannot lose, you see—for with a woman like this, even loss is gain."

Minerva frowned, not understanding, but Quicksilver blushed and turned away.

When she raised her face to her outlaws, the blush had faded. "Go back to Castle Laeg," she cried, "and hold it for me! Will you or nil you, I shall ride with this knight!"

"Our only remedy, then, is to take you back by force," Leander said, frowning.

Quicksilver turned a very cold gaze on him. "Brother," she said, "I love you dearly, and owe you greatly, but I should chastise you sorely if you did. You must make your life, and I must make mine."

"Life?" he said bitterly. "Or death?"

"I shall die boldly, or live sweetly," she told him. "Do not seek to save me from myself, brother, or you might destroy any chance of happiness that I might ever have. Go now, and do not seek to guard me again!" She turned back to Geoffrey. "Let us ride!"

With great reluctance, her bodyguard brought forth her horse—a spirited bay mare—and the outlaws disgorged Fess. Knight and bandit both mounted, and the tall black stallion said, in mental words that only Geoffrey could hear, *I hope you know what you are doing, Geoffrey.*

If I do not, I am sure that you will, he returned. *Bear me on to glory, Fess.*

CHAPTER
~8~

You seem to have extricated yourself from another difficulty, Fess thought at Geoffrey.

Aye, though I think it may be my captive who has extricated me. How did they find us so quickly, Fess?

When you disappeared, they took a moment to recover from the shock, then Leander dispatched runners to the sentries. They do indeed have a network that surveys every route through this forest, though boasting of every foot is a bit of an exaggeration.

'Every route' includes the rivers, then?

It does. A sentry sent word of your arrival almost as soon as you appeared by the riverbank. Her attention was no doubt attracted by the explosion accompanying your appearance.

Quicksilver mistook his long silence. "Are you so angered by a mere challenge when it is not even a defeat?"

"It is irritating to be denied battle, when I have prepared myself for it," Geoffrey acknowledged.

"Aye." Quicksilver seemed to know exactly what he was talking about. "But I could not allow it, you see. I could not risk the lives of my warriors—and my brothers least of all."

Geoffrey swung about in his saddle, staring. "Could not *allow* it?"

Quicksilver stared, confused, then smiled as she understood his meaning. "Has a woman never denied you before?"

"Only in that which it was hers to deny." Geoffrey felt the hot blood mount into his face.

"And never before have you met a wench who could deny you a battle," Quicksilver said drily. "You forget that I am not your common wench, Sir Knight."

"Aye, neither my wench, nor any man's! You are a lady, and do not think I do not know it!"

"Then you know more than I do," she retorted. "I am the daughter of a country squire, nothing more!"

Geoffrey tossed his head irritably, dismissing the objection. "You are certainly no man's wench, if you told me truly in your tale of your life."

"I did!"

"So I thought—but it occurs to me now that you may have had more motive to tell me that tale, and so fully, than merely the desire to satisfy my curiosity."

"That is *all* that I shall satisfy!"

"You are frank in that, but perhaps not in other matters. You kept me in converse so that your bandits might find us, did you not?"

Quicksilver smiled and tossed her head, her long hair swirling about her head and shoulders. "What if I did?"

"Nothing, save that I must always ask myself henceforth why you do what you do. This trail that we follow—will it lead us out of the wood?"

"Aye."

"But will it lead us out if we follow it in the direction in which we are now riding? Or will it only lead us further in?"

Quicksilver smiled again, amused. "It will lead you further in."

Geoffrey nodded, vindicated. "I must ask you everything, must I not? And surely watch each word I say. Come, let us go out." He turned Fess's head.

Quicksilver turned her mare to follow him, eyes sparkling.

As she came up alongside him, Geoffrey asked, "Why do you ride a mare? I doubt not that you are skilled enough in the saddle to handle any stallion."

"You do not think I would trust myself to a male, do you?" Quicksilver countered. "My Belinda is the equal of any stallion in all but sheer strength—and their superior in endurance and intelligence."

Geoffrey nodded, and they rode in silence for a few minutes, Quicksilver casting mischievous glances at him out of the corners of her eyes. It occurred to Geoffrey that she was sure she could escape him whenever she wished, but found him amusing in the meantime.

He had to admit some truth to it. For himself, he found her company entrancing, though he was not all that sure that he could escape her, if she did not want him to. On the other hand, she would find him harder to throw off than she knew.

"So," he said, more to break the silence than to make things clear, "you are a witch."

"As you are a warlock."

"Why did you not tell me that straight out?"

"You did not ask," she countered. "Do not patronize me, knight. You know as well as I that knowledge held in reserve is advantage."

"A fundamental principle of tactics," Geoffrey admitted. "However, now I do ask you straight out: What are your powers?"

"Why . . . the powers of any witch," she said, surprised. "I can hear others' thoughts, and move objects with my mind." Her eyes took on their wicked glint again. "*And* shield my mind from presumptuous warlocks!"

She did not know she was a projective, then—and if she was not about to volunteer knowledge without being asked, neither was Geoffrey. After all, if she knew she had such a power, she might bend him to her will more thoroughly than she already had. Heaven knew she had done enough of that already! "Does your band know of your powers?"

Quicksilver shrugged, making Geoffrey glad he had been watching her. "Some may have guessed—I know not. I have been at pains to hide the fact from my earliest childhood, when my father saw me making my doll move, and cautioned me to let no one know but my mother and himself. I was not always as careful as I might have been, though, and I think my brothers have guessed."

"Well, if one knows, they all do," Geoffrey said, from knowledge of living with two brothers himself. He tore his eyes away from her and watched the curving trail ahead. "You hid it from me well enough—until that arrow bound for my heart swooped down. I must thank you for that, by the way."

"I was glad to do it—the more so since your vengeance might have been more than I wished to see," she gibed. "Besides, my bandits doubtless thought it *your* doing."

"No doubt you made your brothers take the blame for you, too, while you grew. So your sister has not guessed?"

"Not so far as I know; she is seven years younger than I, and I was skilled at dissimulating ere she was old enough to study me. I think she has some witch power of her own, but I am not sure."

Geoffrey doubted that. He thought Quicksilver was probably very sure, one way or another. Studying the road ahead, he said, "This trail twists and turns among positive walls of leaves."

"It does," Quicksilver agreed.

"A score of men could easily be hidden, not three feet from the trackway."

"They could," she acknowledged. "I have sent them home, though."

But Geoffrey did not need to ask if they had obeyed. He was listening to the thoughts all about him, of forest creatures both four-legged and two-legged, and knew as well as Quicksilver that only half her force had gone back to the castle. The other half followed them as silently as a breeze among the leaves, a dozen yards from the roadway on either side, aching for Quicksilver's signal to strike.

Well, there wasn't much he could do about it, except to leave Fess on guard while he slept. Other than that, he decided to ignore them as best he could, until he had decided what to do about them.

He didn't think Quicksilver had decided, either.

Finally, they came out of the trees. Geoffrey tried to hide his sigh of relief—he would have welcomed a good fight, but not when he was so fiercely outnumbered that he might have had to injure a few of the outlaws, and perhaps even kill them because he couldn't take the time to be careful. If they had been thoroughgoing villains, he wouldn't have minded the chance, of course, but he found that he could no longer think of them that way.

Besides, hurting some of Quicksilver's men might have made her hate him, and he was astonished to realize that he didn't want to risk that.

She must have read something of his relief, though, and misunderstood it, for she said, "Do not think that you are out of my domain, simply because you have come out of the greenwood. This land all about is filled with my people."

"Only the peasants, if you have bade your warriors go back to the castle." Geoffrey frowned. "You do not mean that even *they* would fight for you!"

"Every man," she said evenly, looking him straight in the eyes. "Every woman, too, if I asked it of them. I have been a good lord to these folk, Sir Geoffrey."

Geoffrey gazed back into her eyes, frowning. They were dark brown, so dark that they seemed to be deep pools into which he could plunge . . . He shook himself angrily, turning away and forcing his mind back to the conversation. "It would be interesting to put your boasts to the test."

"Why, then, test them!" Quicksilver said merrily, and pointed ahead. "Yonder is a woman—two, though the one is very young. Shall I bid them fight you?"

Geoffrey looked up. Sure enough, a middle-aged woman and a girl had come into sight around a bend in the road— but it was Quicksilver and Geoffrey who had moved toward them, not the other way around, for the woman was bent over their cart, and the girl was holding the horse, which had been unshackled from the traces.

"No, do not," Geoffrey said. "Ask them instead if we may aid them."

Quicksilver gave him a quick, appraising glance, then

followed it with a smile that made him feel he had been rewarded. "As you wish, then." She clucked to her horse and cantered ahead.

By the time Geoffrey caught up, she was bent over her saddle in conversation with the woman, who was curtsying to her, then pointing to the cart.

For a peasant woman, she was remarkably well dressed. Oh, she wore the usual dun-colored skirt and homespun blouse, with a muslin apron over both, and a kerchief to bind up her hair—but none of the garments was patched or ragged, and the cloth was a stronger weave than any he had seen on a serf's back. If this was how Quicksilver's peasants lived, no wonder they loved her.

Of course, the woman could have been the wife of a yeoman—but she was still well dressed for her station.

Quicksilver looked up as Geoffrey reined in Fess. "They have lost a wheel."

"Have they really," Geoffrey said, with a bit of sarcasm. It really wasn't all that hard to see the wheel lying there in the roadway, and the cart leaning down on its axle with the baskets of vegetables higgledy-piggledy all over the roadway. Geoffrey frowned and dismounted to look more closely. "There is no damage that I can see. It is only that the peg that held the wheel has broken off."

"Damage enough," Quicksilver said, with a sarcasm of her own.

"Aye; the wheel is off. This, though, can be mended easily enough, and without a wheelwright or cartwright." He straightened up. "Good day, mistress. I am Sir Geoffrey Gallowglass."

"Oh! And I am only old Maud, sir!" The lady dropped a curtsy. "And this is my daughter Nan."

"Good day, sir." Nan curtsied prettily, with a saucy smile. She, too, wore better cloth than the average peasant lass. She had long brown hair that hung about her shoulders in a thick mass, burnished in the sunlight and held back by a simple band. She was pretty, with the hint of genuine beauty to come, and a figure that proclaimed she had just passed the cusp between childhood and womanhood—fourteen, Geoffrey guessed; old enough to marry, in medieval society, but far too young by any more modern standard. He hoped her mother would let her wait.

"Good day, miss," he said, with a small bow.

"Oh!" Nan gasped, bright-eyed. Geoffrey smiled; a knight bowing to her thrilled the peasant lass. "Should you not be gathering up your mother's produce, pretty miss?"

She blushed at the compliment, but retorted, "Nay, sir, for the horse might eat the vegetables."

Geoffrey nodded judiciously, and forebore mentioning that the girl might tie the horse to a branch. He turned back to Maud. "Well, we must unload the wagon if we are to hoist it up enough to repair."

"Repair!" Her eyes went wide. "Oh! How good of you, sir! But you are a knight!"

"And am therefore sworn to aid those in distress." Geoffrey unbuttoned his doublet.

"Is not such work beneath you?"

Geoffrey smiled as he tossed his doublet over his saddle. "Well, if you see a cartwright passing by, I will gladly leave the task to him—but if you do not, I shall have to manage." He turned to Nan. "Tie that horse, if you would, lass, and seek out a stick of hard wood, an inch or two thick and a foot and a half long."

She was staring at him with very wide eyes, rooted to the spot.

"Nan," her mother called.

Nan shook herself and forced a smile. "Aye, sir, if you

wish it." She turned away, leading the horse, but glanced back over her shoulder.

Geoffrey shook his head and sighed; was it so unheard-of for a knight to do manual labor, that she should stare so? He went around to the back of the cart and began to lift out the baskets.

"How shall we raise the cart to put the wheel back?" Maud asked.

"By lifting." Geoffrey looked up at Quicksilver, and found her staring, too. "I shall have to ask you to step down, lady, and put the wheel on."

She shook herself, coming out of her daze, and snapped, "I am not a lady!" But she dismounted.

"It is for you to say what you are, I suppose," Geoffrey sighed. He hefted a fifty-pound basket of turnips. "How am I to call you, then? 'Mistress?' 'Chieftain?' "

"I am sure you can think of a word," she said drily—then, as she saw the slow grin widen on his face, she snapped, "Though you had better not!"

Geoffrey set the last basket down and flexed his arms, rolling his shoulders to ease the ache—and to revel in the touch of the breeze as it flowed over his bare skin. "To the wagon, then." He turned to Quicksilver. "Will you take up the wheel?"

She was staring at him again, and swallowed thickly before she answered. "Aye." She turned away, but her eyes were the last to leave.

It burst on Geoffrey that her staring had something to do with the huge muscles rolling under the skin of his bare chest and shoulders. He grinned, savoring a moment's revenge, then bent to the fallen axle.

"Will this do?"

He looked up to see Nan holding out a long, thick stick—and staring at him as hard as Quicksilver had. He smiled, enjoying her regard, and took the stick, trying its heft, thumping it into his palm. "Aye, that will do nicely. Hold it till I ask for it, there's a good lass."

"Surely, sir," she said breathily as he handed it back to her.

"How shall you lift the cart?" Maud asked. "I have no rope, and there is no . . ."

Geoffrey shrugged. "It is best to bend the knees, not the back, mistress, and to keep the legs together." He crouched down and took hold of the axle, then stood up, keeping his back straight. "Now, then! The stick, if you will, lass!" Holding onto the axle with his left hand, he held out his right. Huge-eyed, Nan put one end of the stick in his palm. "My thanks," Geoffrey grunted, for the cart was beginning to weigh heavily on his arm. He hefted the stick of wood like a mallet and drove it against the small end of the huge peg that went through the hub of the wheel—luckily, it was the large end that had broken off, or knocking the old peg out would have been much more difficult. As it was, two blows loosened it, and a third knocked it out into the dust. He tossed the stick aside and took the hub in both hands, grunting, "Now, then, the wheel!"

Maud nudged Quicksilver. She gave herself a shake and lifted the wheel, fitting it over the axle. Geoffrey grasped the outside of the hub with his right hand and lowered the cart back down with a thankful sigh. "My thanks. I do not think I could have held it up much longer."

But all three women were staring, and Quicksilver swallowed before she said, "That cart must weigh half a ton."

"Oh, surely only a quarter!" Geoffrey rolled his shoulders and flexed his arms again; the ache was strong, this time. "And I only had to lift a half of that; the other wheel took its share of the weight."

"Did it really," Quicksilver said, with a great deal of breath.

"Now! For the peg." Geoffrey drew his sword, chopped into the end of the hammer-stick, then twisted, and the stick split. He turned it sideways, laying it in the roadway, and chopped again, cutting off a foot-long half cylinder. Then he sheathed his sword, slipped out his dagger, and began whittling.

"Should you not don your doublet?" Maud asked, all motherly concern. "You will catch a chill."

"I am loathe to put on cloth till the sweat has dried," Geoffrey explained. He fitted the peg into the hole in the axle, drew it out, shaved a little more, then fitted it back in. Satisfied, he lifted what was left of the hammer-stick and pounded. A dozen blows, and the peg was in and tight.

"Well!" Geoffrey tossed the stick aside, took down his doublet, and slipped it on. " 'Tis not so fine a piece of work as a cartwright might do, mistress, but I think it will hold till you can come to a village, and have it mended by one who truly knows what he is doing."

"Oh, this is most excellent!" Maud said quickly. "I thank you, Sir Knight! How can I repay you?"

"By aiding another traveller in need of aid, when you come across one." Geoffrey turned back to Quicksilver, who was staring at him, transfixed. So was Nan, who stood right beside her; seeing them next to one another, Geoffrey could only remark on the resemblance, and decided that it boded well for Nan. "You will surely be a beauty," he told her.

That shocked her out of her trance; she blushed. "Oh! Thank you, sir! But why do you say so?"

"Because you looked so much like my lady now," he said, with a nod toward Quicksilver.

That brought *her* to her senses. "I have told you I am not a lady, and certainly not yours!"

"Then what am I to call you?" Geoffrey asked, turning to her. " 'Damsel?' 'Tis too modest for a leader of warriors. 'Captain?' Surely your rank should be higher! 'Chieftain,' perhaps?"

"Why not 'Quicksilver?' " she said tartly.

"Quicksilver! Oh!" Maud clapped her hands. "Are you the bandit chieftain, then?"

"I am." Quicksilver frowned at her. "Or was. Why do you ask?"

"Because if you are, it is you whom I have come to seek!"

There was no movement or gesture you could pin it on, but somehow an invisible mantle of authority seemed to settle over Quicksilver's shoulders. The transformation was certainly there in her voice as she asked, "Wherefore?"

"The village of Aunriddy, mistress! They are beset by bandits!"

"What? Some of my men?" There was instant fury in Quicksilver's face. "If they have harmed a soul, I shall have their entrails out!"

"Nay, nay, not of your band," Maud soothed. "They are a motley crew, and a most ungracious one. They have held sway over the village like tyrants, beating the men and importuning the women, and eating everything in sight, then slipping back into the fastness of their hills until their appetites have grown again. They demand tribute in grain and women; they have already taken what little silver the villagers owned. They hold them in such close durance that it has been half a year before one dared escape to bring word."

"Why, what a pack of mongrels!" Quicksilver raged, but

Geoffrey had caught another implication. " 'They?' This is not your village, then?"

"It is not," Maud confirmed. "We met the messenger on the roadway, and he was nearly done in. We left him some food and water, and told him we would bear word to the bandit Quicksilver."

"You have borne it," Quicksilver snapped. "But Aunriddy! That is not even in my county!"

"Nay, 'tis in County Frith, a day's ride away."

"Why do they not appeal to Count Frith, then?"

"Why," said Maud, "they have. He will not come."

"He fears the bandits," Nan said.

"Not so greatly as they should fear me!" Quicksilver seethed. "Oh, would that I were free again! I should chop those bandits to mincemeat, then chastise that count most shrewdly, for not defending his own!"

" 'Tis for that they have called upon you," Maud said softly.

Quicksilver looked at her, stricken.

" 'Tis for the King to chastise Count Frith," Geoffrey said, "but as to these bandits—why, I daresay I might join you in mincing them."

Quicksilver turned to him, surprised—until she saw the wolfish grin on his face. Then her surprise turned to disgust. "You do not care who you battle, do you? So long as you have a fight."

"You wrong me," Geoffrey protested. "I will not fight the innocent or the good!"

"You have fought me."

Geoffrey should have looked abashed, but the vision of that battle kindled warmth within him. "Aye, that I have," he breathed, "and I shall have the memory of that bout to warm my heart, when all else about it grows cold."

Quicksilver stared at him, shocked, then blushed and

turned away. "I thought you had sworn to take me to the King and Queen!"

"Why, so I have," Geoffrey said, "but County Frith is on the way to them."

"Aye, if west is on the path toward the north!"

"Well, it is closer than the south," Geoffrey said with a shrug. "Come, are you so loathe to fight by my side?"

Quicksilver turned back to him, and if his grin was that of a wolf, hers was that of a fox. "I would rather fight you than *by* you," she said, "but I will take what I may." She turned back to Maud. "Find that messenger and relieve his mind. Quicksilver shall ride to the rescue of Aunriddy."

"But where is your army?" Nan protested.

Geoffrey could have told her that they were only a dozen yards away, but Quicksilver said instead, "I ride with Sir Geoffrey Gallowglass by my side, and it is his boast that he is the equal of an army. What more should I need?"

Nan glanced at Geoffrey with misgiving, but Maud said, quite complacently, "Even so—what more *should* you need? God speed you, then, with the thanks of a poor old widow woman to lighten your burdens—and my blessings upon you."

"Why, thank you, good woman," Quicksilver said softly.

"You are welcome, and well come indeed—and may you go as well as you came." Then Maud gathered up Nan and turned away to the cart. "Come, daughter. We must away."

"Oh, *must* we?" Nan protested, and Geoffrey had to smother a laugh as he mounted and turned Fess's head back up the trail. "So, then, we ride to County Frith."

"Aye," said Quicksilver, "by your leave."

"No," Geoffrey said, "by yours."

A commotion broke out behind them, dimmed by distance. Turning back, Geoffrey saw the cart rolling away down the road, with Nan chattering breathlessly to her mother. They were thirty yards away, but Geoffrey could still hear a few of her words: "He is *gorgeous*, Mother! If she does not grab tight to him, she is a very fool!" Maud murmured something he couldn't hear, to which Nan answered, "Oh, stuff and nonsense! He will, or she is not the man-leader she thinks she is!"

Geoffrey smiled, and turned back to Quicksilver with a raised eyebrow—but she rode with her face set dead ahead, an imperturbable mask. She was blushing, though.

When they bedded down for the night, Geoffrey thought, as he rolled up in his blanket, *Keep the watch for me, will you not Fess?*

Of course, Fess thought back, *though why I should bother when a hundred outlaws are doing so, I cannot think.*

In case they should decide to free their leader, Geoffrey thought drily, *by ridding her of me.* He tried to ignore the blanket-shrouded, curving form beside him in the dark and, to distract himself, thought, *A most fortunate meeting with the mother and daughter, was it not?*

How so? Fess's thoughts were guarded.

Why, thought Geoffrey, *an hour later, and they would have missed us quite.*

Yes, a most fortuitous coincidence, Fess agreed—somewhat drily, Geoffrey thought.

Once again, he could see Nan, side by side with Quicksilver, in his mind's eye. A vision of Quicksilver was not what he needed to put him to sleep, so he concentrated on Nan. *The daughter bears a most striking resemblance to Quicksilver.*

She does indeed.

There was something in the way the robot said it, in the careful noncommittal tone he used, that awoke Geoffrey's suspicions. What was Fess seeing that he was not . . . ? He visualized the two faces again, then the mother's next to Nan's . . .

And his eyes flew wide open. *Fess! Picture the mother Maud's face for me, and transform it backwards twenty years! Show her to me as she was before she married!*

He closed his eyes again, and Maud's face appeared behind his eyelids, then a younger version of the same face next to it, but without the kerchief, brown hair unbound, floating freely about her face and shoulders . . .

She is almost the spit and image of Quicksilver!

No, Fess thought back at him. *It is Quicksilver who is the spit and image of Maud.*

Fess rarely used slang of any sort, and it didn't take Geoffrey more than a moment to realize why the robot had done so this time. *Maud is her mother!*

That would be my conjecture, yes.

Then Nan must be her sister!

That would account for the resemblance, Fess agreed.

Then I have met all the family—save the father, who is dead. Geoffrey relaxed a little, opening his eyes to fix a brooding gaze on the shapely shadowed form beside him. He found he could not think clearly that way, so he rolled over onto his back to gaze up at the scrap of sky visible between the leaves overhead. *Why would they have brought word of Aunriddy's troubles themselves, instead of sending the messenger?*

Fess ignored the rhetorical nature of the question and answered, *Presumably, because they wished to meet you.*

Yes, that would seem clear. Geoffrey frowned up at the sky. *Now, why would they have wanted to do that?*

Why, indeed? Fess said, with the burst of static that served him for a sigh. He reflected that his young master was a positive genius at anything military, but could be singularly dense about anything else—and apparently, he did not yet see that a campaign was forming. Too intent on his own, no doubt. *Good night, Geoffrey.*

But there was no answer; puzzling over a question whose solution was too obvious to see had given Geoffrey the distraction and relaxation he had needed to lapse into sleep. Fess stood by, content to watch—and it was well that he did, for though Geoffrey may have found sleep, Quicksilver had not.

On the other hand, she had no mischief in mind—or none that Geoffrey would have objected to, at least.

CHAPTER
~9~

In the stillness of false dawn, a bird called.

Geoffrey looked up, frowning. "Knows not that owl that he should be abed?"

"So should you, if you were a proper man," Quicksilver retorted.

"No, a proper man would be up and about at this hour. It is the *un*proper man who would still be abed."

"And not alone?" Quicksilver said scornfully. "I am sure you know whereof you speak."

"Trust the voice of experience," Geoffrey agreed.

The owl hooted again.

"*There* is the voice I will trust," Quicksilver retorted. "She, at least, knows what she should be about, and when."

" 'She'?" Geoffrey raised an eyebrow. "How can you be so sure 'tis a hen?"

"Why, by its call," she said, with contempt.

"Indeed! And how is hers different from his?"

"By its tone, of course! Here, the cock owl sounds like this." Quicksilver cupped her hands and blew through her thumbs, producing a remarkably good imitation of an owl's cry. The bird in the bush instantly answered.

"Will she not come to seek you now?" Geoffrey asked.

"No—belike she sought to scold a male who had been out of his bed all night."

"Indeed! And should he not chide her for her vigil?"

"Since it was to await him out of worry, I think not."

" 'Twere best, then, that he not go home. Who could rest in a nest with a quarrelsome hen?"

"Indeed! Well, if she had a grain of sense about her, she would leave the nest ere he comes!"

"At last! We have agreed on something!"

Quicksilver stared at him, nonplussed, then reddened with irritation—but Geoffrey looked up at another birdcall. "That quail, at least, knows his proper hour."

"And his proper task," Quicksilver answered, "which is to greet the sun and find food for his mate and chicks."

"Before the nightcrawlers can ooze back to their beds." Geoffrey nodded. "I have seen them many a time."

"Oh? I thought you had *been* one."

"That, too," Geoffrey admitted. "Should we not stop to break our fast soon?"

"Why? Have you not brought wine enough?"

"When the dog bites me, I bite back," Geoffrey retorted.

She replied that a man is what he eats, and so they rode on in good-natured verbal fencing as the sun rose, and the dawn elbowed its way past the night. After a while, though, both ran out of quips, and they rode side by side in a silence that Geoffrey realized had become companionable, and was surprised to find that he had no desire to break.

After a while, though, Quicksilver began to feel restless—she could not let this arrogant lordling presume too much, so she spoke. "I am surprised that you were so quick to say you would come to the aid of Aunriddy."

"Are you truly?" Geoffrey asked, with interest. "Would *you* turn away from the prospect of a fight in a good cause?"

Quicksilver stared at him, then slowly smiled. "No, I would not! And I suppose it would be too much to ask of you to forego it, either."

"Most certainly," Geoffrey agreed cheerfully. "However, that is only the *true* reason. I have a better."

"How now?" Quicksilver demanded. "You have already told me the true reason, and it is not so good as the false one?"

"Oh, the other is not false. It is simply that even without it, I would ride to the aid of a village beset by outlaws."

"Or a *lord* who was beset by outlaws," Quicksilver said, with irony.

"Or a damsel," Geoffrey reminded her. "Would I had known of your danger, when first you were accosted! But since I did not, I shall have to work out my anger on the outlaws who bedevil Aunriddy."

Quicksilver secretly thrilled to hear him say it, but made sure the thrill stayed secret. "What is this 'better' reason?"

"Why, 'tis simply that such a rescue is my duty. I am a knight-errant, after all, and am sworn to defend the weak."

"Very laudable," Quicksilver said drily, "since it gives you an excuse to go wandering and leave your wife and child at home."

Geoffrey frowned. "I have no wife or child."

Quicksilver hid her savage delight behind sarcasm. "Aye, but when you have, you will be glad of such an excuse to go philandering."

Geoffrey laughed, but quickly sobered, gazing straight into her eyes. "I shall never marry unless I can find a woman who will be so desirable that she will drive thoughts of wandering clear out of my head, making me wish only to stay by her."

There was that in his look and his tone that made Quicksilver quiver inside, but she spoke all the more hotly for that. "There is no such woman, sir, for any man will grow bored with the favors of even the most beautiful female."

"Her remedy, then, is to be a woman of infinite variety," Geoffrey retorted, "so that she is many women in one."

Quicksilver laughed bitterly. "Do you not ask the impossible of her, sir?"

"Why not?" Geoffrey said airily. "She is sure to ask the impossible of *me*."

Quicksilver frowned, and was about to ask—when Geoffrey turned from her, his eyes kindling. "Ah! Is that Aunriddy, then?"

Quicksilver turned to look, then nodded. "Aye."

Below them, the forest opened into a hillside of scrub growth, sloping down into a bowl between itself and other hills. In the hollow lay a village, plumes of smoke rising from its chimneys. Men were trudging out to the fields with hoes over their shoulders, and women moved about the cottages in their morning chores.

"I did not know that we were so close," Geoffrey said.

"I thought it better to come upon them by morning," Quicksilver replied.

"Wisely done, for who knows what may lurk in the night? And from what Maud said of these bandits, I think they are not the sort to wake early." But Geoffrey was frowning down at the village. "There is something wrong about it."

"Oh, naught but starvation and despair," Quicksilver answered.

"Both can be remedied." Geoffrey shook the reins, and Fess moved on down the trail. "Let us hope it is nothing more lasting," he called back to Quicksilver.

They rode into the village side by side, looking about them with sharp eyes. A goodwife saw them and dropped her bucket, hurrying away and shooing her children before her, stopping their complaints with whacks across the bottoms.

"Strangers are not a sign of hope," Geoffrey said.

"I doubt not that too many strangers have shown themselves to be causes of despair." Quicksilver looked up keenly. "Do you know now what seemed wrong to you, from above?"

"Aye." Geoffrey nodded at a tyke who sat playing listlessly in the dust. "It is the children. They do not run and shout at their play, as little ones should."

Quicksilver turned to look, her face darkening. "Aye. They are too weak for such eager sport. They have eaten too little."

The child's mother came running to scoop him up and hurry away with an awkward, limping gait. The tot squalled a feeble protest, then was silent.

"All lack spirit here," Geoffrey said, eyeing the slump-shouldered form of the mother. "Even from the hillside above, we should have been able to hear the men sing as they went out to the fields."

"What had they to sing about?" Quicksilver was looking more and more stormy as they went along.

"Ho! What is this?" Geoffrey reined in and looked up, frowning.

They had come to the village green, if you could call it that—a larger-than-average space between houses, more or less circular, with a few patch-legged stools sitting in the dust. On one of them sat a pretty young woman, tears streaming down her cheeks as older women fluttered around her, making soothing sounds and dressing her hair with flowers and ribbons.

"They deck her like a bride," Geoffrey said, "but why would a bride be weeping?"

"Because she is being constrained to marry a man she does not love," Quicksilver told him, "but I do not think this one goes to a wedding." She clucked to her horse, and it moved up close to the weeping girl.

The women looked up with alarm.

"Why do you weep, maiden?" Quicksilver demanded.

The girl looked up, startled, then gasped in alarm. A woman seated astride a horse with bare legs and bare arms was shocking, even if the scabbard across her back was empty.

"She has cause enough." One of the older women wrapped her arms protectively around the girl. "Let the poor child be."

"Why, so I shall, if others do. Who seeks to torment her?"

"She must go to warm the bed of Maul, the chief of the bandits who beset us, if you must know! He is a crude man, and rough, and takes pleasure in cruelty."

The girl burst into tears, wailing hopelessly.

"You must be a stranger, or you would know of this," a granny said. "Ride warily, mistress, or Maul shall come for you, too."

"I hope that he does!" Quicksilver hissed.

"Do not think your man shall save you from him." Another beldame scowled from Geoffrey to Quicksilver and back. "He is twice your size, young man, and has fifty like him at his back."

Geoffrey nodded judiciously. "The odds are not too uneven, then."

"Aye," Quicksilver snapped, "if you give me back my sword!"

"Here it is, and gladly." Geoffrey took her sword from its lashings and handed it back to her, hilt first. "Now the odds are uneven again."

"Beware, cocksure youth." The granny frowned. "Pride goeth before the fall."

"That it does, and Maul shall surely fall." Geoffrey turned to Quicksilver. "Shall we hunt him, or bait him?"

"Bait him?" Quicksilver looked up in delight. "Why, what an excellent idea!" She dismounted and tossed him the reins. "Let us go inside your hut, Grandmother! Maul shall come for his tidbit today, shall he not?"

"Aye." The granny stared at her, taken aback.

"Well, he shall find her, but not this poor lass!"

Hope sprang in the girl's eyes, but the beldame wailed, "He shall see 'tis not Phoebe at a glance! He shall wreak his vengeance on our whole village!"

"When he has seen my face, do you truly think he will cavil?" Quicksilver shooed them toward the doorway, completely unaware of how conceited she had sounded. "Come, let us prepare him a nuptial surprize!" She turned back in the doorway and told Geoffrey, "You might see to feeding those poor starving babes whiles I dress."

Geoffrey started a scathing retort, but she disappeared into the hut. He shrugged and looked about him. She was right, after all—the children should be fed. A few more hours would make no great difference, but he could not abide to see suffering when he could prevent it.

As he rode around the village green, though, the mothers snatched their babes indoors, leaving only the old and the infirm to sit out in the sun. And infirm they were—a dozen of all ages sat listlessly, spooning thin gruel with hands covered with sores. A nasty suspicion began, and Geoffrey drew up beside one rail-thin middle-aged man whose skin hung on him like a garment suddenly become too large. "Have you no food other than grain, goodman?"

The man looked up, too weary for surprise. "Nay, sir, and no great store of that."

That explained the sores, then, and the lethargy. "Surely you could make your porridge strong enough to eat, not drink!"

"Mayhap," the man said, "though we must make it last till the harvest. Still, I would I dared chew."

" 'Dared'? Why do you not?"

"For fear my teeth might fall out, sir. They seem loose in my head."

"Belike they are," Geoffrey said, and turned away brusquely, hiding his distress at what he saw. It was clearly vitamin deficiency, and apparently the outlaws had taken all food but a small stock of grain for six months or more—long enough for the symptoms to show. Aunriddy was not yet starving, but it was nonetheless dying of malnutrition.

Still, what could he do? Teleport in some tomatoes and dried meat and vegetables and fruit, yes, but how could he tend the illnesses they had now, while he waited for them to heal? He seemed to remember Fess saying something about that in the biology class he had so steadfastly ignored—he had only paid attention to the business about beriberi and scurvy when Fess had pointed out that they were apt to weaken an army besieging a castle. Of healing he knew nothing, except for the rough meatball surgery that might prove necessary on the battlefield—and this did not look like a case of need for cauterizing wounds.

Well, if he knew nothing about healing, he knew one

who did. He called up a mental image of his sister and concentrated on her while he thought, long and hard in the family encoded mode, *Cordelia! Your aid, I pray!*

Cordelia's answer was instant. *What ails you, brother?*

Not I myself, Geoffrey answered, *but a whole village that is suffering from vitamin deficiencies. Babes and aged alike have running sores and live in lethargy.*

There was a pause; this was not what Cordelia expected when one of her brothers called for help. *I shall finish this potion that I brew, then, and bring what medicines I may. What is the cause? Know they no better than to eat naught but grain?*

They do, Geoffrey assured her, *but they are beset by bandits, who take all other food they grow.*

Why, the lice and poltroons! Cordelia answered, seething. *Know you no cure for a plague of wolves, brother?*

I do, he assured her, *and we set a wolf-trap even now.*

'We'? Cordelia demanded. *Who is 'we'?*

Geoffrey almost answered her, then remembered that any picture of Quicksilver he thought of was bound to have his feelings attached—and he wasn't quite ready for his sister to know about those, just yet. *The bandit chieftain whom I was sent to hobble*, he told Cordelia. *I shall speak of her when you come.*

'Her'? Cordelia thought. *A bandit chieftain, and a woman? This I must see! Where are you, brother?*

In a village called Aunriddy, Geoffrey answered, and visualized a map of Gramarye that zoomed in on the Duchy of Loguire, with Aunriddy marked by a large red "X."

I shall fly to you, Cordelia assured him. *Expect me within the hour.* Her thought-stream ended.

Geoffrey frowned. Within the hour? From Runnymede to Loguire, in no more time than that? It was two days' hard riding! Even flying, it should have taken her the better part of a day. How could she manage an hour?

Time enough to ask when she came. In the meantime, there were hungry children to feed. Geoffrey rode to the center of the common, frowning. He murmured softly, sure no one would overhear. " 'Tis a pretty problem, Fess. I must conjure up food enough to heal them, but not so much that the bandits will see it and seize it—and thrash each man and woman till they are sure hidden stocks have been yielded up."

"Then bring only as much as they can hide," Fess answered.

Geoffrey nodded. "Sound advice. Let us turn to it, then."

He dismounted and reached inside his tunic to the inner pocket that served him as a purse. He tossed a heap of pennies onto the ground, then stared at them and thought about oranges. It took quite a bit of concentration, of course—he wasn't *really* turning the pennies into oranges. Rather, he was teleporting the fruit from places where it was, to a place where it wasn't—here—then teleporting a penny back to the source of the oranges, one penny for five, which had been a little more than the going rate the last time he had noticed. He did not want any merchant or farmer to go bankrupt due to his errand of mercy. More to the point, he was a knight, and determined not to rob the commoners. The rich were another matter, but only if they had obtained their wealth by stealing from the poor.

He had to know where the fruit was coming from, of course. He began with those he knew best—the stalls in the market in Runnymede—then moved on to the orchards on the southern coast of Gramarye. He had only seen one or two such, but they were more than enough for the current purpose. He wanted a dozen oranges for each person in Aunriddy, and he got them.

Each orange appeared with a gunshot crack of displaced air; each penny disappeared with a pop. It sounded as though he had lit a string of firecrackers—a very long string, and it brought the village children running out to watch with eyes that grew rounder and rounder as the fruit began to pile up. Their mothers came running after to protect their babes from the strangers, and froze, staring at the warlock and the pile of fruit that seemed to boil up from the ground before him.

At last he nodded, satisfied, and turned to them. "Take a dozen oranges for each person in your family—mother, father, children, and old folk. Each person eat one a day, no more."

The women clutched their children to them and stared out of eyes that had become a little wild.

"Do not fear—'tis real fruit, not made of air or brimstone," Geoffrey said impatiently. "I have not conjured it up, really, but brought it to you from the farms where it grows."

Still they did not move, and Geoffrey suddenly realized that most of them had probably never seen an orange. Tomatoes, yes—though it never occurred to him that neither fruit had been known in medieval Northern Europe, or that his ancestors had performed one of their many improvements on history by bringing citrus fruit to Gramarye. He only knew that these were inland people, whereas oranges grew on the southern coast. If Aunriddy had seen the fruit at all, it would have been as rare treats provided by the lord on festival days—and from the little he knew of their lord, he doubted the Count would have given his peasants anything he could avoid.

He took an orange from the pile, slit the rind with his

thumbnail, then peeled it back and tossed it away. He broke off a section, tossed it into his mouth, and chewed it with every evidence of enjoyment. Then he stepped over to a young woman with three very skinny toddlers and held out a section. Her face creased with the tension between longing and fear, but longing won out; she took the slice, put it in her mouth, and chewed.

Her eyes went round with the wonder of it.

Carefully and slowly, Geoffrey sat down on his heels, separating three more sections and holding them out on his palm. The toddlers snatched them up. Their mother gave a little cry of alarm, reaching to knock the fruit out of their hands, then caught herself and watched, trembling, as they ate.

Geoffrey stood and stepped back, gesturing toward the fruit. The women ran to gather it up. He watched them, seething with anger at the bandits who had made them so fearful, then turned away to another part of the common, flung down more coppers, and began to think of vegetables.

He had just finished conjuring up a heap of string beans when one woman cried, "A witch!"

"No, a warlock!" Geoffrey said impatiently, turning to her. "Can you not tell the difference between . . ."

But she was pointing up into the sky, and the mothers and children were already running for the shelter of their huts.

Geoffrey looked, then looked again. He had expected the broomstick, but had not anticipated seeing two people astride it.

The broom curved in for a landing, and Cordelia hopped off to run to him, leaving her passenger to pick up the stick. "How now, brother! Have you turned grocer?"

"Nay, only merchant!" Geoffrey grinned with pleasure

at seeing her. "And I offer these folk quite a bargain—in truth, 'tis a steal!"

"What, do you not pay for what you take?" asked the tall, broad-sholdered blond young man who came up behind Cordelia.

"Of course I do, but I doubt I'll have luck even giving it away." Geoffrey clasped his future brother-in-law by the hand and forearm with a broad smile. "How good it is to see you, Alain, and how good of you to come to our aid! But we must not put the Crown Prince in jeopardy."

" 'Tis you who showed me the folly of that notion, Geoffrey," Alain said, returning the clasp. "When I am king, I shall have to lead armies; I must accustom myself to the trick of surviving battles ere that time comes." Then, to Cordelia, "You did not tell me there would be fighting here."

"I did not know it." She set her fists on her hips, glaring up at Geoffrey. "Though I should have guessed it, since you were here! Do you mean to fight these bandits, then?"

"Aye," said a voice behind her, "and to beat them into the ground!"

They all turned, to see Quicksilver striding toward them—and Geoffrey caught his breath, for she was dressed as a bride, in village finery and with a wreath in her hair. For a moment, he stood stunned, feeling the eldritch prickling of precognition enveloping his skin; was he looking at his own future? He felt a kind of desire he had never known before, a covetousness to have and to hold the woman entire.

Then he noticed the flash of her calves through the slits she had made in the sides of the skirt, saw the broadsword in her hand, and jolted back to the present; she had made sure the bridal gown did not restrict her ability to fight.

Still, she cut a magnificent figure, Geoffrey thought,

with her split skirt whipping about her, her long legs showing through, her auburn hair swirling about her shoulders, glinting here and there with gold where the sunlight touched it.

Then he realized there was tension in the air, a growing rivalry, emanating from the two women as each saw a potential rival. He moved quickly to resolve it. "Quicksilver, this is my sister Cordelia, and her fiancé Alain." Somehow, it seemed politic to drop the word "prince."

Geoffrey realized that Quicksilver's gaze was lingering on Alain's handsome, open face and broad shoulders, and was astounded to feel a stab of jealousy. To hide it, he hurried to finish the introductions. "Cordelia, Alain—this is Quicksilver, chieftain of the bandits of County Laeg."

"And his prisoner, though he seems to be too gallant to tell you that." Quicksilver did not hold out a hand; in fact, the chip on her shoulder seemed to grow. "It is good of you to come, milady, but we are like to see battle here, and I would advise you not to stay."

"Why, I have seen battle before." Cordelia smiled, amused. "I shall take a hand, if I see a need."

Quicksilver turned on Geoffrey with a frown. "I cannot direct a battle when a woman may upset my plans with her own notions of what will aid!"

"Do you think I know nothing of warfare?" Cordelia countered. "Nay, I will stay aloft, watching for your men who may become too sorely beset, and lend a hand only when I see they are about to be overcome."

"Well, that would aid," Quicksilver admitted, though with great reluctance—and it came to Geoffrey that she did not expect any of her men to be in any such danger.

But Alain picked up on something the others missed. "What men are these whom you will command, Chieftain Quicksilver?"

"Why, the bandits of County Laeg," Geoffrey said slowly, "or half of them."

Quicksilver turned to him in surprise and anger. "You knew!"

"Their steps are silent," Geoffrey told her, "but their thoughts are noisy. Then, too, when I hear an owl hoot after dawn, I discover suspicions—but the more so when you answer it, and it answers you."

Quicksilver's eyes narrowed. "You are perhaps too quick-witted for my own good."

"Oh, I would not be overly concerned about that," Cordelia said with a smile.

Quicksilver turned to her in surprise, and some secret, silent communication seemed to pass between them, for Quicksilver smiled a little, too. "Perhaps, but I am not his sister."

"Praise Heaven for that," Geoffrey breathed, and Cordelia glanced at him in irritation. "No, she is your prisoner."

" 'Tis a rare prisoner who bears a broadsword," Alain noted.

"He has just now given it back to me," Quicksilver retorted, "which he must, if he wishes my aid against these bandits."

"And when the fight is done?" Alain demanded. "Will you give it back to him, then?"

"Will he demand it?" Quicksilver countered.

"Let us win the battle before we deal with the peace," Geoffrey said quickly. "Cordelia has come to heal these villagers, Quicksilver."

The bandit chief frowned. "How are they ill?"

"From poor food," Cordelia told her. "My brother has given them enough to remedy that—if we can persuade the wives to take in that heap of string beans before the crows come for it."

"There is no trouble in that," Quicksilver snapped, and turned toward the huts. "Ho! Wives of the village! Come to Quicksilver! At once!"

The women emerged, wavered for a second, then came hurrying to the chieftain.

"She is not tremendously tactful," Cordelia pointed out in a low voice.

"No," Geoffrey agreed, "but she achieves results."

Cordelia glanced at him keenly. "Brother, do not seek results that you should not!"

"No fear," Geoffrey said softly. "This one is different."

"I had not noticed," Cordelia said drily.

"Had you not? She is magnetic, she is a very dynamo, she is . . ."

"Geoffrey," Alain said softly, "your sister is being sarcastic again."

Geoffrey looked at Cordelia in surprize, then gave her a sheepish grin. "I ride my hobbyhorse, do I not?"

"You do not," Cordelia snapped, "and you had best not!"

The women were hurrying back to their huts, each with an apronful of string beans, and Quicksilver strode back to them. "I have made them swear not to cook them until the bandits have come and gone." She glared at Geoffrey. "How did you bring it here, warlock?"

"Why," he answered, "you should know, witch."

"Is she really?" Cordelia seemed very interested. "But one untutored, no doubt."

"Aye," Quicksilver said reluctantly, "if by that you mean I have had to learn the usage of my powers by myself."

"I did. Know, then, proud lady, that warlocks can move

things from one place to another in an instant, merely by thinking of it; we call that 'teleportation.' "

Quicksilver stared in indignation. "Men can, but we cannot? 'Tis quite unfair!"

"Aye," Cordelia said in a soothing tone, "but they cannot make objects fly just by thinking at them—save themselves."

"Your brother can."

"All my brothers can," Cordelia answered. "They alone among all the warlocks of Gramarye, and 'tis even as you have said—it is quite unfair."

Alain suddenly lifted his head. "I hear the clash of harness."

Everyone fell silent for a few seconds. Then Quicksilver said, "You have good ears—I cannot hear a shred of it. But I hear their thoughts. You have the right of it—the bandits come." She turned to Geoffrey. "Do you take the eastern side of this common, and your sister's betrothed with you, to guard your back."

Geoffrey almost retorted that he did not need anyone to guard his back, then realized that it was a way for him to protect Alain without the Prince being aware of it. He wondered if Quicksilver had been thinking of that, then was quite sure she had.

"Aloft, damsel!" Quicksilver commanded. "I must go sit as bait." And she turned away, to stride to a low stool that stood in the middle of the little common.

Cordelia watched her go with a small smile, then turned away to her broomstick. Alain and Geoffrey were on their way to hide among the huts, and Quicksilver was hiding her sword in the grass at her side. The bandits were in for quite a surprise.

CHAPTER
~10~

The bandits came riding out of the trees, between the huts, and into the village common.

These are wealthy for brigands, Geoffrey thought. *Their clothes are rich, and decked with ornaments.*

But their lace is filthy, and their velvet doublets soiled and slashed, Fess pointed out.

They are slovenly, Cordelia put in from her vantage point above. *Wealthy slovens, but slovens nonetheless.*

The biggest bandit rode at the front and reined in ten feet from Quicksilver. "Ho! What beauty have we here? They have been saving the best till now!"

Quicksilver made her eyes huge and round. "What men are you?"

"Why, I am the bandit Maul, and these are my men." The chief grinned, showing stained teeth with several gaps.

"Bandit?" Quicksilver cried, aghast. "They told me their lord would come to woo me for his bride!"

Maul threw back his head and laughed. His men echoed him. "Why, you have been duped," he said, wiping his eyes. "What are you—some traveller who was passing, and was beguiled into taking the place of the maid I demanded?"

"*You!* Are *you* their lord?"

"In some measure," Maul said, relishing her evident fear. "Not their legal lord, no—he is a craven who will not fight me, so I lord it over this village to my heart's content, and they pay me tribute in food, wine, and women. If they do not, I shall burn their village to the ground, aye, and all their men and old women as well!"

"I am betrayed!" Quicksilver cried, shrinking in on herself.

Geoffrey knew the fear was a pretense, but even so, his blood raged within him, and he ached to feel Maul's throat between his fingers.

"Aye, betrayed, but their lie had some truth in it." Maul swung down off his horse and came toward her. "I am their lord, in a fashion, as I've said—and I do come to woo, though not for marriage." He reached out for her . . .

Quicksilver moved so fast that she was almost a blur. She reached down into the grass beside her, then thrust upward, right into Maul's groin.

Brother, came Cordelia's thought, *are you sure you wish to travel with this woman?*

Maul froze, staring down horrified at the unbelievable gout of blood pumping from him as Quicksilver yanked her sword free. But his anguish lasted only seconds; she leaped to her feet and lunged, stabbing deep into his chest as she screamed, *"Havoc!"*

The sound broke the trance of horror that held Maul's bandits. They were men of violence and brutality, and hardened to the sight of bloody horrors. With one massive shout, they charged down upon the lone woman.

But she was alone no longer; the second she had shouted "Havoc!" Geoffrey had kicked his horse, breaking from the cover of the huts to her side, with Alain right behind him on Quicksilver's mount. They stood now to either hand, swords at the ready.

Her own bandits were just as quick, though unmounted. They burst from the huts all around, from the trees behind.

But the bandits in front were too crazed with anger to pay attention. They rode straight for Quicksilver, swords high . . .

The swords twisted in their hands and stabbed down at them.

The front rank recoiled with howls of superstitious fear, even as their horses reached Quicksilver.

Fess leaped forward, shouldering one stallion aside, and Geoffrey stabbed without compunction, though he did aim for the shoulder, not the heart. The man slumped in his saddle, howling, even as Geoffrey turned to stab the man on his left. He was aware of hoarse shrieks of pain, of outlaws swinging their shields up above their heads to ward off a rain of rocks—and of the quarterstaves that thrust up at them from below. But more than anything else, he was aware of the burning need to keep any of these brutes from coming near Quicksilver. He parried and slashed, working his way along the line, praying that Fess would not have a seizure . . .

Suddenly, the great black horse jolted to a stop, legs stiff, its head swinging down between its fetlocks. Geoffrey barely managed to keep from being thrown by sheer momentum, but he turned at bay, blocking blades that rained at him from every side. In the back of his mind, he rejoiced that if Fess had had to have a seizure, he had waited until he was directly in front of Quicksilver.

On her other side, Alain was hewing mightily about him with sword and dagger. He was already bleeding in two places, but before him was a heap of crumpled outlaws, and their horses were running wild back into the press of their fellows, creating more confusion than Quicksilver's men.

"Will you leave me none for my anger?" Quicksilver cried in frustration. "Nay, then, step aside!" And she leaped past Geoffrey, sword flashing and thrusting, a veritable whirlwind of death in embroidered skirt and bodice, the flower ring still holding to her hair even as her white blouse sprouted stains of her enemies' blood.

"They call for quarter, Quicksilver!" Minerva cried.

"Give them the quarter they gave the villagers!" Quicksilver raged.

"No quarter!" Minerva cried. "No mercy!"

"Nay, save one!" Alain called. "Save one at least! One for the King's judgement!"

"The *King*?" Quicksilver cried, outraged.

Then, suddenly, it was all over. A score of outlaws stood with their hands high, devoid of weapons, either on horseback or a-foot, and Quicksilver's men and women hovered with swords and spears at their throats and chests, each thinking that perhaps this was the one who should be saved for the King.

"The *King*?" Quicksilver turned on Alain in fury. "What service has the King ever done us, that we should thank him? Has he protected us from rape or despoiling? No! Has he protected us from the banditry of Count Laeg? No! Has he enforced the poor man's share of his own crops? No! All we have had from the King is an increase in taxes, so that he may take *his* share!"

Cordelia landed behind Alain and stepped up beside him, but Quicksilver showed no sign of having noticed. "We owe the King nothing!" she said. "No, nothing, and least of all one of these cattle we have just taken by the might of our own arms, not his!"

Alain took it well, standing against the blast of her anger. "Then save one for Duke Loguire's justice."

"Duke Loguire! The King *is* Duke Loguire! Which is to say, there has been no Duke Loguire since the King's father died! Oh, I will own the poor man was safe whiles the old Duke lived, and such villainy as old Count Laeg did, he had to do secretly, so that only we peasants knew of virgins debauched and poachers flogged to their deaths— but not these last twenty years!"

Alain frowned. "There were the Crown's reeves!"

"Aye, each living in fear of Count Laeg, or taking his coin! Nay, if the King had cared for us as he should have, I would not be an outlaw today!"

"If you did not send word . . ."

"It was his duty to know!" Quicksilver snapped. "Or Duke Loguire's, at least! Oh, aye, I know he gave the title to his younger son—but what good is a child Duke? The more so, when he dwells a hundred miles and more away, in Runnymede! What use is he then?"

"He dwells in Castle Loguire now," Alain told her, "and he is not a child any more."

All the bandits went silent. Even Geoffrey stared, amazed, and realized how far out of touch with the events of the Court he had become while he wandered the roads of Gramarye, looking for fun—or wrongs to right, which were one and the same to him. So Diarmid had been installed as Duke Loguire? No wonder his brother was here in the South, to help him settle in—and Cordelia with him!

"Where have you had this news?" Quicksilver demanded.

"At Castle Loguire," Alain said, "from which we have come to aid you."

Quicksilver calmed, eyeing him warily as she prowled about him. Cordelia stepped between them protectively.

"I have heard he is a milksop, this Duke Diarmid," the outlaw chief finally said. "I have heard he cannot lift a broadsword, nor has the courage to order a murderer hanged."

"You shall find him otherwise," Alain replied. "I can testify to his ability with the broadsword . . ."

"With what proof?"

Alain's mouth tightened with impatience, but he pulled up the sleeve of his doublet to show a long white scar. "*That* proof! And this was only from practice, mind you, not done in earnest!"

"Practice indeed," Quicksilver said with contempt. "Has he had more than practice, this dukelet of yours? Has he ever fought in a true battle? Has he ever had to say who will live and who will die?"

"In battle, he has fought beside me," Alain testified, "though 'twas only against a band of cutthroats, not a proper army."

Quicksilver's bandits stirred, muttering with displeasure.

Alain ignored them. "As to judgement, he has never had to sit in the seat himself, but has given good advice to those who have."

"The quality of his governance has not yet been tested, then," Quicksilver said, "nor his good sense, nor his justice. I am not about to bid my outlaws disband and trust to his sense of fairness quite yet."

"None have asked you to."

"Nay, but you have asked me to save one of this worthless rabble to tell lies about me and my band, that this new Duke may be sure we are villains!"

"There are those who can testify to the truth or falseness of his words." Alain glanced significantly at Geoffrey. "I do not ask you to trust yourselves to Duke Diarmid's judgement, but only one of your enemies, that the Duke may know into what chaos his demesne has fallen, and the magnitude of the task he must undertake."

Quicksilver stood glaring at him, unwilling to argue further, sensing a grain of rightness in what Alain said.

"Come, how great a risk is it?" Cordelia coaxed. "You have slain a score of villains, and have a score more to try according to your own code! May not the Duke have one?"

"Only if you bear witness to him of what you have seen in Aunriddy!"

"Why, that I will," Alain said, "and I do not doubt we shall find others who will speak against these bandits."

"And this parish must be taken from Count Frith! He has failed to protect it! It is mine now, to protect and nurture as I will!"

Alain stared a moment, then said, "But you are a royal prisoner."

Quicksilver stared at him, her face emptying.

Geoffrey couldn't stand to see her so forlorn. He stepped forward and asked softly, "Is that what you shall charge before the King? That the title of Count Laeg is now yours, by right of good governance?"

Quicksilver shot him a look of surprize that transformed into gratitude, then as quickly transformed into something else that made Geoffrey go weak in the knees. "Aye," she said, "even so shall I maintain! Let him judge me guilty of thievery when I maintain my cause by Right as well as Might!"

Alain frowned. "There is no precedent . . ."

"Come, my love." Cordelia smiled up at him, taking his arm. "You know full well that anything that *is* a precedent had to happen one first time."

Alain beamed down at her, all sternness disappearing. "Why, 'tis even so! How clever you are, to think it!"

A murmur went through the outlaws, and Minerva stared in surprize, then looked strangely uncertain—but Quicksilver only gave him an acid smile. "I think you are a fool for a woman, sir."

"Aye," Alain agreed readily, "but there is no shame in that, when the woman in question is so wise."

"La, my lord!" Cordelia blushed, looking down, but smiling. "You embarrass me, and in front of so many folk!"

Geoffrey glanced at Quicksilver, and saw the naked longing there in her face before she hid it behind a mocking smile. "How sweet! But whiles you dally, there are men groaning in pain."

"Oh, aye!" Cordelia dropped Alain's arm and stepped past Quicksilver, toward the tangle of wounded. "Come, let us see to their hurts! Leave the binding of prisoners to your men, and aid me!"

Quicksilver stared after her, astounded and confounded.

"Bid your brothers see to the enemy," Geoffrey suggested, "for surely at least one of them is here. Is not the measure of a chieftain how well her band works when she is *not* there?"

Quicksilver frowned up at him. "An interesting notion—and one measure among several, at least. Jory!"

Her bodyguard parted to let her brother step up. "Aye, sister?"

"Bind such of these outlaws as still live, for it would be

wrong to slay them now, in cold blood! You may judge them later, beneath the greenwood tree or at Castle Laeg!"

"It shall be done, Jane." He turned away.

Cordelia halted, looking back in surprize. " 'Jane'?"

"It is for my family to call me that," Quicksilver snapped, "and no other. Let us see to the doctoring, damsel—but I warn you, my surgery is of the roughest sort."

"And mine is of the gentlest," Cordelia rejoined, "so between us, we should be ready for anything we may find. Can you not heal as well as you slay?"

"Aye. Come, and I shall show you!"

The two women strode off side by side, and Alain stepped over to Geoffrey, shaking his head in wonder. "What a spitfire she is! I tell you, Geoffrey, I marvel all over again at this lass of mine, that she can tame even so wild a spirit as this, so quickly!"

"Aye, *she* can," Geoffrey said softly, "but can I?"

Alain turned to him, frowning. "How was that?"

"Nothing," Geoffrey said, aloud. "She may be a bandit chieftain, Alain, but she has had cause."

"So it would seem, from what she said about Count Laeg. She slew him, did she not?"

"Ah," Geoffrey said softly, "so the Loguires have not been as wholly ignorant of what passed in their domain as she thinks."

"Aye, but we should have known the fullness of this ere it came to her rebellion. I will own 'tis that which has made us look more closely."

"And is the cause of Diarmid's coming to Loguire?"

"Aye. Mind you, the lad is nearly twenty, and has long been ready for the office—but Mother would not hear of his being so far from her."

"Ever the case with the youngest," Geoffrey agreed,

thinking of his own younger brother. "But when word of Quicksilver's taking Castle Laeg came, the Queen conflicted with the mother, eh?"

"Even so, and when we heard that Quicksilver had declared the county to be hers, and she its rightful ruler, the Queen won, and agreed to sending her second and last child to attend to the matter."

"With a small army to guard him."

"Aye."

"And his big brother."

"And his big brother's witch-fiancée. Aye."

Geoffrey nodded. "So that is why Cordelia could come so quickly when I called—and why she could bring you with her."

"I will not say it was entirely her own idea," Alain hedged. "I think she was surprized when I volunteered so readily—until she realized that I feared for her safety among bandits."

"You did not tell her that it was also because you wished to study this bandit Quicksilver close at hand?"

Alain shrugged. "Why? I am sure she has worked that out for herself."

"But it is more polite to pretend neither of you knows it." Geoffrey nodded. "And truly, you were more concerned for her safety than curious about Quicksilver, were you not?"

"Oh, aye, but she is more concerned for mine." Alain shrugged off the matter. "No doubt she shall be angered when she sees that I have taken two more wounds—but they are mere scratches, and others are hurt far worse."

"Scratches can fester." Geoffrey turned away to take lint and balm out of Fess's saddle bag. "Come, doff your doublet and let us bind up these wounds!"

"Why, if you must," Alain sighed, and shrugged out of

his doublet. "When you are done, of course, I will bind for you. What of this lady bandit of yours? I am told she slew old Count Laeg; was there any excuse for it?"

"Is self-defense excuse enough?"

"So I had surmised." Alain nodded. "He sought to rape her, then?"

"He would have been pleased if she had submitted willingly," Geoffrey answered, "but she did not—and I gather he was far more pleased with the prospect of rape."

Alain's lips thinned, and it was not with the pain of the balm going into his cuts. "He exercised the *droit du seigneur*, then."

"Not even that. By that law, the lord has the right to each bride's maidenhead, the night before she is wed. Quicksilver was betrothed to no man, nor, from what I hear, were most of the other damsels he took to his bed."

"A thorough rogue indeed!" Alain hissed. "Nay, we should have been far less trusting of our reeves and our steward!"

"Your steward was a good man," Geoffrey said carefully.

"Aye, but he always strove to think well of everybody, never realizing that he might thus be overlooking villainies. Diarmid is more suspicious than that."

Geoffrey remembered Diarmid's cold, analytical insistence on learning all the facts relating to any matter before he made up his mind about it, and felt chilled within. "He is that."

"So the killing was self-defense," Alain said, "though 'twas still a commoner slaying a lord."

"Aye. She was sure the law would not protect her, and for that reason alone, I suspect she was right."

"So she broke the law further, by stealing?"

Geoffrey shrugged. "She felt she had no choice—it was

win rule, or submit willingly to abuse, or die. For a woman alone, that may well have been the case."

"Then the law is vile, and must be changed!" said the future King of Gramarye. "But has she ever set forth to steal, or has she only defended herself and her people?"

"She has never started a battle, if that is what you mean. She has always waited for her enemy to attack first, then has carved him into little pieces. *Then* she has taken his land and castle."

"As it was necessary to take Castle Laeg, in order for her to defend herself." Alain nodded. "That makes more sense than it sounds."

"A great deal more," Geoffrey agreed. "Once she had beaten Count Laeg's troops, she could be sure he would come against her with a larger army, even with royal troops among them."

"And, no doubt, with myself or Diarmid as their general," Alain grunted, "if you had not forestalled her."

"You see? It was even as she guessed. No, surely she needed the walls of Castle Laeg to defend her—and had to chase the young Count from his own demesne, scattering his troops, so that he could not come against her." Geoffrey shrugged. "It was against the law, but it was sound strategy."

"If she were a general for the Crown, we would reward her for it," Alain agreed. "There is less wrong in what she has done than in the circumstances that brought her to it. Yes, there may even be merit to her notion that the young Count has forfeited his county by bad governance, and that it should be hers by right of good governance."

Geoffrey noted that Alain had already officially forgotten who came up with that idea. "It will give her a talking point at law, at least."

"It is certainly the sort of argument that would appeal to

Diarmid. I must say that if it is a choice between changing Quicksilver and changing the law, I can only say that the law is wrong—but it would be a dangerous precedent to lay on the books."

"You worry about the precedent, friend," Geoffrey advised, "and let me worry about Quicksilver."

Alain flashed him a smile. "She is worth the worrying, I warrant you."

"I shall need some sort of warrant, that is sure," Geoffrey said, with a sardonic smile, "though one for her death is not quite the sort I wish." He sighed. "Even if she had been wrong in everything she had done, Alain, surely this battle would have earned her some clemency."

"Putting down a band of vicious outlaws, and saving a village? Aye, and if we add to that her muzzling of the outlaw bands in her forest, I think we may say there is grounds for clemency indeed. That does not mean, though, that she can be exempted from punishment entirely."

"But that the punishment might be crafted to fit the crime?"

Alain gave him a slow smile. "Why, what a fascinating thought! But come, my wounds are bound. Take off your doublet."

"Oh, if I must," Geoffrey grumbled, and they changed places.

Quicksilver held the groaning bandit up with one hand while she took the roll of bandage from Cordelia at the man's right-hand side, unrolled it across his back, and passed it to Cordelia on the left. "That is a most handsome man on whom you have cast the band of betrothal, Lady Cordelia."

Cordelia smiled, trying not to appear smug. "He is indeed, Chieftain Quicksilver."

"There is something of the prig about him, though."

Cordelia looked up in surprize, then decided not to take offense. Instead, she gave Quicksilver a slow smile. "Leave that to me."

"I have no wish to do otherwise," the bandit chief told her. "Indeed, your brother is trouble enough for me."

"Trouble, because you must escape him?" Cordelia asked softly. "Or because you do not wish to?"

" 'Tis unkind of you to say it," Quicksilver snapped, then looked up at her with a sudden, naked forlornness. "Besides, both are part of one problem, are they not?"

Cordelia stared at her, surprized, then managed a reassuring smile. "Problems are for solving, Chieftain. Come, this man is bound—let us go to another."

Quicksilver lowered the bandaged man, ignoring his groan, and stood up, turning to survey the wounded. "That one, I think."

They knelt by a man with a huge gash in his thigh—but even as they did, he surged up, a dagger stabbing toward Quicksilver's stomach as he screamed, "Die, unnatural woman!"

Quicksilver caught his wrist, pushing it aside and twisting. The man screamed and fainted. "So much the better," the bandit chieftain said through tight lips. "They are easier to doctor when they feel no pain."

"Water before unguent." Cordelia began to wash out the wound. "Pay his words no heed, damsel. The woman who fends a man off is all the more woman for that."

"And what *could* make a bandit chieftain a woman?" Quicksilver demanded.

"Why, a man who is worth respecting," Cordelia answered, taking out the jar of unguent, "but only if he arouses in you a desire to *not* fend him off."

Quicksilver was silent a moment, then said, with an

edge to her voice, "You think your brother is such a one, do you not?"

"Many women have thought so in the past." Cordelia watched Quicksilver out of the corner of her eye, knowing the barb would hurt, but also knowing the woman had to be warned. "Even so, he is good-hearted withal, and would never force a woman nor do anything to cause any good person pain, if he could help it."

"There is that in him," Quicksilver acknowledged, "but what good is it, if he is likely to go chasing off after every lightskirt he sees?"

"True," Cordelia sighed. "I long for him to meet a woman who so fascinates him that he shall have no wish to go chasing again." She waited a moment, still watching Quicksilver out of the corner of her eye, then said, "But I fear that no such woman exists, since to hold him, she would have to be as engrossed in the study of warfare as he is—for those are the only two real interests in his life."

Quicksilver looked up, suddenly alert, then frowned. "What two? War, and what else?"

"Women," Cordelia replied.

Quicksilver thought that one over for a time, then said, "Can he love?"

"Oh, yes," Cordelia said softly. "We were all reared in a very loving home, mind you, and half of what ails him is yearning to give love, but finding no woman who is trustworthy."

"None trustworthy?" Quicksilver looked up sharply. "Why, how mean you?"

"He has never met a woman who wanted him for himself alone," Cordelia said simply. "Every wench who has crossed his path has wanted rank and wealth from him—has wanted the High Warlock's son, not Geoffrey alone."

Quicksilver developed a very thoughtful look.

"It is for that reason that he has taken what they offer, I think," Cordelia said, "for it is even as they have sought to do to him ... Well, this one is salved. Give me the bandage."

When they were done doctoring the worst cases, they came back to find Alain rubbing salve into a gash in Geoffrey's chest.

"Why, what a botch is this!" Quicksilver cried in anger. "Step aside, sir, and leave that to me!"

Alain sprang aside a second before she elbowed him out of the way. He looked up at Cordelia in outrage—but his fiancée only smiled, and gave him the smallest of nods. Alain turned back to watch Quicksilver with a thoughtful look.

Her face was rigid as she rubbed salve into Geoffrey's massive pectoral, and her hand trembled ever so slightly.

But when she had finished winding the bandage about his chest, steadfastly avoiding the glow of his eyes as he watched her (well, she sneaked a couple of quick glances, but as quickly looked away again), she stood up, tossed him his tunic, and stepped back, drawing her sword.

Suddenly, Minerva was at her side, there were Amazons all about her, and her brothers stepped up, with fifty bandits behind them.

"The battle is done, sir, and the wounded bandaged," Quicksilver said. "Wherefore should I not leave you here, and go back with my band to defy you at Castle Laeg?"

Alain stared, appalled, and Cordelia developed a look of dread—but Geoffrey only pulled on his tunic and emerged from it smiling. "Why," he said, "because you would rather defy me right here, and right now."

Quicksilver just stood there, her sword raised on guard, staring at him for half a minute. Then she nodded. "You are right—I would. Take up your sword."

CHAPTER
~11~

Geoffrey grinned and reached for his sword.

"Nay!" Cordelia stepped in front of him, hands outspread to shield her brother.

Geoffrey colored. "Cordelia, I scarcely need . . ."

"Oh, do you not?" Quicksilver grinned with delight. "Must the parfit gentil knight be protected by his slender sister? What fun!"

"It has nothing to do with him," Cordelia retorted, "and everything to do with the welfare of your people. Care you naught about your men and women?"

"Leave our welfare to ourselves," Minerva snapped.

But Quicksilver frowned. "This is the trap your brother used, to tempt me into single combat and captivity! Do you think I will fall into it again?"

"Yes," said Cordelia, "because it is still true. Be mindful, damsel, that if you and your band fight Geoffrey now, I shall fight by his side, as shall my betrothed."

Alain grinned and drummed his fingers on his sword hilt.

"Do you think I fear you?" Quicksilver sneered. "Even the three of you together?"

"You should." Cordelia pointed at Quicksilver's sword, and it twisted itself out of her hands. She shouted in anger, then turned to glare at Cordelia.

"We are witch-folk," Cordelia said, "and of no common breed. You stand against two of the most powerful magicians in the land."

"Sister," Geoffrey said, "I think that I should tell you . . ."

"It will not avail." Cordelia held up a hand to stop him. "This has passed beyond you now, Geoffrey. It is my affair, and hers."

"What, sword against sorcerer? Should I therefore quail and be craven?" Quicksilver glanced at her sword, and it flew back into her hand.

Cordelia's eyes widened, but that was nothing compared to the roar of amazement that rose from the bandits— amazement, with an undertone of dread.

"That is what I meant to tell you," Geoffrey said. "She may be self-taught, but she has learned her lessons well."

"I own it will make the match more interesting." Cordelia paled, but stood her ground.

Quicksilver met Geoffrey's eyes and shrugged. "It cannot hurt to let my band know now, for you will remove me from my command of them if I lose." She turned and faced her troops. "Aye, I am a witch! But you know yourselves that there has been scant need of magic in our battles. It is my tactics and your skill that have won us our place! All I have ever done with magic is to make an arrow fly more truly, or a quarterstaff to strike with greater force!"

"Sister," said Jory, "I never knew."

"None of you did, save Mother and Father." She spoke a little more gently to him. "They taught me that above all else, I must hide my powers. Now, though, I face a witch, and if I fight for you, it must be with witch's tricks!"

Geoffrey couldn't take his eyes off her. She stood proud and tall, head flung back, hair tumbling in the breeze; she almost seemed to glow. The sight held her outlaws spellbound . . .

Spellbound. She *was* a projective. "Can she not know what she does?" he breathed to Cordelia.

"Easily," she retorted, "for there is not a one of us does not dream of holding men so, by sheer force of beauty and brilliance of personality."

The outlaws let loose a huge shout of approval that turned quickly into cheering.

Quicksilver stood facing them, eyes glowing with pride. Then, as the cheering began to slacken, she turned to Cordelia, raising her sword to guard in both hands and falling into a fighter's crouch. "Have at thee, witch!"

"And at thee," Cordelia returned, "but with magic alone, and no steel." She glared at the sword, and it tried to wrench itself out of Quicksilver's hands. But she was ready this time, and gripped it firmly, glaring at Cordelia with a hard grin, and the sword blade began to quiver. Cordelia frowned, and the sword twisted—but it twisted back, then began to quiver again.

Is their power so evenly matched as that? Geoffrey thought.

It is, Fess assured him, *but only in telekinesis.*

He was transmitting in the Gallowglass family mode, an encrypted form of thought that he had designed for Rod, so Quicksilver did not hear him—but Cordelia did. She smiled slightly, and the sword kept quivering—but suddenly, grasses began to twine themselves up Quicksilver's leg.

She shouted and leaped aside, slashing at the impromptu twine with her blade—and a flock of birds suddenly plunged at her, filling her ears with shrill scolding and buffeting her face with their wings. Quicksilver gave a yell of anger and leaped clear—straight toward Cordelia, her sword swinging down. It swung with the flat of the blade, though, not the edge, so it clanged most satisfyingly as it bounced off Cordelia's upraised palm. It was all Quicksilver could do to keep the blade from flying out of her hands again—and Cordelia swelled horribly, stretching upward, and turned into a giant bear, filling the clearing with its roaring and raising its huge paws to pounce on Quicksilver.

Her archers couldn't help themselves; with a shout of alarm, they sent a flight of arrows hurtling toward the bear's head.

They passed right through, of course—the bear was only an illusion, and its head was four feet above Cordelia's. But where Quicksilver had stood, there was suddenly a lioness who sprang at the bear with a roar.

The bear disappeared, and Cordelia too.

The lioness landed and whirled about, angry and confused, turning back into Quicksilver.

"So you *do* know you are a projective," Geoffrey said softly.

"I am a shape-changer; what is this 'projective'?" the bandit chief spat. "You might at least be concerned for your sister's safety, knight—and you even more, Sir Alain!"

Both men stood leaning on one hip, arms folded, watching with interest as Cordelia reappeared right in front of Quicksilver.

"Oh, if there were any real threat to Cordelia, I would be wroth indeed," Alain said cheerfully.

"I am a threat to anyone!" Quicksilver snapped, and an eagle flew where she had stood, claws reaching out for Cordelia. But she disappeared even as the bird flew, leaving only a large mushroom behind. The bird tore into the air five feet above the mushroom, though, with a horrible screeching that was answered by a banshee howl—and Quicksilver's sword went spinning up through the air. Minerva dashed to catch it, but Geoffrey was there a step ahead of her, snatching the sword out of the air and saying, in comforting tones, "Fear not. My sister is the gentlest soul alive, unless someone else is threatened."

"But you are threatened!" Minerva cried indignantly.

"No, only Cordelia," Geoffrey returned, "and she likes your chief too much to hurt her."

Minerva stared at him in confusion, torn between the implied insult and the open compliment, then turned to stare at the mushroom, which had suddenly stretched a tentacle upward to wrap itself around the eagle's leg, then turned into a steel chain and shackle. The eagle screamed in rage and turned into a spear that shot out of the shackle, poised overhead, then plunged straight down. But even as it fell, its form beat and pulsed, then turned into a giant, long-stemmed rose, and the shackle turned into a vase.

"Why, even so she is!" Geoffrey cried.

But the rose was trying to pull itself out of the vase. It quivered and surged, but seemed to be stuck. It sprouted thorns, silver thorns that gleamed wickedly, but still the vase would not let it go.

"*That* she is!" Minerva said triumphantly.

"I have known since first I saw her that she must be touched with care and delicacy, or not at all," Geoffrey breathed, his eyes growing as he watched.

Then, suddenly, the vase was gone, and Cordelia stood looking down at the rose as it began to tremble. But it caught itself quickly, standing upright alone, then turned into Quicksilver, who stood there, still crouched like a lioness, glaring at Cordelia and breathing hard. "How dare you, damsel, to show me myself as something I do not wish to be!"

"Lie to me if you wish," Cordelia said evenly, "but never lie to yourself."

Quicksilver stared, pale with rage—but before she could move, Geoffrey stepped up and held out a hand. "Come, mistress mine. You have fought and found no gain; the fight is done, and your freedom once again forfeit."

"I have not been defeated!" Quicksilver cried in outrage.

"Have you not?" Geoffrey sighed. "Come, then, sister, be done with this ere she is hurt. Use your healer's knowledge and your witch's skill to teach her what she must become, to be all that she can be."

"Know you no other proofs but those of force?" Cordelia said in exasperation.

"What matter if I do?" Quicksilver spat. "It is men who decide our fates, men who must be convinced—and the only proofs they know are those of steel and blows!"

"Not all," Cordelia told her, "nor even most—but I will own that those who do wreak the most harm. Very well, then, I will talk to you in their language." She stared at Quicksilver, who glared back—until, suddenly, her eyes rolled up, and she crumpled.

Geoffrey caught her, a split second before Minerva and all her band fell upon them with an outraged shout—and slammed full into an unseen wall, then fell back from it in a tangle.

Cordelia passed a hand over Quicksilver's face, and the

warrior woman blinked, squinting her eyes against the light. "Have I slept?"

"In a manner," Cordelia said.

Quicksilver looked about her as though trying to gain her bearings. "I remember a witches' fight . . . a rose, and a vase . . ." She turned her head and saw Geoffrey's face only inches from her own. Her eyes went wide, held for a half a minute, then looked away and saw that he held her in his arms.

With a howl, she leaped free and stood, breast heaving, glaring from Cordelia to Geoffrey and back. "How did you do that to me!"

"By finding a certain place to push, within your brain," Cordelia told her.

"I must learn it!"

"I will not teach it to one who means to use it for war." Cordelia's tone was iron. "It is healer's knowledge, used to render a person senseless when the healing will cause some minutes of great pain. If you wish to learn it, you must wish to become a healer."

"Why, so I do," Quicksilver said slowly, "as yourself has seen, when together we tended the wounded. But I will not forswear weapons for that."

"Nor have I," Cordelia assured her. "But I shall try your dedication sorely, before I give you such a tool for death as the knowledge of life."

"Oh, will you! And what healing were you doing on me, then?"

"None, I fear," Cordelia sighed, "but I had hoped to. Brother, I must leave her in your hands—I can do no more."

"You have done quite enough!" Minerva snapped.

"Aye, too much." Quicksilver turned slowly to Geoffrey. "And do you have this knowledge she has used here?"

"Not I," Geoffrey said, "for it is even as she has said—healer's knowledge. I know where to press within the mind and body for acts of war, but not for those of peace."

Quicksilver frowned, looking very closely into his eyes. "Why have you not practiced that knowledge upon me, then?"

"Why," Geoffrey said softly, "I would have you come with me willingly and by your own choice, not through threat of torment."

Quicksilver froze, still staring at him as the color drained from her face.

Then she turned back to Cordelia. "Have you tried to heal him, then?"

"Many times," Cordelia sighed, "though to no avail. I fear that must wait for a lass who is far more woman than I, and not his sister, to boot."

Alain stepped up to curve an arm around her. "If she were more woman than you, she would imperil a whole country!"

" 'Tis good of you to say so, my love." Cordelia caught his arm and held it tight. "But I have never yearned to imperil anyone, only to aid and nurture them."

"This, in spite of all the havoc you have wrought," he said fondly, and kissed her hair.

Cordelia shrugged impatiently. "I have a temper."

Quicksilver stood rigid, watching this fond play with a face of stone. Minerva glanced at her with concern.

"It is truly a matter of what one does wish to be," Cordelia informed Quicksilver, "though far more, I suspect, of what one truly *is*."

"As you are truly my prisoner," Geoffrey said, touching her hand ever so lightly. She quivered; then her head snapped around to glare at him. "Truly my prisoner," he said again, "though I have sought to be as gentle as I can in showing you that. Come, let us do no more harm to one another, nor to your folk—and let us go to the King and Queen, as you have promised."

"Aye, I gave my word," she grated, "but if there is a duke in Castle Loguire again, ought I not go to him first? My band and I live within his demesne. Surely 'tis his right to speak sentence upon me before the Crown does."

A murmur of approval went through the outlaws, but Geoffrey frowned, suddenly anxious.

"Bravely spoken, and well said!" Alain cried heartily. " 'Tis even so—you should present your case before your Duke, and go to their Majesties only if you do not accept his justice!"

Geoffrey darted a quick look at Alain, and whatever he saw there must have reassured him, for he turned back to Quicksilver and said, "To Castle Loguire, then. Come, bid your band disperse once more."

"What good will that do?" she demanded.

"For the sake of form, at least," he said, somewhat exasperated. "It is for form's sake that you wish to go to Duke Loguire, is it not? Go bid them disperse!"

Quicksilver flashed him a quick look of amusement. "Why, as you will have it, Sir Knight." She stepped forward, held up her hands, and began to proclaim.

Geoffrey drew Alain aside. "You are sure that this is not the height of folly?"

"Trust our new Duke Diarmid," Alain said complacently.

"And trust your own heart," Cordelia said severely. "Brother, if you let this one get away, you will not only be a fool, but also a miserable and lonely one all your days, no matter how many women you cozen into your bed!"

"I do not doubt the truth of your words," Geoffrey told her. "But it seems I must save her before I can woo her— and before I can save her, I must bring her to Diarmid."

"I did not mean to keep her from escaping prison," Cordelia said tartly.

"I know that well, sister—but for once, I am not sure of victory."

"Are you not, then?" Alain said, with a merry glance.

"I am not," Geoffrey said grimly. "Her body, I know I can capture—but not her heart."

"Trust to truth for that," Cordelia told him.

"Why, so I do," Geoffrey said, "but will she?"

Quicksilver changed back into her own clothing, returning the finery to the maiden whose place she had taken with apologies for the sword rents. The girl assured her the damage did not matter, then embraced her in a profusion of thanks. Somewhat dazed, Quicksilver rode out of Aunriddy beside Geoffrey.

"Surely you are used to the thanks of the people whom you have aided," he said.

"Well, aye, though never before have I had such an explosion of gratitude," Quicksilver explained.

"Have you ever before plucked a maiden from the dragon's jaws?"

"Nay." Quicksilver pursed her lips, considering, then shook her head. "I have not. It has always been at least a day before the deed would have been done, and the women have come to me for sanctuary and shelter. There have been some freed from impending doom by my taking a shire-reeve's house or Count Laeg's castle, but it was never so immediate as this."

Geoffrey smiled. "Sometimes the heart can be overwhelming, even from those whose minds are locked within their skulls."

"Aye." Quicksilver turned to him with a frown. "Which reminds me, sir, to rebuke you for your bullying!"

"Bullying?" Geoffrey stared. "I have won your surrender in fair fight!"

"Is it fair," she said hotly, "when you are a warlock as well as a warrior?"

"Aye, when I fight a witch who bears a sword and knows the use of it!"

"But you know the use of the powers of your mind," she countered. "You have been trained in their use, as I was trained to the staff and the sword. Nay, I did not see how uneven was the match till I stood against your sister! Oh, if only I had been taught as she had, I could have bested her easily!"

Now Geoffrey did feel anger—not for himself, but for Cordelia. "Oh, could you indeed! Do you truly think your mind is so strong as that?"

"Stronger than yours," she said flatly. "Fight me mind to mind, Sir Knight, and you will find that though your body may be stronger than mine, your thoughts are not!"

"When we fought with swords, my greater strength was of little moment; it was skill against skill," he told her. "Naetheless, I am not minded to turn away from a challenge. If you truly think you can overwhelm my mind by strength of thought alone, then strike!"

Instantly, pain exploded in his head. He reeled in the saddle, furious but even now reluctant to truly hurt her—especially where the hurts would do most harm. Instead, he set up a mad tickling at the base of her skull, against the round pink wall of her mental shield, a mouse to gnaw away at it, even as he snapped his own shield closed. Dimly, he heard her cry out, saw her reel in the saddle—no wonder, for the reaction of her thought being so abruptly cut off must have hurt indeed—though it was a hurt he could not have avoided. He remembered the yoga he had been taught, regulated his breathing and calmed his own mind, dimming the pain till he could think, and could pay attention to the world around him again.

Quicksilver was pulling herself back together, glaring at him in anger. He felt the bolt of fury with which she lashed him, but it was muted, dulled by his own mental shield. He waited, timing his own thrust for the moment hers slackened, for he must open his shield just a little to strike out . . .

Her mind's energy ceased abruptly. He realized she was waiting for an opening, and he gave it to her even as he struck . . .

The lash of her own mental bolt was quick and hot, sending a flash of pain through his head—but it was gone as quickly as it had come, for she gasped in shock, shuddering. Well she might—for, fearing to hurt her, he had touched the pleasure center in her brain with a trace of neural energy, only a milliamp or less, but enough to make every fiber of her being quiver with delight . . .

Only long enough for his own shield to close—and as soon as the thrust of ecstasy was gone, she was on him with white-hot fury, thoughts lashing all about him, thoughts of all manner of villains that she compared him to, surrounding him with a flow of mental energy that battered his mental shields. But every thought carried the impress of her personality, every bolt was so completely feminine, so totally desirable, that he found himself trembling with the desire to drop his shields and die in ecstasy . . .

In self-defense, he did the only thing he could; he waited till her anger slackened, then opened his shield and enveloped her mind in the strongest emotion he had ever known—his own aching, yearning, covetous desire for her, mind and body, for the totality of all that was Quicksilver, Jane, Woman . . .

Her own shield could hold only a few seconds against such a barrage. Against anger, against hatred, she could have held all day—but against desire, and most particularly desire so thoroughly imbued with love, no matter how much he would deny the word, she could have no defense, and her own shields melted and were gone.

For a blinding moment, the world went away, the leaves and horses and trackway disappeared, and he was aware only of her all about him, her mind pulsing, quivering with alarm, but with desire also, flashing with ecstasy where her consciousness touched his, and he was exalted, made euphoric by the closeness, by her presence. Here and there, awareness began to mingle, thoughts to share . . .

Then it was gone, and the world was back, and she was staring at him wild-eyed, breasts heaving, frightened though summoning anger to defend herself, but still the world was only her . . .

Finally, Geoffrey found his voice. "Your pardon. I had not meant for that to happen."

"Do not tell me that you are not delighted that it did!" It was an angry accusation, but did he detect a note of desperate longing beneath it?

"Why, I *am* delighted, though I would never do it again without your leave," he breathed—and for a moment, the world was gone again, and her mind pulsed all about his in a luminescent rose-shot pearly haze, drawing, pulling, aching with desire . . .

Then the pearly cloud was gone, and her staring face was back. "You did it again!" she accused.

For once, Geoffrey understood very clearly that he must

take the blame for something he had not done. "I did, and I fear that I will again at the slightest opportunity, for I cannot keep myself within the bounds of my head, when you are so near."

"Then I shall never be so near again!" She turned away, breaking eye contact, more frightened than angry—and she was right, she was gone, or at least her mental presence was, and the world had gone gray all about him, he mourned within, for the life had gone out of the earth . . .

The temptation rose in him, the furious beating lust and craving, the impulse to take by force what he so coveted, but he fought it down, knowing that what he truly sought could never be taken or forced, for it had to be given, or it would no longer exist.

She pushed her horse forward, just a few steps, just enough so there was no chance of their eyes meeting again, and rode ramrod-straight to hide her own trembling. Geoffrey knew she was hiding trembling, because he was—and at that moment, he knew that he would always know what her feelings were, no matter how far apart they might happen to be. It was a foolish notion, and quite impossible even for two telepaths, but it was there.

Then it passed, and the life seemed to come back into the day; its colors revived more brightly than ever. In place of the anger of loss rose the exultation of having experienced bliss, and if it had been only for a moment, that moment was timeless; if worse came to worst, he knew he could live on that moment for the rest of his life.

But he need not, for he rode in Quicksilver's company, and as long as he was near her, there was always the chance that it would happen again. He rode through the forest in the golden light of late afternoon, his gaze caressing every inch of her back, every strand of her hair, his heart singing within him.

She was still brittle, though, even formal, when they camped for the night. "Do sleep on one side the fire, sir, and I'll sleep on the other!"

The temptation rose up in him then, and he yielded to it, not because it was too strong to resist, but because he suddenly did not see why he should. He stepped closer, his hand coming up to touch her waist ever so lightly. "Oh, what need is there of fire, damsel, when the heat of our passion would be light enough!"

"Nay, sir!" she cried, but did not step away, only stood quivering, longing for his touch to deepen. "The fire between us must prevent the fire inside from burning us to destruction!"

"But you have seen the fire within me now," he pleaded, "and know how it *does* burn me, does drive me to distraction with my longing for you—and not just for your sweet, fair body, no, but for your mind also, and your heart, which I know yearns for me as ardently as mine yearns for you!"

"For shame, sir!" She was shocked to hear her voice tremble. "You have looked where you had no right, and use my own feelings to bend me!"

"If there were need for more than my own ardour and yours, I would never seek to bend." His face swam closer. "Nay, damsel, where is the harm in it if two who do burn for one another are united in such a conflagration that it might engulf all their world?"

"I shall burn ere I yield me!" There were tears in her voice now, and her whole body trembled with yearning.

"Thee, only thee," he whispered, "for our duel this afternoon has shown me that only with thee can I begin to approach the heights of ecstasy that are the reward for those of us who must suffer the curse of loneliness that comes from the strangeness of our minds! Oh, if you must suffer that severance, then do not hesitate to take the ecstasy that is yours by right, that those who delight in the normality of the human state and the assurance of community may never know! If you must suffer in isolation because of your difference, revel now in the pleasures that only we can learn! Come to me now, and never seek to draw away!"

She could only stand, trembling, as his lips closed over hers, and as he drank the sweetness of her mouth, she felt herself burning in every limb until she caught fire and, reaching up to press his head against her own, drew on him as though she would drain him of every iota of life force . . .

Until the first, vaguest tendril of his mind touched hers.

Frightened at the surge of desire that surpassed even that of her body, she leaped back, crying, "Nay, sir! Never! Whiles I am your prisoner, no!"

"Never seek to tell me you do not desire me as hotly as I desire you," he said softly.

"Oh, do not torment me so!" she cried in anguish, clenching her fists. "My body betrays my mind and my heart, and never seek to tell me that it does not, for you have no right to know what you have seen!"

"Why, then, I am blind," Geoffrey murmured, "but even blinded, I would know you long for me as I long for you. It is there in the heat of your touch, in the flash of your eyes, in the sweetness of your lips . . ."

"They are none of them yours to know! None of them! Nay, stand off from me, sir! Stand off, and lie down if you must, but lie down far from me, and let the flames blaze high between!"

He stood looking at her, and for a moment, the forlorn aching was so clear in his face that she nearly cried out, nearly went to him, nearly relented—but then, thank Heaven, he composed his features, hiding his longing, and gave her a rueful smile that felt like a benison, and a fall of cool water in the heat of the desert. "Why, then I shall lie far from you," he said, "for I shall not lie to you—though I need tell you no fuller a truth than you tell to me."

She stared at him a moment, not understanding.

Then she did, and indignation came to her rescue, a trace of anger threading through to break the shackles of desire and free her to defy him again. She lifted her chin and gave him her proudest, most disdainful look.

"Know only this," he said, his voice a caress, "that *my* mind and heart are completely in accord with my body."

"So," she said, with full hauteur, "are mine."

"I do not believe you," he whispered.

"What, has a woman no right to a lie?" she blazed. "Nay, sir, sleep you on your own side of the fire!"

"What, with only hot coals to withold me?" Geoffrey said, his gaze smouldering into her eyes. "You would do better to bid me lay my sword between us, milady, for I am sworn to honor that."

"I am not your lady!" she raged. "And I *will* have you sleep on the other side of a wall of flame, or I will have your head! Nay, if you sleep too deep, I will have your head anyway—for I may have yielded me by my vow, but if you seek to keep me so, you must never be sure of me!"

CHAPTER
~12~

Geoffrey studied her for a long moment, brooding; then he nodded. "I believe you, mi . . . Chieftain. But I must sleep, or I shall be too sluggish to fight."

She gave him a smile of harsh satisfaction. "It is a true dilemma, is it not? You must not sleep, so that you may guard against me, in case I attack by night—but if you do not sleep, you will be too slow if I attack by day."

"My remedy, then, is as always with a dilemma, to step outside its terms," Geoffrey said, smiling.

"Outside?" Quicksilver frowned, eyeing him warily. "How can you do that?"

"Why, you assume that you and I have only ourselves to guard with," Geoffrey said. "But you have a hundred men and a score of women warding your slumber, whether you know it or not."

"Aye." Quicksilver's eyes gleamed with amusement. "And though I may have sworn to yield to you if you bested me with your sword, my band has not! Whether I wish it or no, they are quite capable of falling upon you in your sleep and bearing me off!"

Geoffrey nodded. "Therefore I, too, must seek a guardian." He did not tell her that his horse was a better sentry than any human being—though if the mass attack did come, Fess was quite likely to have a seizure trying to defend Geoffrey.

"A guardian?" Quicksilver eyed him with distrust again. "What manner of guardian can you call up on a moment's notice?"

For answer, Geoffrey gazed off into space a moment while he sent a message in the family mode—a very strong message, to penetrate a haze of concentration; a very urgent message, to make the one who heard it come at once, or at least as soon as the work he was engrossed in was done . . .

Air exploded in a gunshot crack, and a slender, pale youth stood there between them, hands holding not a sword but a book. He was fine-boned and wore a dark blue hooded robe over a royal blue tunic and light blue hose. He seemed entirely unprepossessing until you looked at his face, which was so handsome that it made Quicksilver gasp—but more because of its resemblance to Geoffrey than because of its own beauty.

"No need to be so urgent, brother," he said. "I was only reading Einstein, not meditating on his equations."

"Yet," Geoffrey qualified, with a broad smile that held as much of affection as of amusement.

"Yet," the newcomer agreed.

"What monk is this?" Quicksilver demanded.

The teenager turned a clear, limpid gaze upon her that seemed to see and note everything about her, even to the depths of her soul, and Quicksilver fought to restrain a gasp of alarm, for even as he seemed to note every detail of her, he seemed to dismiss it as inconsequential, and to really only be paying attention to something far beyond her, something much more vast, of which she was only a part. She had never felt so small and insignificant in her life.

But his smile was kind. "I am no monk, fair maiden, but only a poor scholar who delights in study and solitude."

"A most excellent scholar, if he were to speak truly," Geoffrey contradicted, "but his false modesty will not let him. Chieftain Quicksilver, be acquainted with my brother, Gregory Gallowglass. Gregory, this is Quicksilver, chieftain of the bandits of County Laeg."

Gregory showed not the slightest surprise at her profession or rank, but only bowed politely. "I am pleased to meet you, Chieftain."

"And I you." *I think,* Quicksilver added silently.

He noted that, as he seemed to note everything else about her, and his lips quirked with amusement. "No, you are not, nor is anyone else who meets me—though women even less than men." His brow furrowed. "I cannot understand why that may be."

Quicksilver could have told him—told him of the feelings he aroused in her, of wariness and revulsion, wariness of a man who could be so completely cold, yet seem so innocent. But she was careful to leave the thought unworded, and kept it in her heart even as she raised mental shields to keep it in—though she found herself doubting that any mind-shield could hold against this man, if he did not wish it. Still, she witheld the thought, and was surprised to realize that it was not out of fear of him so much as from fear of hurting him, for he looked so young and vulnerable, and reminded her so of her own younger brother, of whom she still felt violently protective, even though he was much bigger and stronger than she was, now . . .

She tried to shake off the spell, to pay attention to Geoffrey's words.

"His name means 'sentry,' " Geoffrey was saying helpfully, "or rather, 'watchman.' "

"What difference?" Quicksilver asked, very guarded.

"Why," said Gregory, "it is the watchman who sat atop the ziggurats of ancient Mesopotamia, to study the stars, thereby to comprehend always a little more of the universe, and the God who made it, and thereby, perhaps, some notions of humanity's destiny and purpose—and, therefore, how they should live their lives."

"In a word, 'philosopher,' " Geoffrey explained, "which, to Gregory, is the same as 'watchman.' Any official philosopher would disown him, though, for he seeks to know everything there is to know before he draws any conclusions about humanity or its purpose."

" 'Tis an impossible task," Quicksilver said, dismayed.

"It is," Gregory agreed, "but it is nonetheless vital for that. Indeed, it is the highest praise that one can bestow upon the work, milady, for it ensures that there will always be a cause for striving, always a purpose in life, and never a moment's boredom."

He was an alien creature indeed, and daunting. To defend herself, Quicksilver fastened on the one word he had said that really mattered. "I am not a lady!"

But she wished she hadn't said it, for that keen glance seemed to penetrate right through her again. "Nay, you speak falsely," Gregory said, "for it is clear to any with eyes to see, that no matter what you were born, it is a lady that you have become—and that, through your own goodness and striving."

Quicksilver could only stare at him, speechless.

Geoffrey chuckled. "Argue with me if you will," he said, "but never argue with Gregory—for he will *not* argue, but only explain to you, quite reasonably and calmly, why you are wrong. Worse, he will go on to explain, in far more detail than you wish, what the truth is."

Gregory turned, smiling gently at him. "Come, brother! You wrong me—and praise me overmuch in the same breath."

"Do I so?" Geoffrey countered. "Like Gilbert and Sullivan's King Gama, Gregory, you always tell the truth, whether people want to hear it or not. Therefore do they hold you to be a most disagreeable man!"

" 'And I can't think why,' " Geoffrey quoted, with a smile of amusement. "Ah, well, brother, there is an easy remedy for that." He turned back to Quicksilver. "If you do not wish to hear the answer, do not ask the question."

"I did not," she said quickly. "Nor will I, either!"

The youth's brow furrowed, and he turned to his brother. "Then why did you bring me here?"

"To guard my slumbers," Geoffrey answered. " 'Bare is the back without brother behind it.' "

Gregory stared at him, then gave his head a quick shake and stared again. "Do I hear aright? Geoffrey Gallowglass will spend the night with a beautiful woman, and wishes to be *guarded*?"

Quicksilver smiled with grim satisfaction.

" 'Tis even so," Geoffrey said, chagrined.

" 'Tis not my charms from which he seeks protection," Quicksilver said, "but his own sword, in my hands."

"Indeed!" Gregory swung back to her. "Then how do you come to be in his company?"

"I am his prisoner," she said grimly. "The King feared

to start a war by sending his own soldiers against me and my band, so he sent your brother alone."

"Ah, now I remember hearing of the bandits of County Laeg!" Gregory nodded. "I had wondered why their chieftain had taken the name of an alchemist's element." He turned back to Geoffrey. "Dine, then, and sleep, and I shall guard."

Quicksilver stared. Why hadn't he asked? Did he really know why she had taken the name of the silvery liquid? Even his brother had not heard the true reason! And if Gregory did know, how had he managed to guess it from no more evidence than seeing her?

She decided it would be a good idea to sway Gregory to her side—and certainly it would do no harm to make Geoffrey jealous, perhaps even drive a wedge between the two brothers. Who knew? She might even be able to beguile Gregory so thoroughly that his vigilance lapsed. She knew her own worth as a warrior, after all, but she had known her own power as a woman far longer.

So, during the dinner, she overcame her own revulsion and offered Gregory a bit of roasted partridge. "Come, sir, eat!" She held out a drumstick and fluttered her eyelashes.

"Hm?" Gregory looked up with a start. "Oh. I thank you, maiden, but no. I am fasting this week." And he sank back into his reverie.

"Surely you must partake of something!" She rose to kneel, leaning forward, drumstick held out on both hands as an offering, cleavage fully exposed, smiling her sweetest, head lowered a little so that she might look up through long lashes . . .

Gregory lifted his head again, and his eyes met hers. She just barely suppressed a shudder; he was looking at her, but *not* at her—as much through her as though she had not been there. "Nay, thank you, maiden. Too much food would cloud my thoughts." And he was gone again.

She stared, astounded. No man had ever dismissed her before, most especially at her most flirtatious. She turned away in a huff to plump down by the campfire again—and looked up to see Geoffrey watching her with amusement.

She could have torn his eyes out for that.

"If you can stir his interest from the airy realms of thought to the vital presence of womankind," Geoffrey said softly, "all my family will thank you."

She turned away, face burning.

When Geoffrey had buried the remains of the meal, she had calmed down enough to ask him, "Has he never shown any interest in women, then?"

"Neither in women, nor in any of the things of this world," Geoffrey told her. "Even the monks in the monastery are too much concerned with the toils of daily living to sustain his interest long."

She frowned. "Does he strive for sainthood, then?"

Geoffrey shook his head, exasperated and, for the first time since she had known him, totally at a loss. "He pays no more heed to religion than any of us do. He says he solved its puzzle years ago, so it holds his devotion, but no great interest."

"Solved its puzzle?" Quicksilver stared. "God is infinite, and your brother says he has solved His puzzle?"

"Not the puzzle of God," Geoffrey corrected, "but the puzzle of religion. He is most emphatic in that distinction. He says that God is not a riddle, but a mystery, and Gregory refuses to seek to understand that mystery until he has all the facts."

"But one can never have all the facts about God!"

"So Gregory says," Geoffrey agreed. "To him, that is the highest praise that he knows."

Quicksilver turned to stare at the youngest Gallowglass, sitting with legs folded and back straight, gazing off into space. "He loves puzzles and mysteries, but has no interest in women?"

"I cannot comprehend that, either," Geoffrey said, sighing, "but for his part, he says he cannot comprehend my interest in battles."

"Or women," Quicksilver added.

"Oh, I think I may finally have grown past that," Geoffrey said, entirely too casually. "By your leave, Chieftain, I must sleep. I trust you shall, too."

Quicksilver would see him hanged rather than let him have a good night's sleep—perhaps hanged literally, for a groggy Geoffrey might be one it would be possible to beat. She sat up awhile, dressing her hair, carefully sitting right where neither Geoffrey nor Gregory could avoid seeing her. She leaned her head over to brush out her fall of rich auburn, twisting and contorting her body as she did. She didn't see Geoffrey's eyes open, but after a while, he turned over, as though in his sleep. She smiled and rose, going past him to take a ribbon from her pack, then sat down in full view of him again (and, beyond him, of Gregory) and arched her back, reaching up to part her hair, then began to braid it. She smiled with satisfaction when she heard a very faint moan coming from the mound that was the supposedly sleeping Geoffrey, and took pity on him, going back near the campfire to plait her other braid—but doing so fully in the light of the fire, still with her back arched, sitting in profile to Gregory.

She wished she hadn't.

It wasn't that he did anything to offend her, nor even gazed at her lasciviously. That was the trouble—that he did not. He sat there as though he had not even noticed her, gazing off into space.

Finally, exasperated, she rose with a stamp of her feet and marched away, around behind him, and stood with her arms folded and her back to the men. She would not violate her word of honor; she would not signal her bandits to come and bear her away; but she knew that, by her posture and attitude, they would infer that she no longer wished the company of Geoffrey Gallowglass.

Of course, that was anything but true. Still, he was obviously not interested enough. If he were, he would have followed where she led, not the other way around.

Minerva and Jory took the signal, sure enough. In minutes, dark forms bearing steel and staves had surrounded the campfire. Quicksilver looked up to find herself facing Minerva. "Do them no lasting hurt," she breathed.

Minerva turned to look at Gregory with contempt. "A fine sentry is he, to sleep while he wakes!" She looked up at Jory and nodded.

The outlaws moved silently toward the two brothers. Cudgels swung up and smashed down . . .

And jarred to a halt.

They didn't bounce, as though off an invisible shield; they slowed abruptly, then stuck fast, as though in a mire of tar. Minerva and Jory both pulled back on their weapons, but they would not come. They tugged harder, but both cudgels resisted. Finally, in exasperation and almost in unison, they dropped their sticks and whipped out their swords.

"No!" Quicksilver cried, but too late—the blades were already flashing down . . .

And sticking. Tight. Not as though in tar, but as though they had chopped into a very hard wood, and would not now come loose again. Minerva and Jory tugged as hard as they could, threw all their weight against their hilts, but they would not come loose.

The bandits muttered with superstitious fear, but they raised their weapons . . .

"You must not harm them!" Quicksilver hissed.

Finally, Gregory looked up from his trance. "Do not fear, maiden. They *cannot* hurt us."

Total shocked silence fell on the band; even Minerva and Jory froze.

"You have known all along what they did?" In her shock and, yes, fright, Quicksilver almost forgot to whisper.

"I have—though it was not worth breaking my stream of thought. Your own anguish, though, is."

"My anguish? What know you of my anguish?" Then Quicksilver, glad to feel outrage, demanded, "And how can you be sure I am a maiden?"

"Why, it is evident," Gregory told her.

"Evident! By what signs?"

Gregory shrugged, with a trace of irritation. "Too many to mention, too numerous to even register consciously. Like will to like. It takes one to know one. What more need you know?"

She stared at him, speechless. So did the rest of her band, men and women alike; they had never heard a male openly and willingly acknowledge the fact that he was a virgin—not unless he was a priest.

"Go back to your camp, now." Gregory turned slowly, taking in the entire band as he spoke. "You shall not prevail, for I shall not sleep, and while I am awake, your weapons shall not strike. I would not have you lose your rest to no purpose."

He was so confoundedly gentle about it! So gentle, and so polite!

"We shall not go without our chief," Minerva said nervously.

Gregory turned to give Quicksilver a searching, and very thorough, look. It made her skin writhe, for there was no admiration in it, nor even interest—just a one-second examination to determine her state of existence. "She is not chained, nor do I hold her caged," Gregory said, then to Quicksilver, "What holds you?"

"My word," she said.

Gregory just gazed into her eyes a minute, with that look that seemed to see far more and far less than it should. Then he nodded. "Then you are bound far more tightly than any shackle could hold you. I can do nothing thereby."

"Then we must steal her away!" Minerva insisted.

Gregory considered the statement, then shook his head. "Geoffrey would not wish it."

"Oh, would he not!" Minerva said angrily, and aloud. She ignored Quicksilver's frantic shushing motions and stepped up to seize her chief around the waist, to lift up . . .

Quicksilver stuck fast.

Jory saw and came running to throw his arms about his sister, too, and help pull. A dozen more of the bandits crowded around, male and female both, tugging frantically. Quicksilver bit her lip against a cry of pain.

But Gregory heard her mind and said, not loudly, but with a voice everyone heard right next to his or her own ear, "Desist. You are hurting her."

They dropped Quicksilver as though she were a hot rock and leaped back. "Let her go!" Minerva said angrily.

"No," Geoffrey said simply.

Enraged, Minerva spun away, seized a battle-axe from another bodyguard, and swung it down at Gregory's head.

"No!" Quicksilver screamed.

"No indeed," Gregory agreed, looking up at the whetted

edge that was stuck fast in mid-air eighteen inches from his face. Behind it, Minerva struggled to pull it free, cursing furiously, red in the face.

"We have come back to where we began," Gregory said. "It is fruitless. Go away."

"Fruitless indeed!" Quicksilver snapped at him. "How many men would it take to overcome you? A hundred? A thousand?"

"*Too* many," Geoffrey said. "They could not all come at him at once, and I would chop them down from behind."

Quicksilver whirled. He was leaning up on one elbow, smiling, still under his blankets. He did not even think them enough challenge to get up and draw his sword!

"Oh, there is no fairness in you, in any of you!" Quicksilver raged. "There is no justice, no equity, in fighting a Gallowglass, is there? For even if I should manage to work out a way to settle with one of you, the others would pile in and vanquish me utterly! No, you are unfair, unjust, you with your magic and your thought-hearing and your skill at swords! There is no winning against a Gallowglass, because Fate has endowed you with gifts denied to the rest of us! No opponent has a chance against you, against any of you, for you will all come at us in a gang!"

"It is even so," Gregory said quietly. "There are six of us, and we have you outnumbered."

She spun about, staring in fury—but the look on his face was bland, even serious; if he had mocked her, he seemed unaware of it.

"I have never known him to use sarcasm," Geoffrey said, "nor to boast."

Quicksilver turned her back on Gregory with a shudder. "He is inhuman!"

"Now, that he is not!" Geoffrey was on his feet suddenly, fists clenched. "He is a good man, one of the best, and he has done you no wrong save to keep you from wronging me! Yet you have wronged *him*, who is the gentlest and best of boys!"

Quicksilver stared at him, amazed at his anger. Then she spun about to Gregory, and saw the signs of hurt in his face. Even as she watched, he smoothed them out, hid them—but now she knew they were there.

Minerva stared, shocked. So did Jory, and all of them.

"It is you who have wronged him, Madam!" Geoffrey snapped.

She turned to look at him, and now she knew the tone, knew the look—it was the elder brother defending his little brother, as Leander and Martin had done for her, as she had done for Jory and Nan. Suddenly contrite, she turned back to Gregory—and saw him suddenly not as a heartless, imperturbable monster, but only as Geoffrey's little brother. Her heart broke open; compassion flowed. "Oh, I am so sorry! You have done nothing but aid your brother, nothing but defend yourself against me and mine! Nay, there is nothing inhuman in you, save your strength." That wasn't quite true—she also could have mentioned his apparent lack of a sex drive—but she was able to bite her tongue, for once. And she was repaid, in a sudden beam of gratitude from Gregory that seemed to light up his whole face. It held her transfixed for a moment of sheer surprise.

Then it was gone; he closed his eyes and bowed his head courteously, saying, "I thank you, Chieftain Quicksilver. I spoke aright before; you are all that a lady should be."

For some reason, she felt completely and very oddly flattered.

She turned to her band, waving them away. "Back to your campfires! Away! I cannot thank you enough, good friends, for seeking to free me from a road to the gallows—but I can see it is not to be done this way. No, away, and I thank you with all my heart!"

Unsure and looking askance, they nonetheless began to slip away into the woods, until finally only Minerva and Jory were left. Quicksilver gave Minerva a little nod of assurance, and she went.

"Sister . . ." Jory pleaded.

"Nay, you must leave me, too, brother," Quicksilver said, low. "Do me the courtesy to believe that I know what is best for me—and that I have enough sense of honor to keep my word, once it is given."

"Why, I shall trust in that fervently," Geoffrey said.

Quicksilver felt her heart flutter, but Jory frowned at Geoffrey, puzzled, and Quicksilver wondered, impatiently, if her brother would ever lose his essential naïveté. "I am well for now, brother," she said, "and I go to do what I must. I thank you deeply. Good night."

Jory turned to glare at Geoffrey. "If you harm my sister, I shall never rest till I have slain you!"

"You are a man of honor," Geoffrey returned, "and worthy to be a knight."

Jory only glared at him a second longer, then turned on his heel and strode away.

The woods were silent for a minute.

Then Gregory stirred and said, "You should sleep now, both of you. There will be a long ride tomorrow."

Quicksilver looked up with a frown. "When will *you* rest?"

"I do even now," Gregory assured her, "for my vigil gives me as much rest as your slumber. Nay, fair lady— good night."

"He speaks truth." Geoffrey lay down again. "I have seen him stay awake in this fashion every night for a week, and at the end be as well rested as though he had slept the whole sennight." Then, more softly, "I thank you for your compassion, lady."

"I am not a lady!" she snapped.

"Do you still maintain that?" Geoffrey sighed. "Ah, well, then I must suffer it. Good night to you, fairest of the fair."

"And to you, unfair and inequitous," she returned—but she did lie down again. On her own side of the fire. "And I may be a gentlewoman, but I am not a lady!"

Geoffrey sighed again, and called out, "What did Emerson say to it, Gregory?"

" 'What you are, stands over you the while,' " Gregory quoted, " 'and thunders so that I cannot hear what you say to the contrary.' "

Geoffrey nodded, satisfied. "Haunt my dreams, fair one. Good night."

The next morning, Geoffrey took Gregory aside and asked, "What do you make of her, brother?"

Gregory frowned, musing. "To speak objectively . . ."

"Can you speak in any other way?"

Gregory smiled, almost affectionately. "Well, then, to speak objectively and judiciously, I would say that she is brave, capable, and worthy—but is also gentle and sensitive. Moreover, she is a very beautiful woman with a soul that is so dynamic as to shatter the hardest of hearts."

"Was mine so hard, then?"

"Nay, nor was hers. She can be rash and hot-tempered, aye, but she is also compassionate and tender."

"With all my hopes, perhaps," Geoffrey said softly.

"All indeed." Gregory nerved himself up to speak plainly to his older brother, since that was the only sort of talk he really understood. "Clearly and to the point, then, brother—I would say she is the finest woman of our generation that I have ever met."

"Of our generation?" Geoffrey smiled. "And who is the best woman of any, pray?"

"Why, our mother, of course." Gregory smiled, eyes twinkling. "And I am sure that someone once told Father what I now tell you—you are already ensnared."

"That much, I know."

"Then if you do not bind her to you while you can, you will live to regret it, and curse the fact that you do."

Geoffrey nodded, his gaze locked on Gregory's. "You advise me to hold fast to her, then."

"Aye, and let no one take her from you."

"Including the Crown's justice?" Geoffrey frowned. "What should I do, then? Turn bandit?"

"You are seriously considering that, are you not?" Gregory gave him a penetrating glance that made even Geoffrey brace himself—but it faded into musing, and Gregory said slowly, "It would be much better if you could shield her from the Queen's justice, and turn her to the King's service."

Geoffrey smiled. "One might say that you have it the wrong way around."

"One might," Gregory agreed, "if they did not know Queen Catharine and King Tuan."

CHAPTER
~13~

They hadn't been riding for more than half an hour before an elf popped up on a low-hanging branch in front of them. "Warlock's sons!"

Geoffrey reined in. "Hail, Wee One."

The elf dropped down onto Fess's head. He froze, round-eyed, then sprang back up onto the branch. "Faugh! Cold Iron!"

Quicksilver swung about to stare.

"I am not." Geoffrey held up an arm.

"Nor I," Quicksilver said quickly. She held up an arm, too. "Speak to me, Old Thing!"

The elf glanced at her, then smiled and sprang down onto her horse's head. The mare went rigid, but before she could bolt or rear, the elf started murmuring soothing words in some forgotten language—forgotten by humans, at least, but the horse seemed to understand it well enough. She swivelled an ear toward the elf, listening, then began to relax. He stroked her head with a diminutive hand, coaxing, soothing, and she settled placidly.

Quicksilver stared. "You *are* magical."

The elf smiled. "We have ever had sway over dumb beasts."

Quicksilver smiled, too. "Is that why Sir Geoffrey hearkens to you?"

Geoffrey looked up in mock indignation. "Here, now! Who but lately feared the Wee Folk?"

"Only because I had rarely seen them," Quicksilver said complacently, "and never closely, nor to speak with."

"But seen them you had." Geoffrey turned, frowning. "How is it you did not tell me that the bandit chieftain was a woman, back in Runnymede, Wee One?"

"It did not signify." The elf shrugged. "Male or female, what matter? She was their chief."

"I assure you, it mattered to me," Geoffrey said drily. "How is it you now choose to ride with her, then?"

"Walk," the elf told the mare; then, as they began to move again, he told Geoffrey, "She is prettier than thou art."

Quicksilver smothered a giggle.

Geoffey tried to look injured. "If you have no kinder words than that, you had better state your business, and quickly."

"Mortal folk are so impatient," the elf sighed. "Well, then, brusque one, know that a witch hath lately begun to use her magic to gain power over the peasants of her parish. She hath affrighted the Count of the district, and doth even now raise forces to go up against the shire-reeve."

"Why, even as I did!" Quicksilver turned to frown at Geoffrey. "Do not expect me to aid you in this!"

"I think thou wilt," the elf countered, "for she doth not use her power for the people's good, but rather for their oppression. They mocked and spurned her for many years, seest thou, and she doth seek revenge."

Quicksilver sat up straight in surprize, then frowned. "Perhaps . . ."

"How now, brother?" Gregory asked. "Do you make a habit of setting such matters to rights?"

Quicksilver turned to stare. How was it that Geoffrey's own brother did not know? Could he really be *that* indifferent to what went on about him?

"I am a knight-errant out of idealism and boredom," Geoffrey told him. "Surely, Wee One. I shall undertake to show this witch the error of her ways. But you did say she gathers forces? A band of warriors?"

"Aye—first a bodyguard, but it has grown so numerous that it verges upon becoming an army."

Geoffrey frowned. "How is it you Elven Folk have not simply put this witch to sleep? Or . . ."

Gregory coughed discreetly into his fist.

Geoffrey glanced at Quicksilver and finished, ". . . or otherwise dealt with her according to your own taste and fashion?"

Quicksilver felt a prickle of apprehension envelop her back. What ghastly punishments did the Wee Folk practice, that Sir Geoffrey feared to offend her delicate sensibilities? Her mind instantly conjured up so many horrible tortures that she did not even scold him for it.

The elf sighed. "Ay de mi! 'Tis so hard to judge you mortal folk! She doth humiliate the women of the villages, aye, and send the men to double their work—but she doth trouble not the children, nor doth levy any greater tax than the peasant folk have formerly paid; indeed, she has lightened that burden. In sum, we have not smitten her because we think she may be, at bottom, a good person, and could be swayed to be a force for Right and Justice."

"Here is no simple matter of chastising a wrongdoer." Geoffrey frowned. "Why do you seek to send me? I am no judge!"

"Yet in this instance, *I* may be." Quicksilver held up a palm to stay him. "Perhaps this witch is worth your study—or mine. What is her name, Old Thing?"

"Moraga," the elf told her. "She is a peasant born, so owns only the one name."

"It is enough," Quicksilver acknowledged.

"We shall undertake it," Geoffrey sighed.

The elf grinned. "Blessings on thee, mortal folk! And blessings there shall be, for we of the Folk shall watch!" He sprang back up into the branches before Quicksilver could protest that such spying might not be exactly what they would want.

Instead, she turned on Geoffrey. "Why, a fine lackey are you! Are you a mere errand boy, to go hither and yon at the bidding of one not a tenth of your size?"

"Small in stature, yet great in power," Geoffrey reminded her, but Gregory frowned. "Why, how is this, lady? You but even now spoke of undertaking this matter yourself."

Quicksilver turned a black look upon him. "Never marry. You think far too much of what is right, and makes sense."

"Quicksilver!" Geoffrey barked, shocked. She swung about to him, eyes glittering with the anticipation of battle . . .

But that confounded boy held up a hand to restrain his brother. "Never rebuke one for speaking truth, Geoffrey. It is only one reason among many why I should never marry."

Quicksilver stared at him, appalled, and the dread of the alien crept over her again.

"As to his being a lackey, damsel," Gregory explained, "he goes not out of fear of the Wee Folk, but out of respect for the law."

He was stealing a perfectly good argument away from her, and moreover one which she could easily abandon at any time, because she knew it was really without basis. In anger, she turned to Geoffrey and snapped, "So you will go wherever you are bidden by any careless lord who happens by, simply because he invokes the name of the law?"

But Geoffrey only seemed to be amused. "The King of the Elves is scarcely just anybody 'who happens by,' and the messenger spoke for him. Moreover, that King, too, is one to whom I owe fealty."

"Indeed!" she said, fairly dripping with sarcasm. "And have you, then, sworn fealty to a mannikin?"

The infuriating young man actually smiled wider at that! Worse, he exchanged a glance of secret amusement with his brother!

"No, I have not sworn obedience," he said, turning back to Quicksilver, "but I have favors to repay—and a bond that I choose to honor and accept."

"A bond, forsooth! What manner of bond is this, that it could hold between a mortal and the King of the Elves?"

Geoffrey shrugged. "What matter, so long as it *does* hold? After all, it holds both ways—he will aid me as much as I aid him. Besides, would you truly choose to defy the Elven King without a really strong reason?"

"I will defy any who try to order me about," Quicksilver replied hotly, "for Sir Hempen and Count Laeg had the right to do so, under the law, but they abused it most horribly, and sought to abuse me even worse!"

"Aye, I know that well," Geoffrey said, suddenly somber—even sympathetic, which she found maddening; had he no sense of the right time or place?

"There is no law so great that it cannot be perverted to the use of selfish and evil folk," Gregory said gravely, "but the poor folk would suffer far more, with no law at all."

She wished he would be quiet, and let her argue with Geoffrey in peace!

"But would you forswear an obligation that you had taken on freely?" Geoffrey asked, and he seemed suddenly very intent upon the answer, entirely too serious for a good, enjoyable spat. She forced herself to drop the spirit of play she had been trying to kindle and said reluctantly, "No."

Geoffrey sat back in his saddle with a smile.

He seemed entirely too complacent, so Quicksilver said quickly, "Only if it were not forced upon me in any way, and I had undertaken it willingly!"

"Then beware of those who make you wish to bind yourself to them," Geoffrey said softly.

She turned on him hotly, about to retort that she must then beware of him, but caught herself in time. Instead, she turned his own words back on him and said, "Then had you best not beware of me, sir?"

"Oh, no," Geoffrey said softly, his eyes glowing. "No, most surely not."

He nudged his horse closer, leaning from his saddle to take her in his arms and kiss her. Appalled, she pushed him away. "I am not a show for the avid, sir! Your brother is watching!"

"Gregory," Geoffrey said, never taking his burning gaze from hers, "begone."

There was a gunshot crack as the younger warlock disappeared, and Geoffrey's face was coming closer, and she would have resisted longer, but the memory of yesterday's kiss rose up and overwhelmed her, so that she did not push him away, but let her lips part as soon as his touched, and let herself be lost in the sensations that his kiss drew swirling up from within her.

But when her body began to ache for his touch so strongly that it frightened her, Quicksilver broke away to slap him. Her palm cracked against his cheek, and his head rocked—but even so, he caught her hand before it could leave his skin, and stroked it, saying, "Even that harsh touch is a delight, when it comes from your hand, O sweet one!"

"I am not sweet but bitter!" She yanked her hand back, blushing furiously. "Bitter toward men, and most sour toward you!"

"Oh, no," he said softly, "for your kiss is nectar—nay, mead, for it intoxicates me quite!"

"Then be drunk alone!" She turned away and rode ahead, thinking a peremptory summons: *Gregory Gallowglass! Come back!*

Air exploded behind her, but she did not look back, only rode ahead with grim satisfaction.

"Your pardon, brother," Gregory sighed. "This was one female summons I thought it best not to refuse."

"That is quite understandable, my sib." Geoffrey grinned wickedly, watching the shapely, extremely upright back before him, swaying with the movements of the mare. "I would never be able to resist her either, if she bade me 'Come hither.' "

They knew when they had come into Moraga's domain by the looks the peasant men shot them, where they worked in the fields. They were apprehensive, yes, but not exactly terrified—and they looked up at Geoffrey with a glimmer of hope.

Quicksilver was not at all sure she liked that.

She assumed Geoffrey would pay his respects to the local lord, or at least to the Crown's shire-reeve, but he did not. Instead, he turned to Gregory and said, "Lead us to the witch, brother, if you will."

An abstracted look came over Gregory's face, as though he was listening to some music they could not hear. Quicksilver felt her back prickle with eeriness again, and found herself straining her own mind to hear whatever it was that Gregory did—but she could detect only the ordinary, very common thoughts that always filled her mind when people were about. The clamor would have driven her crazy if she had not learned how to shut it out when she wanted—and the battles between husband and wife would have angered her to murder. Resolutely, she closed her mind again, relieved that, at least at the moment, no village girl was being harassed by vulgar swains.

Now that she thought of it, that was odd in itself. Perhaps there was something to be said for Moraga's form of revenge.

Gregory led them to a meadow. Quicksilver looked up at the sound of hoofbeats, and saw a troop of armored horsemen pounding toward them. She turned to Geoffrey with a frown. "Why do the lord's knights ride?"

"We have come too late," Geoffrey returned. "Whether Moraga's forces are ready or not, the lord attacks."

"We must aid her!" Quicksilver swung back toward the knights, reaching for the sword that was not there, then crying out in frustration. "Give me my blade!"

Without a word, Geoffrey passed it to her, but his gaze stayed on the horsemen. She stared at him, indignant that he took her obedience so much for granted that he did not even feel he had to guard against her! She was about to raise her sword to teach him a lesson, when she realized . . .

That he was trusting her.

"Let us not ride if there is no need," Geoffrey said softly. "Nay, let us see the power of this Moraga."

Quicksilver darted an anxious glance at the tons of metal that pounded toward the trees. "Only if you give your word that we shall pounce if they seek to harm her!"

"We shall pounce most shrewdly," he promised her. "Gregory, be ready to strike."

"Gs, watts, or BTUs?" Gregory asked.

Quicksilver felt a moment's giddiness. Was this how witches talked?

Before Geoffrey could answer, the knights snapped back in their saddles as though they had been hit with lances that knocked them down. They fell, and their horses kept on running, then realized they were lighter, and turned back to stand over their masters, as well-trained war-steeds do.

Now the foot soldiers came in sight, a band of men running, pikes and halberds waving—until they saw their leaders' horses riderless. Then they stopped so quickly that Quicksilver thought they must have run into a morass.

One of them, though, plucked up the courage to dash ahead and help a knight back up to his feet. "Moraga!" the knight screamed in fury and frustration. "Peasant witch! It is Count Nadyr who speaks! Show yourself, coward! That we may see our foe, and strike!"

There was no answer.

"Coward! Miscreant! Vile witch!" he screamed. "Fatherless, misbegotten mandrake's spawn! Farrowless sow! Raddled hag!"

Still there was no answer.

Quicksilver was red with anger. "Calls he himself a nobleman, and uses such terms on *any* woman?"

"I despise his ethics," Geoffrey agreed, "though I must admit it is a sound tactic."

"She seems to know, that, too," Quicksilver said, with irony. "She does not answer, but lets him rant." She gazed off into space a moment, listening with her mind, then shook her head. "I find no trace of her."

"She hears him," Gregory assured her. "She delights in his rage."

Quicksilver almost shuddered. How could he know? She solaced herself with admiration for Moraga.

Finally, the Count gave up in disgust, and beckoned his footmen. Seeing nothing further happening, they approached, albeit somewhat hesitantly, and he sent them about their business with blows and curses. They helped the knights to their feet, then boosted them back into their saddles.

"We are mounted again, and her purpose undone!" Count Nadyr shouted. "Onward to the village! We shall take again what is ours—for I doubt she'll have the courage to show her face!" He turned his horse and rode away, brandishing his sword. His men followed him, with considerably less enthusiasm.

"Sir Geoffrey," Quicksilver said, "are you sure we fight on the proper side in this conflict?"

"Not at all," Geoffrey said, thin-lipped, "though I mistrust any who defy the law."

The sword went flying from the Count's hand. Something struck him out of his saddle.

Quicksilver smiled. "Well done, witch!"

"I saw what smote him, this time," Gregory said. " 'Twas a rock, a common rock."

"She is a telekinetic, then," Geoffrey said, "and one of might and skill."

The footmen had crowded back in superstitious fear; the

companions could hear their furious clamor. A few of the knights rode forward hesitantly, though, and took up station to either side of the lord. They barked to the men, beckoning, and a dozen came forward to heft the count back into his saddle—or across it.

"He is unconscious, then," Geoffrey said.

Gregory nodded. "The rock struck his helm."

"Then he will be fortunate if he wakes," Quicksilver said, in a tone that indicated the nobleman would be better off dead.

The knights turned away, accompanying their lord in silence, riding back the way they had come. After a moment, the soldiers followed.

When they were almost out of sight, Gregory's face suddenly turned abstracted, and he slipped off Fess's rump, striding away across the meadow.

Geoffrey looked up, startled. "Gregory?"

"Come," the youth commanded, and strode ahead.

Quicksilver bridled, indignant at being ordered about—but there was something in Gregory's tone that did not brook delay, so she swallowed her resentment and rode beside Geoffrey, following his brother.

Gregory led them to a large old apple tree, two feet thick in the trunk, its branches tangled and gnarled. Unripe fruit glistened among its leaves.

Gregory came to a halt and called, "Moraga! Come down!"

There was a pause, just long enough for Quicksilver to wonder if the young man had taken leave of his senses. Then the leaves began to rustle with more than the wind, and a pair of stockinged legs appeared, descending to stand on the lowest branch. A long dark skirt dropped down to cover them, with a voluminous blouse above it, and a very plain-looking, very ordinary peasant girl's face above that. She had mousy hair, thin, short, and bound close to her head by an embroidered circlet—her only sign of ornamentation. She was plain, very plain, but not quite bad-looking enough to be ugly. Her nose was definitely too large; she squinted with nearsightedness; her cheeks seemed too full. Certainly they were far too pale, as though she had grown up inside a cave. "Who calls me?" she demanded.

"Gregory Gallowglass," the youth answered. "You acted without honor when you did not appear in answer to Count Nadyr's challenge, Moraga."

The very ordinary face came alive with anger and bitterness. "Honor! Honor is for the rich and the idle! We cannot afford honor, we who must labor from sun to sun! For us, honor is a word men use to cozen us into dying so that they may live!"

"Why, how dare you speak so!" Geoffrey cried in indignation.

But Moraga was running at full steam, not about to stop for him. "Honor? Did he have honor when he rode against me with a dozen knights and fifty footmen at his back? Nay! Do not seek to cozen me—knight! Honor is for fools!"

"'Honor is all that prevents the strong from exploiting the weak!" Geoffrey proclaimed.

"Is it?" Moraga sneered. "I tell you truly, it was one of Count Nadyr's knights who dishonored *me*! Where was his protection of the weak, then? Where was his chivalry? What did *he* know of honor?"

"Oh, I do not doubt that he knew *of* it," Geoffrey said with contempt. "He could not have won his spurs otherwise. But he chose to disregard it, and is not worthy of his rank."

"A knight alone seldom degenerates so far, brother,"

Gregory pointed out. "At the least, his lord should have punished him when he learned of the crime."

"Truly spoken," Geoffrey acknowledged. "Therefore, his lord did not learn of the crime—or did not choose to punish it."

" 'Tis more likely the lord set the tone for his men, is it not?"

"It is, most surely," Geoffrey said, in tones of utter censure. He turned back to Moraga. "Does Count Nadyr have so foul a reputation as his knight, damsel?"

But their discussion had given Moraga time for thought. She turned to Gregory. "You are a stranger!"

"Aye, to you and to this parish," he agreed.

"How, then, did you know my name? How did you know who I am?"

"The Wee Folk told us of you." Gregory was very bad at lying, so he didn't bother.

"The Wee Folk!" Her eyes widened. "Did they lead you to me, then?"

"Nay," Gregory replied. "I had only to follow the aura of your thoughts; as it grew stronger, I knew I was coming closer."

Her eyes went round. "But my thoughts were shielded!"

Quicksilver shrank away inside herself. If Gregory could detect Moraga's thoughts in spite of her shield, what might he have read of Quicksilver's?

His answer reassured her, at least a little. "I could not read your thoughts," he said, "but only their aura. Think of your mind as being like a ship that sails the ocean, leaving a wake behind. Follow the wake, and you come to the ship."

Even Geoffrey eyed him sidelong. He *thought* he knew what his brother was talking about—but in what medium did human thoughts leave residual waveforms?

Obviously, in one Gregory could detect, and Geoffrey could not. It sent prickles up *his* back.

"You are a warlock, then!" Moraga accused.

"Well, a wizard," Gregory hedged, "for I am more concerned with study than with action. It is my brother who is a warlock." He nodded at Quicksilver. "And this lady is his prisoner."

"As you would no doubt make me!" Moraga cried, and a rock shot up from the ground, straight toward Gregory's head.

Quicksilver gave a shout and a dive, to catch the rock, but missed. Geoffrey lashed out a kick—but before boot hit rock, the stone crumbled, and Geoffrey's foot slashed through a cloud of dust.

"You would have injured your foot, brother," Gregory explained.

"Cheat!" Moraga cried, and a small boulder lifted up from the base of an oak.

Gregory frowned at it, and it exploded.

"Down!" Geoffrey threw an arm about Quicksilver and pulled her with him as he hit the ground. He managed to twist about, so that he landed first, breaking her fall.

"What seduction is this?" she demanded, face inches from his.

Geoffrey groaned. "Do not tempt me in mid-battle!" He struggled, and Quicksilver threw herself up to her knees with a look of contempt.

Geoffrey was on his feet in time to see shards of rock bouncing off an invisible sphere that seemed to surround Moraga. She stared, shaken, but rallied and sent two long, straight branches whipping and drubbing at Gregory.

"Nay, this is *my* affair!" Geoffrey cried, and took hold of one of the sticks with his mind. He was surprised at the strength of Moraga's mental hold, but pulled it out of her grip with a single sharp twist. She cried out, clapping her hands to her head, and the other staff fell to the ground.

"You are warlocks!" Moraga cried. "You cannot move things with your minds!"

"We can, for we are Gallowglasses," Gregory said. "Hybrids, of a sort."

" 'Tis unfair!"

"Oh, it truly is!" Quicksilver cried fervently. "If they can do all that we can, surely we should be able to do all that *they* can!"

"Yield you," Geoffrey said sternly.

"Never!" A vine ripped itself from a tree and went spinning toward Geoffrey's head. He frowned, and suddenly, he was gone—but in his place reared a giant snake that caught the vine in its teeth and cast it aside. Moraga narrowed her eyes even more, and a forked stick came hurtling toward the snake—but the serpent transformed, and the stick bounced harmlessly off a hollow tree.

"Burn, then!" Moraga shrieked, and fire blossomed at the base of the trunk. The tree went up in a roaring blaze, and Quicksilver cried out, running blindly toward the flames, hands outstretched—until she heard Gregory's voice in her ear. "Fear not, maiden—my brother is well, no matter what you see." Quicksilver skidded to a halt, looking about frantically, but Gregory had disappeared, too; where he had stood, there was only a circle of mushrooms.

"Be food, for I am not fooled!" Moraga cried, and a wild pig came trotting out of the woods, snuffling its way toward the mushrooms.

But the hollow tree had disappeared into ash, and the pig suddenly struck its nose against something that made it retreat with a cry of pain. Quicksilver looked, and saw a fallen spear glittering in the grass.

Moraga glared at a rock, and it looped up into the air,

falling straight toward the spear—which disappeared. Quicksilver looked about, beginning to feel as though the world had gone fuzzy. She could see neither spear, nor Geoffrey, nor mushrooms . . .

But she did see a broad old stump right beneath the apple tree, and she was sure it had not been there before, and there was a hollow log decked with a flowering creeper that she had not noticed earlier either . . .

"I am not deceived!" Moraga glared at the log, and it began to smoulder . . .

The stump turned into Geoffrey, who reached up and caught the witch's ankle. She screamed, pulling away, and the log ceased to smoke; in fact, it turned into Gregory.

Geoffrey yanked, and Moraga fell screaming from her branch—straight into his arms.

"Do not dare!" Quicksilver sprinted, and was standing right across from him in an instant, glaring over the struggling woman into his eyes.

"Why, I would not have harmed her in any event," Geoffrey assured her, "but for you, O fair one, I shall loose her." He set Moraga's feet on the ground and let go. She backed away, wild-eyed, but stumbled and would have fallen if Quicksilver had not reached out an arm to catch her and stabilize her. "They have treated you most unchivalrously, damsel!"

"Unchivalrously!" Geoffrey cried indignantly. "She sought to smash us, burn us, and shred us, and all we have done in return is to pull her down from her perch!"

"A knight does not strike a woman, sir!"

"Nor have we," Gregory reminded her. "Indeed, I deflected all the shards from the exploded rock, so that they would not touch her."

Quicksilver looked up and shrank away, toward Moraga. Where had he come from?

" 'Tis in full accord with chivalry," Geoffrey said, "to prevent a woman from striking, when she seeks to—and that is all we have done."

"But how did you change your shapes?" Moraga cried.

Geoffrey shrugged impatiently. " 'Tis a child's game."

"We did not truly change, damsel," Gregory said, "only cast the thought of different forms into your mind. Even as my brother says, 'tis a game we played at in childhood."

"Is that truly all?" Moraga narrowed her eyes, and seemed to gather herself.

Gregory looked up at Geoffrey in alarm. "Must we truly hurt her? Is there no other way to make her cease?"

CHAPTER
~14~

"Oh, this is insane!" Quicksilver cried. "Stop it, stop it now, all of you! Surely witchfolk should make common cause, not fight one another!"

Moraga hesitated, her glare lessening. "There is some truth in what you say—but they *are* men . . ."

"Aye, men, not brutes of the sort that despoiled you! Nay, I will warrant that they are gentlemen in the truest sense of the word! This one has had me in his power these three days, and has never offered me harm save to defend himself, nor ever sought to touch me except when I tempted him most unmercifully! They will not hurt you, so long as you do not seek to hurt them! A truce, I beg you, for I do not wish to see you suffer more, nor them either!"

"If you are sure." Moraga stepped a little closer to her, but definitely seemed to relax a little.

For her part, Quicksilver was amazed at herself for playing peacemaker. She had never done it before—in fact, she had always been more than ready for war, awaiting her enemy's attack with relish.

"Are you a witch, too?" Moraga asked.

"I am," Quicksilver admitted.

"You scarce have need of it, if you can fight as well as a man!"

Quicksilver smiled gently. "God does not ask if we need these strange powers of mind, damsel, nor if we want them—He gives them to us at birth, to cope with as we may. For myself, I would rather use force of arms."

"Is it for that reason you have become an outlaw?"

Quicksilver smiled. "Nay—all I wished to be was a wife and mother, even as my mother was." Out of the corner of her eye, she saw Geoffrey look up, suddenly intent, and smiled with glee inside—but went right on talking to Moraga. "I turned outlaw because a lord sought to force me, and I would not submit to him."

"Why, even as was done to me! Though I was beguiled, not . . ." Moraga glanced up at the boys, then quickly away.

"Was there none to teach you the use of your powers?" Quicksilver asked gently.

"Nay—and I thought I was some sort of monster, foredoomed and foredamned, so I kept my powers secret all my days."

Quicksilver nodded. "It was thus for me, too. And I was paid for my discretion with my neighbors' friendship."

"Well, with their companionship, at least," Moraga said bitterly, "though 'twas companionship heavily seasoned with condescension, for I am no beauty."

Quicksilver's smile was brittle. "Had they accorded you the place of future spinster, then?"

"Aye, for no lad showed any interest in me. I lived with

my parents till they died, then eked out a meager living by spinning."

"A spinster indeed," Quicksilver murmured.

"Aye—though I had learned something of herb-lore, and moreover, had made use of my powers to aid healing, and my neighbors became friendly indeed when I began to cure their ills. Then I caught the eye of Sir Gripardin, the knight on whose land our village stood." Her face hardened. "I knew it not, but he had learned that I was a witch—a poacher had espied my practice at moving things by thought, when I had thought myself hidden in the forest, and had sold me out when he was caught and brought before Sir Gripardin. That, and my healing, gave him all he needed to know. He feigned love for me, though he never quite spoke the word, or truly said the word 'marriage,' either. At first, I thought only that he meant to practice the *droit de seigneur* on one who had no lover, husband, or parent to protect her, and prepared to sell my virtue dearly—but I was quite undone by sweet words of flattery and made no demur when he invited me to his bed. He used me with gentleness and tenderness, and I was so overcome with love that I never thought to question when he asked me to brew up potions by the hundredweight. I knew he sold them for gold, and was thrilled to think that, together, we might become rich—but 'twas he who gained riches, then spurned me from his bed, for he had no further use for me, nor need to cozen an ugly wench. Nay, he sent me packing home, penniless and covered with shame, to endure the jibes and taunts of they whom I had thought to be my friends."

Her voice caught on a sob, and Quicksilver embraced her impulsively. "Why, what a rogue was he! No matter what you did to him, he deserved far worse! And your neighbors deserved small credit, either!"

Moraga nodded, swallowing tears. "I was now shunned by those I had thought to be my friends, because I stood revealed as a witch, and a fallen woman."

Gregory nodded gravely. "Those who had looked upon you with comfortable condescension now feared you."

"And Count Nadyr gave you no justice?" Geoffrey demanded.

"Justice for a witch?" Moraga said, with a bitter smile. "Surely you jest! Oh, I appealed to him for redress, but he supported his knight and turned me away. In anger, I turned to revenge. I began by tormenting Sir Gripardin with supposed haunting, and by stealing his gold from his strong room when he was gone from his manor house—for I had learned well how to make things move by thought alone, I assure you."

"I have had experience of that," Geoffrey acknowledged. "You have."

"You impoverished him, then," Geoffrey inferred.

"No more than he deserved," Quicksilver said, thin-lipped.

"Did he not seek to move against you?" Geoffrey demanded.

Moraga smiled with vindictive satisfaction. "He tried to have the shire-reeve arrest me, but I defeated both himself and his constables. His men rejoiced, for they had hated his service, and swore themselves to mine."

" 'Twas then you began to think of ruling the parish," Gregory said.

"Indeed I did! Now it was *I* who sent the false knight packing, and the shire-reeve too, with his own men. I confess I lorded it over those who had treated me first with condescension, then with rebuke—and, oh, my vengeance tasted sweet!"

"I trust you did not abuse them truly," Quicksilver said, frowning.

"No. Oh, I repaid their insults and jibes with my own, but I lightened their taxes, and was still quick to heal the sick, of course."

"Of course," Gregory said, in tones of wonder. Geoffrey glanced at him in concern, but Little Brother's face was all bland calmness.

"Did you sell charms to those who sought them?" Quicksilver asked, remembering the wise woman of her own village.

"Nay, I gave them—but first I gave counsel to those who came for charms. Mocking or not, healing or not, I made it very clear to everyone that it was now I who ruled them."

"Count Nadyr could not long abide such a challenge to his authority," Geoffrey said, frowning.

"He did not," Moraga confirmed. "He sent three knights with a dozen men against me—and at their forefront rode Sir Gripardin. I overthrew them all, making the ground turn to mire beneath them, then into a pit, and as they fell, plucked each man's helmet from his head and struck him senseless with a flying rock." She smiled with a vindictive satisfaction that made Geoffrey's blood run cold. "But he who had used and misused me, I burst the buckles on his armor, shelled him quite, and summoned quarterstaves to beat him until he dropped, senseless. Then I pulled each of them from the pit, closed it up again, and watched them ride home, chastened."

Geoffrey nodded gravely, thinking meanwhile that this woman was a very strong telekinetic indeed, if she had really done all she had described.

Really, Fess's voice reminded him in family thought-mode, and Geoffrey felt a little better. Yes, she could have been making it all up—smart tactics, in her current position. Come to that, he really hadn't seen any of the army she claimed to have recruited. He wondered if any of the people she governed had seen it.

"Did you then lay claim to the county?" Quicksilver asked.

"Nay, only to the parishes that adjoined mine."

"Only *half* the county, then," Geoffrey interpreted.

Moraga tilted her chin up and shrugged. "They had declared me outlaw, and I had risen above it to the status of a rebel. I saw that if I were going to do it at all, I might as well do it openly."

"And you set up rule?" Geoffrey asked.

"I did. I appointed a woman to be mayor over each village, and made it clear to all that she had no choice in the matter—she was to administer the village as I told her, or suffer the consequences of my wrath. All had husbands and children; none of the village folk questioned why they did as I bade them."

"Well, yes—but do none wonder why your mayors do not seem to go in fear and trembling?" Quicksilver asked.

Moraga turned to her with a slow smile. "Perhaps they do. Who will question it?"

" 'Tis well done," Gregory said judiciously. "You protect your lieutenants from blame or charge if you fail, yet ensure their loyalty if you succeed."

Moraga turned to him with a short, grim nod. "That is even as I intend. You see well, lad—and clearly."

Geoffrey frowned at the term "lad," but it didn't seem to bother Gregory at all.

For her part, Quicksilver wasn't sure whether what she was seeing was real—but as Moraga told them her tale, her defenses lowered, and she came alive with enthusiasm. The more vibrant she became, the more attractive she seemed to become. Surely it was all in Quicksilver's mind, and only the wariness of a potential rival, though poor plain Moraga certainly could be no competition at all.

But she *did* seem to be becoming prettier, and the suggestion of a figure actually seemed to be emerging from her voluminous garments as the wind blew them against her skin, showing curves that might well be more voluptuous than obese.

Quicksilver gave herself a shake. It *had* to be her imagination.

"Since then, you have conquered other villages?" Geoffrey asked.

"And set my mayoresses in them. Aye."

"This, in the space of only a few days?" Gregory asked.

Moraga shrugged impatiently, "I must strike quickly, or the knights will strike me down."

"Does not the Church condemn you?" Gregory asked. "After all, they have some claim to these parishes, too."

"The pastors have not had time to send to the abbey to ask the Abbot what they are supposed to think," Moraga answered, "and I do not think they will, for I have made it very clear that I will not bother the clergy if they do not bother me. My quarrel is not with them, after all."

"Amazing, that we should discover two female rebels so much alike in so short a time." Gregory's tone was mild, but the glance he gave Geoffrey was significant, and both heard Fess's voice. *So amazing that the possibility of random coincidence is negligible.*

"I must admit that I have heard of you, lady," Moraga said to Quicksilver, "and I own I have sought to do as you have done."

That would account for it, Fess admitted.

Geoffrey looked up with alarm, and Quicksilver felt her heart sink—she knew that he was suddenly seeing her as setting a dangerous precedent, and that if she were not punished, disaffected women might rise in rebellion throughout the land. She feared she had lost his support suddenly, and the shadow of the noose seemed to fall about her neck. She stiffened, squaring her shoulders, bound and determined that he would not see a trace of fear or grief in her. If his love had no more foundation than that, or could be swayed so easily as by the animation of this very plain country wench, why, he had never been worth having in the first place!

But within her, something mourned.

"So Count Nadyr proclaimed you outlaw, in all the towns?"

"Aye," she said bitterly, "an outlaw, with my life forfeit to any who wished to take it. He set a price on my head, then marched against me with his knights and soldiers. You have seen the result for yourselves—though I will own I had not expected so easy a victory, and am somewhat suspicious of it. Still, I am glad my men did not have to strike, so that they are still clear in the eyes of the law."

"You care most amazingly for your people," Gregory noted.

She turned to him with a bitter smile. "Aye. That is another way in which I differ from the lords."

She said it with a glare that made it a challenge, and Geoffrey reddened. Quicksilver stepped in quickly, though she was no longer sure why. "It is a tale that strikes a chord on my own heart's strings, for it is much like my own."

"How?" Moraga turned, frowning—and her squint had entirely disappeared. "Were you despoiled by a knight?"

"Nay, but only because I struck harder and quicker than he," Quicksilver told her. "I was a villager myself, damsel, the dutiful daughter of a squire, waiting for adult life to begin. I was well liked, though, and loved my village in return, cherishing the thought of living thus all my days. Indeed, I looked forward to becoming a wife and mother, to being fully a woman . . ."

Even now, Geoffrey looked up alertly, a little surprised and very much interested. She noted it with bitterness, glad that she had realized in time how feckless he was, and went on. "But I was revolted at the thought of climbing into bed with any of the boys I knew. Nay, I fear I had only contempt for the callow youths who lusted after me, but could not stand up to me. I found that I could beat any of them—could even best the knight who sought to take me by force. I began to see that they were no better than I myself, and were lords only by accident of birth."

"Nay," Geoffrey said, frowning. "They were born as they should have been; 'twas *you* who were born in the wrong station, by accident."

She glanced at him, puzzled. "Thank you, Sir Knight—I think." She turned back to Moraga. "Despite what he says, damsel, I found most of them to be no better than my village swains. I began to think that I should be a lord myself."

"I said you were a lady," Geoffrey purred, but she no longer trusted the glow in his eyes, and went on. "At last my father died, and without his protection or that of a husband, I found myself far more vulnerable than I would ever have thought. My count summoned me to his bed, with a troop of soldiers led by a knight, to make sure I came."

"Why, the caitiff!" Moraga cried indignantly.

Quicksilver gave her a grateful smile. "I determined to sell my virtue dear, and went along to the lord's bedchamber, then fought him off—and slew him."

"What a pity!" Moraga's lip curled.

Geoffrey frowned, unsure, so Quicksilver smiled warmly. "Is it not? I made good my escape—and knew that I was an outlaw. I could not go back to my village, and knew that with the outlaws of the greenwood, I must become either their base slave, or their master." Her smile widened. "By luck, skill, and Heaven's grace, I triumphed. The rest, I think you know."

"Aye—but not what went before! I had only heard that you were a forest outlaw who had welded the bandits of the greenwood together into an army, and marched against a knight, then his lord!" Moraga gave her a smile that was blinding in its admiration. "Oh, you have wrought wonders, lady!"

Quicksilver returned the smile, but was shaken by how much it had transfigured the plain, dumpy woman—plain no longer, but suddenly almost beautiful, and her clothes seemed actually to have shrunk upon her, revealing a figure that was lush indeed.

"We should be allies," Moraga said, "and should begin by overthrowing these arrogant boys who seem to have come to put us in what they deem to be our proper places!"

Surely it could only be the deep emotions the story stirred that made her face more lovely! Quicksilver knew it was not just her imagination, though, because she could see how Geoffrey was gazing at Moraga in fascination—though, of course, his younger brother was not. Quicksilver was surprised to find that she had to throttle a measure of jealousy, and told herself sternly that Geoffrey was not worth it, that his own behavior proved that!

But she was alarmed to find that she did not believe herself.

Gregory was speaking now. "Your place is with the

Queen's Witches, Damsel Moraga, and ever should have been."

"Aye, even so!" Geoffrey agreed—fervently, Quicksilver thought, and why not? That way, he would always have the woman close to hand! And, she reflected sourly, she definitely did mean "hand."

But Geoffrey was still talking. "You are tremendously gifted, if what we have seen is any measure—not only in magic, but also in administration. Why should you carve out a petty kingdom here in the hinterland, when you could be instrumental in ruling a large one? You would find Runnymede very much to your taste, I think, for the Queen pays her witches well, and there are many shops in which to spend your money—seamstresses and modistes, milliners and artisans, and troupes of players performing in the innyards! You would be among your peers, among folk like yourself, not tolerated with condescension that depended upon hiding your gifts, but regarded with honor as one of Queen Catharine's Witches!"

He sounded, Quicksilver thought, like a procurer, trying to persuade a giddy, restless country girl to go to the city, where he could have his wicked way with her and enslave her to his purposes.

"The thought is tempting," Moraga said slowly, "but I tell you frankly that I do not trust either you two young dandies, nor the Crown. What assurance have I that I will not be clapped into prison?"

"Chiefly," said Gregory, "that the prison has never been invented that can hold a witch of your power for long."

"How, then," asked Moraga, "do you deal with evil witches who will not amend their ways?"

"With death," Gregory told her, his gaze level, and Quicksilver shuddered.

" 'Tis true," Gregory admitted, "though we have found

very few who would not yield to clemency, and the Queen's promise."

"You would have to stand trial," Gregory informed her, "but you have slain no one yet, and your conquests can be overlooked, if you undo them. By your own testimony, none of those who have served you will suffer, for you have been careful to take all the blame to yourself."

"Indeed," said Moraga, with a thin though wary smile. "But I think that I have shown you that I am not a witch to be trifled with."

"That is true," Gregory allowed, "but you prevailed so long because we wished to arrest you, not slay you."

"Oh, did I really! And if you despaired of capturing me, how would you kill me?"

"Oh, probably like that." Gregory pointed to a tree, and it exploded. Splinters rained to the ground.

Quicksilver stared at the growing heap of tinder, shaken to her core, then glanced at Geoffrey, and was glad to see that he seemed shaken, too. "Brother," he said, "Father told you not to toy about with nuclear fission like that."

"I have learned to control it most excellently, I assure you," Gregory said with a shrug. "I split only a few atoms in the center of the trunk."

"What are they talking about?" Moraga demanded of Quicksilver.

"I know not," Quicksilver said nervously, "but if they offer you clemency, I would advise that you accept it." She glanced at Gregory and felt a chill deep within her.

"I think that I shall," Moraga said slowly, but it was at Geoffrey she was looking now, and Quicksilver did not like the gleam in her eye.

"Excellent!" Geoffrey slapped his knees and stood up. "Come, then! Let us go, ere your Count recovers and comes back with twice the number of men! None are dead in this coil yet, and it were best to keep it so!"

Moraga stood up, looking apprehensive. "Do we go to Runnymede, then?"

"Aye," Geoffrey said, "but first we must go to your own Duke."

"My Duke!" Moraga cried. "There is no Duke Loguire, not truly! If there were, and he had been a good man, I would have had redress at his court!"

"He is grown now, and has this week taken up his place," Geoffrey told her.

"I know him—he is a good man," Gregory assured her.

At least, Quicksilver knew he meant it as assurance— but for her, coming from Gregory, it had just the opposite effect.

Not so for Moraga, though. "Well, I will trust to your word, then," she said slowly, "and come to judgement before this 'good man' of yours. But woe unto you, if you betray me!"

And, no matter how she felt toward the woman, Quicksilver found herself saying, "Amen to that. Betray her, and you shall have two of us to contend with."

Geoffrey looked up at her—not in anger, she saw, but in hurt. "Do you trust me so little as that?"

The implied vulnerability shook her, and Quicksilver chose her words carefully. "I trust you, Sir Knight, or I would not be here, no matter how many times I had given you my word. Yet this new Duke I know not at all, and therefore cannot trust at all."

"Why, that stands to reason." Gregory nodded, approving, and Quicksilver felt as though she must have done something wrong, if he thought it was right.

But she was far more concerned with his brother's attitude. Were they to be companions in arms, then, even if they were not to be lovers? Somehow, she doubted that—and knew that she could tolerate it not at all.

Geoffrey turned to Gregory. "Brother, since there are two powerful witches to escort now, will you stay with us? I may need to sleep again."

"Ay de mi!" Gregory sighed. "I did so wish to go back to my studies—but the bonds of blood are greater than the lures of books. Yes, I will come."

So they set off for Castle Loguire, two witches, a warlock, and a wizard. Moraga turned into a veritable bubbling fountain, keeping up a constant stream of chatter, then drawing both young men into telling her about themselves and their upbringing, their adventures and their triumphs. She managed the almost impossible feat of monopolizing them both, and Quicksilver fell behind, seething with a growing resentment and wondering if the woman really could be turning into a stunning beauty even as she watched.

Beauty or not, it seemed she could not make up her mind as to which Gallowglass she preferred. Quicksilver hoped fervently that she would settle on Gregory; it would do him a world of good—and Quicksilver, too.

By the time they came to Castle Loguire, she had finally admitted to herself, openly and in so many words, that she had fallen head over heels in love with Geoffrey, and had believed that he had fallen in love with her, too; that was why she had found it so much fun to torment him with her presence. As a consequence, she was now thoroughly wretched. She felt sure that his interest had been mere lust after all, and rode with a sick, leaden feeling through a darkened day; even the caresses of the sunlight could not warm her bare shoulders. Almost, she rode quietly off the road; almost, she went back to the waiting, protective arms of her brothers, her bodyguard, and her band, who she was sure were riding through the trees to either side of them, out of sight and out of hearing, but never out of mind.

Almost. Not quite. The game was not completely played out yet.

So she rode, with full knowledge, over the drawbridge and under the great portcullis in the cliff face that was decorated with a hundred arrow-slits, the mountain that the first Lord Loguire had honeycombed for his home.

She felt as though she rode to her death.

CHAPTER
~15~

There was no real courtyard in so subterranean a place, of course—but Quicksilver was amazed to discover that they came out of the entrance tunnel into a wide open area, large enough to assemble a whole army (as it no doubt had, many times). It was filled with light from the lower two rows of arrow-slits, even though archers stood near every tenth one.

Quicksilver dismounted and let a groom take her horse as she looked about, awed by the cathedrallike grandeur of the place. It was the largest building she had ever seen, and in spite of the bustle and clamor of a working castle, gave an air of great serenity. So *this* was the ancestral home of the current King of Gramarye! It explained the good repute of his reign.

She shook herself. No, that was ridiculous! It was Queen Catharine who had inherited the throne, not her husband. If there was any truth to the tales of their good government, surely it was her doing, not his!

"My lady."

Quicksilver spun about, words of denial on her tongue—but they froze there, for Geoffrey took her hand and bent over it, then looked up into her eyes with admiration (yes, but admiration was not love—was it?). "I must leave you now, for a short while," he said. "I have sent word to the new Duke, and he will receive us in two hours' time—in full court. You may wish to take the chance to wash off the dust of the road, perhaps to rest a little—and if you wish fresh garb, it shall be provided."

Full court! Quicksilver most definitely *did* want fresh garb, and something a bit more elegant than her daily battle-dress.

But had Geoffrey been hinting that she was too crude for the eyes of a royal prince?

Quicksilver remembered his sudden fascination with Moraga, who was behind him, gaily chatting up his little brother. Quicksilver drew her chill chieftain's mask over her features. "I thank you, Sir Knight." Then anxiety broke through, lending her words a sharper edge than she intended. "And what of you? Will you desert me, now that you have delivered me up to justice?"

"I shall be at the court," Geoffrey promised.

"Aye, to see me condemned!"

"I can give no assurance how the Duke will decide," Geoffrey admitted. "However, I may hazard a guess that Queen Catharine's son will favor a bandit who has shown concern for the common folk, and has magic to boot."

"Not magic enough to captivate you!"

"Oh, that you have," Geoffrey said softly, "but chivalry is stronger than love, for love is self-indulgence. Never fear—you shall be treated as befits a royal guest."

"Aye, though I am still a prisoner!" And she stalked away, feeling very thoroughly betrayed.

A serving-maid led her to a chamber with two of the arrow-slits that had looked so small from outside, but here were five feet high and eighteen inches wide, flooding the room with sunlight. A copper tub filled with steaming water stood in a corner on bare flagstones; the rest of the floor was covered by two carpets. Quicksilver stared at them in wonder—she had only seen a carpet in Sir Hempen's manor house, and in the Count's bedchamber; she had never thought to dwell in a room that had even one. A tapestry adorned the wall, with a splendid picture of a gorgeous bird rising up out of flames, and a great four-poster bed.

That sight chilled Quicksilver. Who was planning to share that bed with her?

No one, for if any tried, he would die, or she would!

"Thank you!" she said to the maid. "Leave me, now!"

"Why, as you wish, my lady . . ."

"I am no lady, but only the daughter of a squire!"

The girl recoiled, and Quicksilver instantly regretted her temper—but the maid said stoutly, "The Duke has bade me address you as 'my lady,' so I shall! There is a gown laid out for you on the bed, my lady, and others in the wardrobe, if that one does not strike your fancy."

Quicksilver darted a quick look at the bed, then looked again. Her eyes widened. "Oh, that will do, and most wondrously! I thank you, lass!"

" 'Tis but my duty," the girl said, somewhat reassured. "Shall I return in the half of an hour to dress your hair, my lady?"

Quicksilver turned to glance at the sheet of polished steel that hung on the wall. (A mirror! An actual mirror!) She fluffed her hair thoughtfully, arranging it around her shoulders, and delivered her verdict. "No. I shall wear it as I always have, and he who has not the sense to see its beauty, so much the worse for him!"

"Why, as you say, my lady," the maid said, round-eyed. "But I shall come back in an hour with some food to break your fast, then to lead you to the Great Hall."

"I shall be glad of it," Quicksilver said unwillingly, and knew she would be very glad indeed of some company, any company, when that time came. "Now leave me."

"As you wish." The maid curtsied and went out the door.

Quicksilver sprang to bolt it, then turned slowly back to dabble her fingers in the heated water, marvelling. Delicious perfume filled her nostrils—the bath was scented! Never had she bathed in heated water before—and with perfume! With sudden decision, she banished apprehension and slipped out of her clothes. Let condemnation and execution be hanged—she would revel in life while she had it! She stepped into the water, shivering with delight, then lowered herself slowly in, closing her eyes to treasure the caress of the warm, oiled foam all about her, leaned her head back against the copper, and breathed in the heavenly scent.

Bathed, her hair clean and dried, she sighed with regret and took up the weary burden of clothing again. Her gaze fell on the beautiful dress laid out on the bed, and she smiled with sardonic amusement, reflecting that she might as well take the chance to wear so beautiful a gown, for she might never have the opportunity again.

If she lived long enough for the question to arise . . .

"What did you expect?" she asked herself angrily, "He is a lord's son, after all, and you merely the daughter of a dead squire!" But the obvious sense of it didn't make her bitterness any less, and the thought of his betrayal was still an icicle through her heart. She had seen mere lust so often! How could she have mistaken it for love? How could she have been willing to risk her life on the hope that he might love her, might save her from both outlawry and the noose, might want to *marry* her?

There, the word was said, she had taken it out and looked at it—and didn't it look ridiculous! For a moment, anger flamed up in her, anger at the cruel God who could withold the right man from her, then show him to her only to yank him away, leaving her with a rope about her neck. He, only he, had been a man she could truly admire, could truly feel a soul's bond with, could . . .

Love . . .

And he might as well never have been born, for all the good he did her!

There is another, somewhere, something within her said, *one who will love you, who will be of your own station, who will marry you.* But she squashed the thought instantly and with every ounce of the huge weight of misery, anger, and bitterness that was in her, for when she tried to look at the whole affair with a clear head and the veil of romance ripped from her eyes, she doubted heavily that there could ever be another man like Geoffrey Gallowglass.

She turned back to the garments with resolute defiance. While she lived, she would live to the fullest, and let him beware who sought to hinder her! She thrust the thought of Geoffrey's treachery from her with a grim determination to enjoy every second that was left to her, and pulled on the shift, revelling in the touch of silk, then took up the gown. The velvet stroked her arms and legs as she pulled it on, and she found herself delighting in the gorgeous dress as much as she had in the bath. She turned to look into the mirror and froze, staring in astonishment. A lady looked back at her, a lady born and bred, tall and elegant, with a cloud of glorious auburn hair restrained by a simple brazen band, in a gown of green and gold that enhanced her figure amazingly. She smiled, caressing the fabric and feeling much more confident. Let Moraga grow as beautiful as she might—Quicksilver knew that she herself was more than a match for her rival!

But she knew that it was not Geoffrey alone for whom she must be a match. She turned to the wardrobe and searched. Luck was with her; she found a pair of hose left from some previous male tenant—a child, at a guess, for they fit her snugly enough. Then she tested the seam about the waist of her dress, making sure that the skirt would rip away easily. If the Duke's decision was to hang her (as it probably would be), she intended to die fighting instead. Her sword had been taken from her, true, but she was quite sure she would be able to snatch a weapon from a guard.

A sudden, faint tug at her mind alerted her; Geoffrey was near. She told herself that she did not care, then cursed herself for a liar. Oh, if only she truly did not care! Then she would . . .

She stiffened, sensing another mind's touch, one with the caress of allure, calling, inviting—to Geoffrey! Moraga! The hussy was trying to steal her man! Never mind that she already had, well enough to wake Quicksilver from her folly—she was bound and determined that the shrew would not have him! All her hurt boiled up into anger, and she burst out of her room.

The guards at either side of the doorway looked up, startled, then gave a shout and leaped to stop her. She whirled about, lashing a vicious kick into the shin of the first man, then snatching his pike from his hand as he opened his mouth to shout. She swung the butt up at his partner's face

as the man came running. He jerked to a halt and swung his
halberd up to block—and she swivelled her weapon down
to jab him in the stomach. As he doubled over, she spun
back just a little too late, for the first guard had limped
close enough to catch her arm, blood in his eye, and his
fingers dug deep, sending a shoot of pain up her arm. She
clenched her teeth, stamped on his foot, and, as his mouth
opened in agony, clipped him in the chin with the butt of
the pike. As he fell away, she pivoted back to his partner,
but the man was rolling on the ground, struggling for
breath. Quicksilver curled her lip and stalked away, reflecting that no matter what they had been told, the fools had
never expected a woman to fight back. It had made them
easy meat—but they were not to her taste . . .

She went after the hunk of beef that was.

They stood on a stairway landing in a pool of light colored by stained glass, one of the very few real windows,
chatting with animation and every sign of pleasure, which
cut Quicksilver to the quick.

"But I shall be tried!" Moraga insisted. "You cannot
deny that!"

"Well, you have broken the law," Geoffrey admitted,
"so at the least, the Duke shall have to give you a hearing."

"Hearing? You mean he will listen?" Moraga had tears
in her eyes.

"To be sure, he will listen!" Geoffrey moved closer,
hand reaching up for Moraga, to give comfort. Moraga
turned into the curve of his arm, and Quicksilver saw, with
shock, that the woman had somehow become quite lovely.
Perhaps it was the visitor's gown that had been supplied
by the Duke, even as her own had—but this one clung to
a figure suddenly revealed as voluptuous, and the pudgy
face had somehow thinned, becoming firm-cheeked, small-

chinned, heart-shaped, and with large eyes framed by a rich black mane. Her lashes were long and full, her lips even fuller, and very red. Quicksilver halted for a moment, stunned by the metamorphosis. Surely pretty clothes and a decent hairstyle could not achieve that much of a transformation!

Then anger surged as she realized just how deep Moraga's deception must have reached, and she lanced a quick, feather-light probe into the witch's mind. She read a brief flash of thought—the determination of a beautiful woman to gain Geoffrey's trust by appearing plain, then once she was close to him, making herself more and more attractive, stimulating his interest as much by touches of thought as by beauty—a telepathic temptress!

Then the thought closed off abruptly as Moraga spun about with a gasp of surprize that quickly transmuted to outrage.

There was more there, but Quicksilver had not had time to read it—nor did she truly care. All she really needed to know was that a scheming female had deliberately stolen her man from her, probably the only male ever born who would have been man enough for Quicksilver, and she swooped like a hawk on a snake.

What Moraga saw was an avenging Fury in a fine gown of velvet and brocade, with a tall pike in hand. She may be excused if she shrank in fright. She may be, but she did not. She fixed Quicksilver with an acid glare, and the bandit chieftain felt a sudden stab of pain in her head. "You would, would you, witch?" she cried, and stabbed back with a mental lance of her own, hafted with hurt of treachery and barbed with all the rage of that injury. Moraga cried out and shrank away, hands pressed to her head, then suddenly lunged at Quicksilver, hand cracking across her cheek. The pain startled her just enough for her mental guard to drop, and suddenly she saw not Moraga, but a fiery demon, and instead of Geoffrey, a venomous snake. The little girl within her cried out in fear and burrowed deeper—but the grown woman erupted in a fury she had never known. "You would cast illusions, would you, witch? Then let us see your true nature, that we all may know!" And with the strength of all her anger and frustration and bitterness, she ripped aside the mental veil of illusion and showed the woman as she truly was.

She was even more beautiful than Moraga, and just as voluptuous. Golden hair cascaded down around her shoulders; a face of elfin beauty stared in outrage from two huge blue eyes. The waist was tiny, the bones delicate, the figure superb . . .

Then it was gone, and in sheer self-defense, Quicksilver cried, "Why, how is this? I tear away one illusion only to reveal another! Is there no truth in you?"

"Yes, and it is this!" Moraga stabbed a finger at her, and pain exploded behind Quicksilver's eyes. She sank to her knees, dropping the pike and clutching her head with a cry of agony . . .

"Enough!" said Geoffrey's voice, and the pain was gone.

Quicksilver looked up incredulously and saw Moraga red-faced and straining, fists clenched, standing apart from Geoffrey, eyes squeezed shut as she fought to lash out at Quicksilver again.

The bandit chieftain scrambled to her feet. "Loose her! I shall deal with her myself!"

"No," said Geoffrey, "for I wish no blood spilled on your way to trial—either of you!" He turned to glare at Moraga. "Do you wish to be hanged for a new crime, when you might be found guiltless of the old?"

Moraga stilled, stood frozen a moment, then gave

Geoffrey a stunning smile. "Why, you are right, as always. I thank you for saving me again! But if you will excuse me now, I shall go, for I must repair the ravages this wanton has wrought!"

"Wanton!" Quicksilver cried in indignation, but Moraga only brushed past her with a quick, venomous smile and went on up the stairs. Quicksilver turned to follow, but Geoffrey's hand restrained her, ever so lightly on her forearm. "Nay, sweet lady. Stay, and do not pursue a fight not worthy of you."

Quicksilver turned on him, anger at Moraga transmuting instantly to anger at Geoffrey's perfidy. "And you, sir! Will you gaze longingly at me, then turn to cozen any other pretty maid who happens by? Is there no faith in you?"

"There is." His eyes were glowing into hers again. "Pardon me if I took pity on a stray, or if I did let myself enjoy her conversation and her presence. I assure you, 'twas nothing of any depth, for I knew her for what she was."

"Oh, did you indeed!" Quicksilver spat. "Then you may know it alone, for you surely know not truth when you see it!" Even that did not assuage her outrage, though, so she went on. "You need not look so smug, sir! That witch meant to entrap you if she could and, if she could not, to geld you, in your mind if not your body!"

"I do not doubt it for a second," Geoffrey assured her. "Indeed, I saw it in her mind as you fought. I must thank you, lady, for my life." And he stepped forward to take her hand and kiss it.

Quicksilver stood frozen in shock; then, before her emotions could betray her, she snapped, "Aye, you will thank me for *your* escape—but you will not lift a hand to ensure mine!" And she spun on her heel and stalked away, back to her chamber where the two guards were just now reviving. She tossed the halberd back down between them with contempt. "Here—not that it will do you any good!" And she swept on into her chamber, leaving them to gawk at her, stupified.

One look in the mirror was nearly enough to reduce her to tears. Her hair was dishevelled, her face red with exertion and alarm. Fortunately, her gown did not seem to have suffered at all—and there was a box of rice powder close at hand. She washed her face, dried it, and powdered, then rearranged her hair, scolding herself all the while for having bothered to go to Geoffrey's defense, when he had only been about to get what he richly deserved.

Still, she found herself wondering why that kiss on the hand had so nearly enfeebled her.

Fool! she told herself, put down the powder puff, and surveyed her reflection critically, then turned and looked back over her shoulder to check the rear view. Satisfied, she allowed herself a single, gloating smile—he might sell her out to her enemies, but one look at her, and he would regret it sorely.

She threw the door open and announced to the guards, "I am ready!"

"Most timely, milady!" the maid said, wide-eyed. "I was just now coming to lead you. A body would think you had heard my thoughts!"

"Who knows but that I did?" Quicksilver said airily. "Lead on!"

The maid turned away, and Quicksilver swept after her, with a single haughty look over her shoulder at the guards.

To the stairway they marched—but as they came to it, a middle-aged man and woman joined them. "Hold," Quicksilver said to the maid. "Age goes first."

"Scarcely aged," the lady said, amused, "but I thank thee, damsel." She was round-faced, with a gentle smile and lively eyes. Her red hair was bound up with pins, as much silver as flame, and her husband was even more gray, but still had a full head of hair. He was hawk-faced and craggy, but seemed to look kindly upon the bandit girl—for a girl she suddenly felt to be again; he was so like her father! Not in his looks, no, but in that clear aspect of the warrior, mellowed and blended with the spouse and parent. "You are a knight," she heard herself saying, "and a father."

He gave her a little bow. "I am honored by both titles, my lady, but more by the second. Thank you."

"Do you come to the Court?" asked the motherly woman.

"Aye, whether I will or no!" Quicksilver gave them a hard smile. "Know that I am a prisoner of Sir Geoffrey Gallowglass, and that he is about to see me hanged for my crimes."

"Surely a knight would not so abuse a sweet damsel!"

"I have known more knights who gave abuse than succor," she said—but the lady reached out to touch her arm with a look of such sympathy that suddenly, Quicksilver could no longer hold back the tears. They burst forth, and the lady wasted only one quick look of surprize before gathering the girl into her arms. "There, now, love, let the tears fall, for thou'lt be much better able to face the Duke, if their weight is spent from thee . . . there, now, there." She murmured more inanities until Quicksilver's tears slackened, and she managed to push herself away from the comforting bosom. "No! No, I thank you, milady, but I must not . . . I have ruined your dress . . ."

" 'Tis only linen, and the tears will dry." The old dear smiled with amusement again, and touched Quicksilver's cheeks with a handkerchief. "There, now, dry your eyes, and tell us the manner of it as we walk."

She did—she had absolutely no reason to trust these people, except that they seemed so kind, so understanding. Besides, what matter if they betrayed her? She was done already.

"So Sir Geoffrey has betrayed thee, then?" the woman asked, beginning to look a bit severe.

"Oh, he has given me no promise," Quicksilver said, "nor asked even as many favors as I would wish, curse him! Yet I thought I saw a promise in his eyes, felt a pledge from his lips . . . No! It was my own foolishness, nothing more!"

"Perhaps not," the woman said gently. "It may be that he meant more than he said; there are men who do."

"I doubt that he is one of them," Quicksilver said, with irony. "Strong he may be, but silent he is not."

"Trust him a little longer," the woman coaxed. "He may not have forsaken thee quite." She looked up at her man. "Husband, what sayest thou?"

"Only that if he lets such a gem as you slip away from him, he's a fool," the man said.

"You know not what I have done!"

"I don't think it would make much difference," he said firmly. "I know a good heart when I see one. But tell me this, maiden—would you want him so much, if he *did* ask for your hand?"

"Oh, yes!" she breathed, and felt the fluttering within her. "It is unkind of you to make me reveal so much of my heart, sir." She could feel the tears again.

"Yes, I'm afraid I've always been unkind in my blindness," he agreed. "But do think carefully before you answer, maiden—you might not want to be bound to so restless a wanderer as he."

It conjured up a sudden vision that made her tremble, and she said softly, "Be sure, sir, that if I were his and he mine, he would never be restless again."

"So thought I, once," the lady said with a sigh.

"Well," her husband said, "it was *mostly* true."

"Aye," she agreed, "mostly."

He had a very strange way of speaking, Quicksilver thought.

"We are here," the maid said.

Looking up, Quicksilver was astonished to see the huge oaken doors of the hall before her. Somehow, though, she found that she was no longer anywhere nearly so frightened as she had been. This nice old lady and gentleman had calmed her. She straightened her shoulders and actually found that a smile came unbidden to her lips, felt the fire of battle-joy light her eye. "Let us go to the fray!"

The doors swung wide, and in they went among a babble of noise, for the Great Hall was thronged with courtiers, and the tapestries muted little of their noise, for the walls were too far away. The ceiling was lost in the gloom, for the light of a hundred torches and candles did not reach so high.

Above them on a dais stood the Duke's great chair—or should have; even higher than that stood two thrones, and on them sat a man and a woman, both with silver hair mingled with golden, both with regal bearing. The Duke's chair stood beneath them with a slight young man sitting in it, leaning forward with his elbow on his fist.

With a shock, Quicksilver realized that the King and the Queen had come to visit their younger son.

In a panic, she spun about, looking for Geoffrey. There he was—talking to the nice middle-aged couple she had been chatting with on the way down! As she watched them, the older man stepped a little to the side, a torch lit his features—and she caught her breath. Side by side with Geoffrey, the resemblance was unmistakable. She had been talking with the High Warlock and his wife—worse, with Geoffrey's parents! Oh, what must they think of her for speaking so shrewishly about their son!

Hot on the anguish came anger. They could have told her, they could have identified themselves! Never mind that they had probably feared to embarrass her—what did they think she felt now, seeing them with him?

But they had seen she needed comfort . . .

They moved on, stopping to have a word with Gregory—and again, the resemblance was clear. Lady Gwendylon cast a jaundiced glance at Moraga, but the witch did not notice—she was too busy giving Quicksilver a gloating look. Quicksilver glared back.

Then Geoffrey turned and saw her. His eyes went round and his breath hissed in between his teeth and, for a moment, he looked positively haggard with longing. Only a moment—it faded into a sort of numbness before he finally wrenched his gaze away from her, and Quicksilver smiled, relishing her revenge.

He came up to her, still a little dazed—and still hungry. She trembled at his nearness, cursed herself, and found a barb for her tongue. "Well, sir! Have I met all of your family now?"

He looked up at his parents in surprise, then turned back to her, smiling. "Not quite. My eldest brother Magnus is far away from here, too far to come back to meet you, I fear. Other than that, though, you have met us all, yes—even my brother-in-law-to-be." He nodded, and Quicksilver, looking where he indicated, saw Alain standing behind Cordelia—who was chatting with the nice middle-aged couple. Once again, the resemblance struck her—but this time, between mother and daughter.

And . . .

Between Alain and the man on the throne!

She cursed herself for a fool. The whole kingdom knew that Lady Cordelia was betrothed to Prince Alain. Why had she not remembered it?

Because it was one thing to hear of them so far away, and another to see them right before you, with no luxury, no teams of retainers, no courtiers—just a sister and her fiancé. Again, Quicksilver cursed herself for a fool.

Trumpets blew, and the whole Court stilled. A herald stepped up to the foot of the dais on which the thrones stood and called out, "Duke Diarmid now holds his court! Let any who have grievances step forth to speak of them!"

"I!" Count Nadyr stepped forward. "I bring charges against this witch Moraga, my liege! Charges of banditry, charges of brigandage!"

The herald glanced up at the people on the thrones; they nodded, and he turned back to Count Nadyr. "State the charge!"

Count Nadyr gave a brief, lurid, and highly biased account of Moraga's few days of activity. He painted her as a villainous upstart who had cropped up from nowhere, tyrannized his peasantry, and pounced upon his law-abiding, peaceful knights with absolutely no cause other than pure greed and lust for power. When he finished, he stepped back, and the King finally stirred. He turned to the Queen and said, "Most singular."

"Aye," said Queen Catharine, "if he is to be believed."

"Majesty!" the Count cried, affronted. "Would a nobleman lie?"

"Not if he knows what is good for him." Her glance was steel; then she turned back to her husband. "Nonetheless, husband, we are guests in this demesne. I am minded to leave this judgement to its rightful lord."

"Then so we shall." King Tuan turned to his younger son. "What say you, Duke Diarmid?"

The slender lad stirred himself, and Quicksilver felt nothing but contempt. Could this man hold the whole Duchy of Loguire in order, this stripling, this boy? Why, he seemed scarcely old enough to shave!

Then his gaze fell upon her, and she stared, shaken. There was wisdom in that gaze, and determination—but even more, a tinge of that alien, remorseless quality that was so strong in Gregory. *Yes,* she found herself saying, *he can hold his demesne—and Heaven help anyone who defies him!*

CHAPTER
~16~

The new Duke lifted his head, looking out over the crowd. "Who speaks for this woman?" he asked, in a tenor that was high and clear, but surprizingly resonant.

"I shall," Gregory answered, and Quicksilver's mouth twisted. Surely the Duke had known that beforehand! She was witnessing a ritual, and wondered if the ending were already known, as well as in any ritual.

A stab of fear chilled her vitals as she realized that the same could be said of herself and her own cause.

The Duke was nodding. "Speak, then. Is there truth in what the Count charges?"

"Truth in the facts he has presented, my lord, but not in the manner of it."

"How dare you!" cried Count Nadyr, his hand leaping to his sword—but Gregory only turned that clear, cold gaze on him, and he froze in place. "I speak of the facts you have presented, my lord, and they are few enough:

viz., that the woman Moraga did declare herself master of a village; that she did defeat the knights and footmen you sent against her, with magic; and that she did then lay claim to six more parishes, defeating yourself, and your household knights and men, with more magic. That much is true; your conjectures about her reasons for doing this are wrong."

"Do you say I lie?" Count Nadyr cried, but wild-eyed; his hand was on his sword, but his fear of the wizard was plain for all to see.

"I do not," Gregory said simply. "I said you were wrong."

"Then what is the truth of it?" Duke Diarmid demanded.

"Let us hear the tale afresh, but from the woman's view." Gregory turned aside with a slight bow. "Damsel Moraga, will you tell what did happen to you?"

Moraga did—and once again, she seemed to be dowdy and insignificant when she began, but as she spoke of her lover's abandonment of her, anger built, and she began to gain beauty and attraction; when she told how she had punished him, she became voluptuous; and as she finished her tale, there wasn't a male eye in the Court that was not fixed upon her, spellbound.

Except for Gregory, Diarmid, Alain, their fathers—and, most amazingly, Geoffrey! He darted quick glances at her, yes, but also kept glancing at the Duke, at his sister, at Their Majesties, and at Quicksilver. She marvelled that he had managed to escape the witch's spell, then suddenly understood how—he saw the whole event as a battle, and his love for a good fight was greater than his lust for beauty! She felt her admiration for the warrior kindled anew, even as her bitterness over his betrayal increased.

Unless . . .

No! How cruel he had been to kindle a spark of hope within her, there on the stairway landing, and how that spark had burned and twisted in her heart, even as she had scolded herself for a credulous fool, to be tempted to believe in him again! She would not think well of him, she *would* not!

Moraga was done, bowing her head demurely and clasping her hands. Duke Diarmid nodded judiciously. "There is far more to this than Count Nadyr knew of—I trust." He cast a keen, penetrating glance at the Count, then turned away even as the nobleman was pulling himself together to look offended. "She verifies the few facts he did present, though her motives seem diametrically opposed to those he attributed to her. Master Gregory, is there proof as to which of them spoke more truly?"

"Aye, my lord." Gregory lifted his head, calling out, "Wee Folk, will you speak?"

A buzz of shocked conversation broke out, then cut off abruptly as an elf jumped up onto the arm of the Duke's chair. "Why did you not simply ask me at the outset, mortal man?"

Duke Diarmid inclined his head gravely toward the mannikin. "It is our way, Wise One. Each must have his say. Now we ask that you have yours."

"Why," said the elf, "what the woman says is true, for there were those of our people who saw most of it."

Moraga blushed furiously.

"She was always a good-hearted soul," the elf went on, "and would not believe us when we told her she was being duped. But when that louse of a knight betrayed her and spurned her, she wept for the whole of a day and into the night, until she slept. We were minded to touch her in the night, to bring her forgetfulness, but our chief bade us withold yet awhile—and in the morning, when she came out of her forest hut, she was a different woman quite: no longer meek, but defiant; no longer forgiving, but bound on revenge; no longer mild, but a Fury incarnate. We cannot truly blame her for what she did, for the knight deserved every bit, and more." He turned to dart a sinister glance at Count Nadyr. "And so did the Count, for he knew of his knight's perfidy, and did naught to stop him. Indeed, he demanded one part in five of the knight's treacherous gain!"

Moraga whirled toward Count Nadyr, enraged, but Gregory's hand on her arm witheld her. "We are in the Duke's court, damsel, where you may demand redress, rather than inflicting it yourself." He turned back to the Duke. "My lord, this woman calls down your justice upon those who have wronged her!"

The whole Court burst into amazed chatter. The accused had suddenly become the accuser!

Duke Diarmid waited it out, chin on fist, unblinking, unmoving. One by one, his courtiers glanced at him, looked again, stared, and fell silent. When the whole room was still, King Tuan stirred and said, "What is your justice, my lord Duke?"

"This is my verdict," Diarmid said, in a voice that carried to every corner. He sat up straight, hands on the arms of his chair. "The woman is wronged, and nothing can ever restore what she has lost, either in body or in heart. Yet she has taken her revenge by herself, and needs to see no more suffering in the treacherous knight." He turned, fixing Sir Gripardin with a severe glare. "I, however, do. I cannot have a knight who is untrue to his vows, here upon my land. Your belt is forfeit, Gripardin, and you are a knight no longer."

The room burst into incredulous clamor again. It was unheard-of for a knight to be stripped of his rank!

Diarmid waited till they were done, then called out, "Take you to a monastery, and pray for a year's space, for forgiveness and enlightenment—and if you do not, you shall hang!" He waited for the next hum of conversation to ebb, then went on. "In a year's time, you may come forth from the cloister, and seek for a knight who will take you as his squire. If you are sufficiently fortunate in that regard, and prove yourself worthy, you may again rise to knighthood."

"What . . . what of my house and goods?" the knight stammered.

"Your house and land are your lord's, given to you to hold in trust for him. They revert to him now, to assign to one more worthy."

The room was ghastly quiet now; he had just hit every aristocrat and gentleman where they really lived—in the living.

"Your personal goods you may take away with you," Diarmid allowed, "save the gold you did wring from a gullible woman's work. That shall be restored to her." He swung about to glare at Count Nadyr. "Every penny! Even the fifth part that you kept, my lord!"

Count Nadyr glared in fury at the boy half his age who was suddenly in authority over him.

"As for yourself," Diarmid went on, "you are guilty of complicity in defrauding the woman Moraga—but of complicity only. You shall therefore comply in your knight's punishment, ensuring that he goes to the monastery, and does remain there one full year. You shall also ensure that none who were forced to serve the woman shall be punished therefore."

He fell silent. Count Nadyr stood glaring at him, hand on his sword—but after a minute or so, he bowed stiffly. "You are gracious, my lord."

"I am glad you realize that." Diarmid's voice was still severe. "I shall punish you no more than this. Get you gone, my lord, to govern your people with justice and kindness." The way he said it made it no empty formula, but a command, and an implied threat.

Count Nadyr stood stiffly in outrage, then forced himself to bow and turn—but he could not hold it; he spun back, crying out, "Is the woman to be punished not at all for her rebellion and theft?"

"All that she stole from you has been restored already," Diarmid answered, "and she was punished mightily for her rebellion before it ever took place. Indeed, had she not been so abused, I doubt she would ever have risen against you. In her sudden conquests, my lord, you reaped only what you had sown."

"Shall she go free, then?" the Count blared in exasperation.

"She shall—but she shall go to Runnymede, there to speak with the Queen's Witches and discover if she may become one of their number. If they and she decide that she may, she shall apply to the Queen, to enter her service."

Moraga could not restrain a cry of delight, clasping her hands together, eyes shining.

Count Nadyr gave her a black look. "Is this justice?"

"It is," Diarmid said, in a voice like granite.

Count Nadyr glared at him—but could not escape seeing the older man behind him, the one with the crown on his head. It seemed to remind him of something; he glanced at Diarmid's brother, which was unfortunate, because that made him also aware of the pretty young witch who stood at Alain's side, and her parents who stood behind her—as a family, probably the most powerful single force in the land. He bit down on gall, swallowed it, managed a last, curt bow, turned on his heel, and strode away. The crowd parted for him, then closed again after the ex-knight who followed him numbly.

There was no conversation, no talking at all. Every person of privilege was shaken by the new Duke's version of justice.

"Go your way," he told Moraga, "and never break the law again. Master Gregory?"

Why only "master"? Quicksilver wondered. Why not 'my lord,' or some other exalted title?

Gregory stepped forward. "Lord Duke?"

"I shall ask this of you," Diarmid said, "that you escort this woman to Runnymede. That much I will concede—that she be taken to meet the Royal Witches, not sent there on her own recognizance. Damsel, you are not to think of yourself as free of the law's shadow until the Queen has accepted you into her service, or given you some other obligation, however it shall serve her."

Moraga stared at him, wordless, until Gregory leaned next to her and murmured something. Then she came to herself with a start and dropped a curtsy. "I thank you, my lord. I thank you from the bottom of my heart! You are merciful, more merciful than I could have hoped."

"Well said." Diarmid nodded with approval, but he still seemed to see her only as a subject, not as a woman. "I have great hope for your reformation. Master Gregory, I thank you."

Now the hum of conversation broke forth as the courtiers relaxed a bit, relieved.

Diarmid turned to look back at his parents. "My liege! Does this justice meet with your approval?"

King Tuan only nodded, for it was the Queen who was the true sovereign here—but she nodded, too, and said, "It is meet indeed, and meted well. We concur in your judgement, Duke."

"I thank Your Majesties." Diarmid inclined his head, then turned back to the crowd. Now his gaze sought out Quicksilver, and she braced herself against the chill of that glance—but hope burst loose in her heart. The Duke might be merciful—if Geoffrey did not fully betray her!

If . . .

Duke Diarmid nodded at the herald.

"Let the bandit Quicksilver stand forth!" the herald cried.

"Why, here stand I!" Quicksilver felt her temper rising again, and fought to restrain it—but they had no right to pillory her like this, no right!

"Damsel Quicksilver," the herald orated, "you stand accused of theft of land and goods, of rebellion against Count Laeg, and of murder most foul, murder of Count Laeg the elder, murder of his knights and footmen!"

"I slew Count Laeg in defense of my virtue," Quicksilver snapped, not waiting to be told to speak. A pox on their rules! "Any others I slew, I slew in self-defense, for they would have taken me to hang!"

"Nay," said Duke Diarmid, "they would have brought you to the Count for justice."

"As I said, to hang!"

"Nay, for you could have appealed to me."

"Appealed?" Quicksilver's lip curled, never mind how coldly he looked upon her. "I, a simple squire's daughter, appeal to the Duke for judgement against a lord? Even if the law allowed it, how would you have heard my cry?"

The courtiers were dead silent, aghast at her impertinence—but Duke Diarmid only nodded gravely. "There is truth in what you say. But you fled to the greenwood. Could you not have fled to me?"

"Aye," she said, "but could I have come to you alive? Or would I have been taken and slain ere I could find my way to this castle?"

"Why, I know not," Diarmid said, with deceptive mildness. He turned to Geoffrey. "How say you, Sir Geoffrey?"

"She could have come here to you, if you had been here when she was first beset," Geoffrey agreed readily, "and if she had known it—and if no one had sought to stop her." He turned to young Count Laeg. "*Did* you seek to stop her, my lord?"

"Of course I did!" the young man cried. "Of course I sought to avenge my father's death! Was not that my right? Was not that my duty?"

"I shall judge that," Diarmid said, with a hint of irritation, "when I have heard what happened. Sir Geoffrey! Can you make any sense of this wrangle, sir?"

"I can, but only because I have heard the whole of the tale." Geoffrey turned to Quicksilver with a grateful sigh. "Now, maiden!"

An incredulous murmur swept the court.

"I *am* a maiden!" Quicksilver cried in anger. "He who would give me the lie, let him come with his sword to try me!"

"Lies are not tested with swords, but with proof." Diarmid's voice cracked like a whip, and his glare seemed to pierce through her. "It is truth I demand of you, maiden, not blows! Speak clearly now, and to the point—and do not waste my time with challenges or threats!"

She stared at him, quite taken aback, then began to rally, but Geoffrey stepped close and murmured, "He is like my brother—the only thing that really angers him is poor logic. Tell him your history, I beseech you, gracious one— tell it as clearly as you told it to me."

She gave him a narrow glance, but decided he was making sense, and turned back to Diarmid. "Well, then, milord Duke, the tale truly begins when I was newly come to womanhood." She paused, expecting him to stop her, to tell her she was filling his ears with useless chatter, that she should begin the tale with the Count's murder—but Diarmid only nodded and said, "Go on."

Quicksilver glanced at the face of his mother, above and beyond him, and what she saw there gave her heart to continue. "The boys of the village would not leave me alone . . ."

It was hard at first, in front of so many people—hard to admit, to speak openly, of the stolen caresses, the touches from behind, and she began to realize just how sympathetic and sensitive a listener Geoffrey had been. But when she had managed to speak of them once, she found she could speak of them again, and her voice gained force and clarity as she went on to tell of Sir Hempen's harassment, of her father's death, of the old Count's summons—and of her defense that had left him dead. But once begun, she found she could not stop—nor was there need, for Duke Diarmid waved aside every attempt to interrupt or to stop her. She rolled on, explaining how her only chance of survival had been to establish her own rule over the bandits of the forest, how she had stolen back the household goods that Sir Hempen had robbed from her mother, how she had taken his cattle and horses in punishment. Then she went on to relate how she had stolen from his tax collectors and from rich merchants, yes, but had given much of the money to the poor folk who had been ground down to yield every penny they could. Then she explained how it was defeat the shire-reeve and defeat the Count, or die.

Finally, she ran out of breath, ran out of anger; finally, she could let the story lie. She lowered her eyes, amazed to discover how much lighter she felt, as though she had put down some great burden. Had she been carrying such a weight all this time?

The Court stood in silence, spellbound.

Then young Count Laeg erupted. "She lies! My lord, she lies and wrongs my good father's memory!"

Quicksilver's head snapped up, a denial hot on her lips, but Geoffrey was already speaking, quietly but firmly. "She speaks only truth."

"Oh, and how shall you prove that?" Count Laeg demanded. "Where is your elfin witness now? The Wee Folk cannot come within our castle, for it is hung about with Cold Iron!"

"Wherefore?" Geoffrey said simply.

Count Laeg stared, taken aback. "Why ... because ... because ..."

"Because you want no witnesses to what you do?"

The Count could only stare, tongue-tied.

Diarmid nodded. "It is well asked. For myself, I have always found that they who seek to bar the Wee Folk are not to be trusted, and have wickedness in their hearts."

Count Laeg swung to him in outrage, but Diarmid snapped, "We shall proceed. Sir Geoffrey, what proof can you offer?"

"The testimony of Quicksilver's mother and sister," Geoffrey answered. "You have heard how they figure in the tale. Let us confirm this much of it, at least. I have asked the Wee Folk to summon them."

Quicksilver spun to stare at him, amazed. He gave her a little nod, then turned to look at the woman and girl who were stepping forward from the midst of the crowd. He gazed at them for a moment, then turned to Quicksilver with an impish smile. "Have *I* met all of *your* family now?"

"Aye," she said. "You have even met my horse."

"Perhaps I should summon her to bear witness." Geoffrey turned back to Maud and her daughter. "Good woman, have you heard the story this young lady had to tell?"

"I have indeed, Sir Knight," Maud said with dignity, while beside her, Nan's eyes danced with excitement.

"And is there truth in as much of her tale as you have witnessed?"

"Aye, and I do not doubt the rest! I assure you, Sir Knight, that if I had known of the effronteries of those village swains, they would all have borne fat ears!"

A ripple of amusement passed through the hall, and Nan turned beet-red. "Mother!" she hissed, in an agony of embarrassment.

"You have taught your daughter well," Geoffrey told her, "and I thank you for your testimony."

Maud took that as as dismissal, gave him a little bow, and stepped back, hauling Nan with her, who lingered to give Geoffrey a mischievous glance before she hurried after her mother.

"That much, then, is so." Diarmid nodded. "As to the elves, they may have been excluded from the castle, but I mind me that they were probably throughout the village and the greenwood." He raised his voice. "Wee Folk, if you would be so kind, we would be glad of the benefit of your witness!"

The crowd murmured uneasily; traffic with the Wee Folk was quite unpredictable. They might help, but they might also bring disaster.

An elf-wife hopped up on Diarmid's chair arm. "Twice in one day! Canst thou not ask all thy questions at one time, Lord Duke, so that we need not be troubled twice?"

"I thank you for your troubles and courtesy." Diarmid

bowed his head gravely. "Tell me, goodwife—have you heard this woman's tale?"

"Aye, twice now—first when she told it to the knight who doth accompany her."

Now it was speculation in the murmur that went through the hall. Diarmid hurried on. "Is there truth in all that she has said?"

"Every word," the elf-wife said firmly, "and she has told all that she knows—up to her meeting with this bawcock of a Gallowglass."

Rod Gallowglass looked up, interested.

"But she has spoken little of her life after he defeated her in their duel, and began to ride the road here," Diarmid inferred.

"Exactly." The elf-wife fixed Quicksilver with a stern glance. "She has not."

"She is not on trial for any deeds done while we travelled here," Geoffrey said quickly.

"Oh, is she not?" the elf-wife said airily. "Well, mayhap not in this court." She turned back to Diarmid. "Is there aught else thou wouldst know, Lord Duke?"

"Much, but nothing else regarding this case." He bowed his head again. "I thank you, goodwife."

"Thou art welcome, my lord." She hopped down and disappeared.

Diarmid lifted his head. "The facts are spoken, then. I hold the woman innocent of the death of Count Laeg, by virtue of self-defense."

The great hall went up in a roar of furious comment.

Quicksilver glanced sidelong at Geoffrey, her heart thrilling. He had not abandoned her after all!

The hall quieted, and Diarmid said severely, "However, I must still hold her guilty of theft, of stealing many times, both by herself and by commanding others—and of resisting a royal officer when he sought to arrest her. I will excuse her the deaths and injuries that she and her folk wrought when they fought off the Count's knights and footmen, for not to do so would surely have led to her death—it may be against the law, but it can be understood, even forgiven. The injury to a royal officer, however, cannot be countenanced."

The hall was very quiet, and Quicksilver's heart was bleeding. She glanced at Geoffrey, hoping, hoping . . .

"My lord," he said, "I beg your leniency."

"It may be granted," Diarmid allowed, "if I hear good reason. Wherefore should I give it?"

"Because she is in herself a most admirable woman, my lord, good-hearted and generous to the core, more the victim of foul men than a villainess herself. This may be seen in her rule of the peasant villages she conquered and held, for, though she was stern in her justice toward the strong who preyed upon the weak, she was gentle and wise in her care of the poor. Even after, as we journeyed here, she aided me in the putting down of a band of outlaws, true rogues, who preyed upon the folk of the village of Aunriddy. Further, she aided my brother and me in bringing the witch Moraga to this court, for justice. Already she has begun to render service to Your Grace, and is worthy of your indulgence. Accord her mercy, restore her to your favor, and she will be a source of strength for the Crown and the realm all her days."

"It may be so." Diarmid steepled his fingers. "But I must have more substance than your word alone, Sir Geoffrey."

Quicksilver, though, did not. Inside, she was melting rapidly.

The Duke raised his head, calling out. "Who speaks in favor of this woman!"

"I!" Cordelia stepped forward. "I, and my fiancé!"

Diarmid looked up without surprise. "Do you speak for this woman, brother?"

"I do," said the Crown Prince, and the room was a-buzz with gossip again.

Diarmid waited it out, then asked, "What do you know of this woman?"

"Only what a shield-mate may learn, for we fought side by side against the bandits of County Frith," Alain said. "I can say without doubt that she is strong-hearted, intent on doing good, on defending the weak and punishing the wicked. She is indeed a lady grown, though mayhap not a lady born."

Diarmid nodded, and looked down at Cordelia. "And you?"

"She has helped me to heal," Cordelia said, "both the folk who had fallen ill as a result of the depredations of those bandits, and the bandits themselves, when they had fallen to her and her band. She is compassionate and gentle to those she deems within her care, kind and understanding—and once her word is given, she is loyal to it, and to whomever she has pledged it."

"Strong virtues indeed," Diarmid said, nodding. "So she used herself and her bandits to defeat a band of brutish outlaws. From this may we see her loyalty to the Crown and to the force of Right, as well as the moderation of justice of her own rule over the villages she took and held."

He raised his face to the courtiers. "I judge this woman to be right and virtuous, and a pillar upon which the Crown may lean. She shall not hang."

The crowd went wild, and Quicksilver went weak at the knees. She concentrated very strongly on simply staying upright, holding hard to the arm that reached out to support her—then realized it was there, and followed it up to Geoffrey, whose eyes were glowing into hers again.

For once, she was speechless.

The tumult slackened, and Diarmid called out, "She may not be free of all punishment, however! Hear now my sentence—that she must send her bandits to Runnymede, there to toil for some years in the Royal Army!"

It was wise, Quicksilver realized—it removed her outlaws from the chance of Count Laeg's vengeance, at the same time that it put them under the Crown's control. For herself, she had no great argument with being closer to Geoffrey for a few years . . .

"Yet she herself shall not abide there long," Diarmid proclaimed.

Quicksilver looked up, alarmed.

"She shall ride the roads and paths and trackways of this kingdom for five years! She shall ride as a knight-errant rides, defending the weak and curing the ill!" He turned and looked up at his parents. "That is my verdict, Majesties, and my sentence upon her! Is it to your liking?"

King Tuan nodded judiciously, but Queen Catharine said, "She has been an outlaw, and a desperate one."

"True," King Tuan said, "but she has begun to atone for her banditry, in putting down a band far worse than her own."

"But she did steal half a county."

"Aye, but she did as little damage as she might, in hewing her way to power, save in striking back at those who came against her, intending to deprive her of life, liberty, and virtue."

"I do not doubt that," Queen Catherine agreed, "and her peasants were well governed withal. Still, we cannot have her loose in our kingdom on her parole alone. She must ride in the company of a trusted knight, one who will accept responsibility for her and hold her tightly within his own regard, to ensure that she does not seek to flee to the greenwood again."

"Well thought, Majesty." Diarmid bowed his head, then turned back to them.

Quicksilver stood holding her breath, taut as a tripwire.

"Sir Geoffrey," Diarmid said, "will you undertake to ride with this woman five years, and keep her within the law?"

"My lord," said Geoffrey, "I will."

"And you, lady?" Diarmid turned to Quicksilver. "Will you accept the justice of this court, and the company of Sir Geoffrey?"

Quicksilver turned to stare at Geoffrey, saw not only the desire and longing in his eyes, but, yes, surely, the love, too. "My lord," she said, her voice growing faint, "I will."

Never taking his gaze from hers, Geoffrey reached out and took her hand—and right there in front of the whole Court, he asked, "And will you marry me?"

She stared at him, swallowed, and fought against every urge within her as she said, loudly and clearly, "Nay, Sir Knight, for I could not wed a man who cannot understand me well enough to know why I have called myself 'Quicksilver.'"

"Why," Geoffrey said, "it is because you are bright and quick and enticing—but if a man should try to catch and hold you, you would be gone, for you would slip away through his very fingers." His voice sank low, caressing, wooing. "Do I not know you, then?"

She could not answer, for her throat had gone too tight; she could only nod.

"And will you marry me?" he asked again.

She found her voice, enough to whisper huskily, "Nay,

for I cannot be safe abed with a man unless he loves me so dearly that he will kneel to me, to beg my favor."

Slowly, Geoffrey knelt, never taking his gaze from her face, never losing his slight, glowing smile. On bended knee, he asked a third time, "My lady, will you marry me?"

"My lord," she said, "I will."

EPILOGUE

Moraga followed the maid back to her chamber, chatting excitedly about her pardon, and the thrill of going to Runnymede—but as soon as the door was closed, she tore her dress off and threw it in the corner with a curse. Howling with rage, she snatched the bowl off the washstand and swung it back to hurl against the wall . . .

And saw Grommet standing there in the sunlight from the arrow-slit.

She froze, face going empty, shocked not so much at having one of her agents see her in her shift, but at having him see her with all masks dropped. She recovered quickly—what had he really seen, after all? Only the beginnings of a tantrum, and Heaven knew they had all seen her in that before, in full spate. She flung the bowl with all her might, shouting an obscenity. Grommet ducked with a yelp; the bowl flew where his head had been, and shattered against the wall.

"All right, all right!" he called from behind a chair. "Next time, I'll knock!"

Moraga/Finister caught herself on the verge of a laugh and held it down to a smile of vindictive satisfaction. "Oh, of course you can't! Mustn't have the servants seeing me let you in, must we? Well, what are *you* doing here?"

"Waiting for orders," he said, coming out from behind the chair.

Come to gloat, more likely—but she didn't say it aloud, only shrugged. "The plan remains unchanged. We go along with the Gallowglass as far as we can."

"Just a different Gallowglass," Grommet said, with a gleam of a smile—until Finister glared at him; then he went deadpan. "You have to admit, chief," he said nervously, "that this mission has been a bit of a failure."

"Failure?" Finister gave a quick, forced laugh. "Not a bit! I'm all set to infiltrate the Queen's Witchforce now! And I'll be right next to that reptile Gregory with the perfect opportunity to bewitch him, as we ride back to Runnymede."

"True." Grommet frowned; he hadn't thought of that. Then he rallied a bit and took a chance. "But you didn't pull Geoffrey away from Quicksilver, did you?"

"No," Finister admitted, "not yet."

" 'Yet,' " Grommet agreed, but for the first time, he really doubted it. "You really think you can steal him?"

"Why not?" Finister tossed her head with a smile. "I've stolen everything else this kingdom has to offer—and Geoffrey Gallowglass has far too many hormones for his own good." She turned to look into the mirror, poking stray tendrils of hair back into place, willing her confidence to return. She stepped back, hands on her hips, swivelled them experimentally, and smiled more genuinely as she heard Grommet stifle a moan. "As you said once before, Grommet—where there is bachelorhood, there is hope."